Chantal's Call

Book 1: The Women of Atherton
A novel

Traci L. Bonney

© 2012 by Traci L. Bonney
Published by JTH Books through CreateSpace.com
First print edition

ISBN-13: 978-1475115352
ISBN-10: 1475115350

Author's Note: This novel is a work of fiction. Names, characters, places, and incidents are either products of the author's imagination or used fictitiously. All characters are fictional, and any similarity to people living or dead is purely coincidental.

Cover designed by Traci Bonney using royalty-free photos from MorgueFile and Dreamstime.
Cover photo (top): From MorgueFile.com, by user ecerroni (file name IMG_50051.jpg)
Cover photo (bottom): From Dreamstime.com, "Kudzu Along the River" by Tim Markley (Tsmarkley)

The font used in this print edition is High Tower Text, a free font downloaded from FontZone.net. The font used on the cover is Chocolate Box Decorative, one of the fonts included in MS Word.

PROLOGUE

"Whew! I'm not used to this muggy weather yet." Chantal pulled her wavy auburn hair into a ponytail, wiped sweat off her brow with her hand and dried it on her jeans leg. "I forgot what September in Mississippi is like."

Sue grinned and donned an Atherton Warriors baseball cap, tucking her curly brown hair into it and slipping on a pair of aviator style sunglasses. "That's what you get for running off to Kansas, cousin." She put two large nested plastic bins in the bed of her old red Chevy pickup and checked the contents of the top bin – water bottle, cell phone, sunscreen, boots, gardening gloves, two pair of cutters and two spools of twine. If all went well, the bins would be filled with kudzu vines by the end of the day.

"Ready to go? I want to get as much done as we can before the day gets too hot." Sue climbed into the truck and Chantal followed, pulling sunglasses over dark brown eyes and settling in for the bumpy ride back down the dirt road she'd just traveled to Sue's cottage.

"Where are we going today? There's a ton of kudzu in these parts."

"A few days ago I spotted a place on the riverbank that looks promising. I thought we'd start there." Sue glanced at Chantal. "I'm glad I can harvest without a bunch of government interference. Believe it or not, fiber artists I know in other states have to get permits to cut kudzu. You'd think the states would welcome any help they can get controlling the stuff."

Shania Twain's "Feel Like a Woman" came on the radio. Sue cranked up the volume and started singing along as the truck flew over the dirt lane toward the paved county road that ran parallel to the Mississippi River.

Chantal harmonized with her cousin for a verse and a chorus, then asked, "What got you into fiber art full time? I thought you were doing okay as an accountant."

Sue turned down the radio. "Even with the extra effort involved in running my own business – filling online orders, working shows and festivals, the actual basket weaving and making of papers and jellies and whatnot – it's so much more satisfying than simply crunching numbers all day.

"And believe it or not, the money is better. Between Internet orders and the Kudzu Fest six weeks ago, it was a very good summer for me. That's why I needed to go out today – with the Fall Festival coming up at the end of October, I need to refresh my vine stockpile and make more baskets, paper and wall hangings. I still have plenty of soaps and kudzu blossom jelly, but I'm running low on the other items."

Pulling off the road at the patch she'd chosen to harvest, Sue cut the ignition and turned to Chantal. "A couple of things to remember – keep your gloves on at all times; you never know what you'll run into in these vines. Speaking of which, watch out for snakes – sometimes you find cottonmouths in kudzu. I haven't seen any yet, but you never know."

"Snakes? You left that out of the sales pitch, girl." Chantal pulled on her boots and hopped out of the truck, casting a slightly alarmed glance around the area.

"Would you have come?" Sue grinned, geared up, retrieved the bins and waded into the sea of green. "Let me show you what to look for and how to harvest it." She handed Chantal a pair of cutters and a spool of twine, then separated the bins and handed her the empty one.

Sue took hold of a vine that was about the diameter of her pinkie and traced its length almost to the ground. Making a cut and gently tugging on the vine, she pulled it loose from the tangle of overgrowth, then coiled it, tied the coil gently with twine from the spool she'd hung from her belt, and dropped the coil into the bin.

"Be patient as you're pulling the vines loose. Kudzu grows up to 18 inches a day in summer, so it won't damage the rest of the plant if you break the vine off, but it might make the cutting useless for weaving."

Chantal nodded and started harvesting, using the technique Sue had shown her. Satisfied with her cousin's efforts, Sue moved a bit away. Working slowly and steadily, she harvested several small young vines, then turned her attention to some bigger ones for basket handles.

A particularly entangled older vine drew her deeper into the patch. Inching forward and humming a Faith Hill tune, she bumped into something in the undergrowth. A rank, rotten/sweet smell rose and Sue shifted to the left a little, trying without success to skirt the obstacle. Since kudzu covers anything in its path, Sue assumed it was a decaying tree trunk or log.

Tugging the last of the vine free, she stumbled and fell forward. Instinctively reaching out to break the fall, Sue touched something soft. Even through gardening gloves, it didn't feel like a rotting log...

Sue felt bile rise in her throat, jumped up and stumbled backward, away from the partially decomposed corpse of a tall, thin man in ragged jeans and a grimy t-shirt. She turned aside a few feet away from the body and threw up, then stripped off and dropped her gloves and reached for the water bottle and cell phone.

"911? I'm out on Highway 11 about two miles south of Johnston Road. There's a corpse in the kudzu..."

Her next call was to Chantal, who tried to run to Sue's aid but tripped in the snarl of vines and had to resort to goose-stepping. When she finally arrived, ready to give Sue a comforting hug, she found her cousin shooting pictures of the dead body with her cell phone camera.

"Cous? What in the world...?"

Sue turned troubled emerald eyes to Chantal. "Something about him seems familiar."

CHAPTER 1

"I understand, Brigitte, and I'm sorry you can't make it. I hope we'll see you soon." Hanging up the phone and sighing, Helene Atherton turned to Chantal. "Your little sister has a prior engagement, my dear. She won't be joining us for dinner tonight. Again."

Chantal shook her head and gave her mother a brief hug. "Mother, I know how disappointed you are. I'll try to get together with Brigitte sometime next week and find out what's keeping her away so much." She pulled back and started to leave. "I need to dress for dinner; I'll be back at 6 sharp."

Helene patted Chantal's shoulder. "Thank you, darling."

"For what, Mother?" Chantal turned around.

Helene cleared her throat. "For remembering what's important to me and caring enough to honor our traditions."

Chantal paused, searching her mother's expression for any sign of the manipulations that were second nature to Helene. Seeing nothing but genuine pain over Brigitte's continuing withdrawal from the family, Chantal walked back to embrace her again, but in that instant Helene's matriarchal façade quietly slipped back into place as she turned toward the staircase in the foyer. "Don't be late, dear. We're having steak au poivre tonight."

Biting her lower lip, Chantal watched her mother sashay up the stairs to her suite. Helene Atherton, born Helen Smith, *sashayed* everywhere. Chantal suspected if Helene had her way, she would probably wear the antebellum dresses reserved for use during the Spring Tour of Historic Homes every day. Firmly convinced of her status as a Southern belle, Helene played to the hilt her role as wife of the town's leading citizen. Add to that her lifelong love of all things French, and Helen had dubbed herself Helene, who named her children Chantal and Brigitte.

Chantal chuckled wryly but quietly so as not to offend her departing mother, who had excellent hearing. Leaving the foyer, Chantal walked through the house and out the back door to the garden, meandering across the yard to the corner where her cottage was located.

When she moved back home and gave up a job as a journalist at a small daily newspaper in Kansas, Chantal made separate living quarters one of the conditions of her return. Her mother wasn't happy, but agreed with the arrangement.

What Helene knew that Chantal didn't at the time was there was no other housing available in Atherton, so to honor their agreement, Helene had a small cottage built on the grounds of the family estate. This gave Chantal a living space separate from her parents, while keeping her close enough to be called upon quickly if something else should happen to Martin, Chantal's father and the reason she had agreed to return in the first place. Martin had suffered a heart attack six months earlier, around the same time his executive assistant retired, prompting Helene to call her oldest daughter home.

So now, back in her childhood hometown only five months, entrenched in the latest family dramas and working at her father's bank, Chantal reconsidered the wisdom of her decision as she paused at the cottage door. *Wonder if my old job in Kansas is still open?*

CHAPTER 2

Brigitte sat on the edge of her armchair, fidgeting with a cup of tea as her gaze darted around the room. Chantal was no less tense but feigned nonchalance, relaxing into the chair opposite her sister and sipping a latte as she observed Brigitte's agitation. Chantal was amazed Brigitte had even answered her cell phone, let alone agreed to meet her at Fuzzy Logic, the town's only coffeehouse and Internet café.

Fuzzy Logic was owned by a former high school classmate of Chantal's, Josefina Madison. Jo had attained a dual degree in business and computers at an out-of-state university, then returned to help bring Atherton into the 21st century. Having been bitten by the Internet bug during her college years, Jo decided her hometown needed to be wired. Since no one else caught her vision, she had to be content with opening a bookstore, Cover 2 Cover, with an in-house coffee shop. When the local cable company began offering Internet service, she brokered a deal to become the town's only wifi hub. Everyone who knew her thought she was wasting her money; what did a small town like Atherton need with an Internet café?

Jo's vision paid off in a big way when business travelers found out there was a wifi hotspot in town, since the local hotels either didn't offer Internet service or charged for it. Now, five years later, Fuzzy Logic was doing so well she was contemplating selling Cover 2 Cover and working out a deal to continue running the café as a separate business. The café had an entrance adjacent to the bookstore's, so customers didn't have to go through one to get to the other. That option was available to them, though, and bookstore browsers often did wander into the café to spend some time reading their purchases over a cup of whatever.

Jo hadn't been able to line up a buyer for Cover 2 Cover yet, but she was always on the lookout for the right person. Lately she'd been eying Chantal, who had firmly refused to consider the idea of becoming a business owner. She said it was because her father needed her at the bank, but the truth was, she wasn't sure she wanted to make such a commitment to a business or to the town itself. In the back of her mind, she nourished the notion that once dear old dad was healthy enough to manage on his own, she would start looking for another reporting job somewhere outside the area.

Meanwhile, she had to try to mediate between her drama queen of a mother and her rebellious younger sister. She set her cup down on the table between the sisters, noticing that Brigitte's agitation seemed to grow the longer they sat, as if she were afraid to be seen there – whether in the café or with her sister, Chantal wasn't sure.

"Okay, spill," Chantal finally said. "You're more nervous than a cat on the Cracker Barrel front porch during the Sunday lunch rush. What's going on in your life? Why are you avoiding us all of a sudden?"

"I'm not avoiding anyone," Brigitte retorted. "I've been busy with church stuff."

"Church stuff?" Chantal raised her eyebrows. "I haven't seen you at church since I got back into town. What church stuff have you been doing?"

"Didn't Mom tell you? I left the family church and joined a new outreach-oriented organization. Christians United for Peace, CUP for short. We have three services a week – Wednesday night and Sunday morning and night – plus a Tuesday night prayer meeting and Thursday night small group meetings. I host a small group meeting at my house." Brigitte lived in the left half of a duplex on the edge of town.

"CUP, huh? Isn't that the group our church's former youth pastor went out on his own and started?"

Brigitte nodded. "Joseph is a dynamic leader and totally committed to the vision God has given him for this new work. He's scouting out property in the county so we can build a church and whatever other buildings we may need to do the work God has planned for us. Meanwhile, we're meeting at the old Starlite drive-in theater outside town. We've set up a big tent with folding chairs for the church services, and our music minister is Billy Judson, the guy who deejays all the weddings and big events, so he has his own sound equipment already. When the chairs aren't in use, we store them in the former concession stand. It's kind of primitive, but it works for now."

Chantal noticed her sister became more animated and less nervous as she talked about her involvement in CUP.

Determined not to shatter the fragile connection they were building, Chantal avoided voicing her skepticism.   Joseph Zacharias was a relative unknown; he had moved to town a year earlier to take a position as youth pastor at Atherton First Baptist Church, the largest mainline denominational congregation in the area, then abruptly left after six months to start his new group.

Since the Athertons had helped found First Baptist, it was exceedingly rare for family members to attend some other church. Brigitte's choice to affiliate with CUP was unheard of; no Atherton had ever joined a nondenominational congregation. Chantal could imagine the scene it must have caused between Brigitte and their mother, and she began to understand her sister's avoidance of the weekly family dinners.

Taking a deep breath, Chantal said, "Sis, I'm glad you've found something you're so passionate about. Let's face it, an office job isn't very satisfying for most people; we both know it." Brigitte was in a similar position to Chantal's, but across town at the attorney's office founded by their uncle, Lawrence Atherton. "Sure, we've both been blessed with a work schedule that gives us Friday afternoons off, but otherwise, office work is – well, it's somewhat monotonous, isn't it?"

Brigitte grinned ruefully and nodded. Chantal continued, "So I'm glad you've found a church home you're happy with and that takes up so much of your down time. But Brigitte, we're all Christians in our family. You don't have to cut yourself off from us, do you? And according to what you said, you have Mondays,

Fridays and Saturdays free. You could come to dinner with Mom and Dad once in a while, couldn't you?"

Chantal watched for a reaction, and what she saw was a puzzle – Brigitte's expressions portrayed the emotional spectrum of a soap opera in mere seconds. "Brigitte, we're not asking you to give up the duplex or come back to First Baptist, just to visit with us once in a while. I've been home five months, and this is only the third time we've seen each other." Chantal sighed and took another sip of latte. "I miss you, girl; we all do. Think about it, okay?"

Brigitte swallowed, started to say something, then shut her mouth. Her face continued to reveal some sort of internal struggle, making Chantal wonder what her little sister really was doing in her off-work hours. As quickly as the storm of expressions arose it subsided, and Brigitte was smiling and nodding again. "I will, Chantal. I miss you too, sis. I'll try to make more time for the family, okay?"

The sisters stood and hugged, and Chantal watched Brigitte leave. The second she walked out the front door, Brigitte's cell phone rang. Chantal saw Brigitte fumble with the phone and flip it open, put it to her ear, blanch, and look quickly around as if searching for someone. Brigitte started walking away from the café at a rapid pace, talking animatedly the whole time. Chantal followed her outside in time to hear Brigitte exclaim, "I didn't tell her anything! I swear I didn't!"

Chantal broke into a sprint, but by then Brigitte had reached her car and peeled out of the small off-street parking lot, nearly sideswiping a sedan as she entered Main Street. Chantal could only stand on the sidewalk and watch as her sister sped away. She saw Brigitte drop her cell phone onto the passenger seat as she drove off, so Chantal grabbed her cell phone and pressed 4 on the speed dial. The phone rang four times and went to voice mail: "Hi! It's Brigitte here – I'm not actually here, but you know what I mean. I can't be reached at the moment, but please leave a message. Here comes the beep – you know what to do!"

Chantal slammed her phone shut in frustration. *Can't be reached, indeed.*

CHAPTER 3

"Okay, Sue, lunch tomorrow sounds good." Chantal snapped shut her cell phone and thought about their trip into the kudzu. It had been a week since they'd seen each other, and Sue hadn't returned any of Chantal's calls in those seven days. Understandable, though; finding a corpse in the kudzu would traumatize almost anyone, but falling on top of it? Chantal shuddered. If she'd been working that part of the patch that day, she would probably go hermit for a while too.

At least Sue had retained enough presence of mind to move away before tossing her cookies. Chantal doubted she would have been able to contain herself long enough to do that. And then to snap photos of the corpse while waiting for the cops to arrive? Chantal didn't know whether to be impressed or horrified at her cousin's decision to study the dead guy's face and try to remember where she'd seen him before. One thing was sure, though – Chantal was amazed at Sue's ability not to lose it and run away screaming and crying, as she had wanted to do.

Now that Sue was over the shock of her discovery and finished dealing with the sheriff's department, she seemed more than ready to reconnect with her closest relatives. She had all but jumped at the chance to meet Chantal at Taco Loco, their mutual favorite when it came to mostly authentic Mexican food. Owned and run by longtime friend and former classmate Luis Irias, the restaurant's offerings came closer to the real deal than anything else within a 30-mile radius of Atherton. Sue and Chantal had arranged to meet there at noon the next day, a Friday.

Plugging the phone into its charger base, Chantal went back to cleaning house. Since the cottage was on her parents' property, the family's housekeeper could have done it, but she insisted on doing the work herself, much to her mother's dismay. Aside from the fact that Chantal felt it would be pretentious to have a maid cleaning a living space barely 800 square feet in total usable area, she really enjoyed cleaning day. She found the work therapeutic, as she often tried to explain to her mother.

Picking up the dusting wand she had left on the coffee table, Chantal began cleaning books one by one. When she reached her stereo perched on the second shelf from the top of the bookcase, she dusted it and turned it on, selecting the jazz playlist on her mp3 player. Turning up the volume, she began swaying along with a Cool Springs Jazz Quartet/Juju Song rendition of "Song in My Heart." As the tempo picked up and the piano melody line grew in complexity, Chantal pirouetted from the bookcase to the desk and began arranging papers, dancing along with the music.

A laugh stopped her in mid-sway. She looked through the office door, tensing instinctively. Although she'd left the front door open to get some fresh air into the cottage, few people Chantal knew would walk in without knocking. Not expecting company, she realized she'd made it incredibly easy for someone to break in and rob her.

The tension ebbed from her neck and shoulders as she saw it

was Sue, not a robber, who had decided to pay a visit. "Hey, girl!" she exclaimed, dropping the dust wand on the desk and rushing to hug her cousin. "I thought we weren't getting together until tomorrow."

"I hope you don't mind."

Chantal thought Sue held on a little longer than normal, but considering what they had been through, perhaps they both needed it. Realizing she was clinging to her cousin, Sue disengaged with a sheepish grin and stepped back. She plopped onto Chantal's blue microsuede sofa. "Since the story broke in the *Atherton Gazette*, the sheriff's department released me to talk about what happened. Before, they didn't even want me talking to you about it, and you were there." She shrugged and raised her eyebrows. "But now apparently it's okay, so can I dump on you for a while?"

"What are cousins for? Want some tea?" Chantal moved into the small kitchen and reached into the refrigerator for the cut glass tea pitcher she had swiped from her mother's pantry. She showed it to Sue. "Remember this?"

Sue smiled. "How much tea did your mother pour from that at those parties she was always hosting when we were kids?"

"Gallons. But she doesn't use it anymore, so I snagged it." Opening the cabinet between the refrigerator and sink, she pulled out two tall tumblers, also liberated from the main house, and poured each of them a glass of sweet tea, which she garnished with sprigs of fresh mint. She gave the glasses a swirl as she walked back to the sofa, where Sue sat on one end with her feet curled up under her. Taking up a similar position on the opposite end, she said, "So? What happened with the sheriff's department? Tell me everything."

"Remember the two new deputies that came out and took our statements? They've been given the case, so they talked to me some more and said they might need to interview you too." Chantal cut her eyes away from Sue, who grinned at the blush that suddenly colored her cheeks. "I thought so! That Marcus Thibodaux is one fine lookin' man, my friend," she commented. Chantal laughed and tea almost came out her nose. *Leave it to Sue to be scoping out prospective dates while being interviewed for the discovery of a dead body*, she thought, shaking her head and grinning.

Sue looked puzzled at Chantal's outburst. "Well, he is. I think he liked you too..."

"Oh, no, don't you start now!" Chantal exclaimed. "Ever since I came back to town, Mom has been trying to set me up with every eligible bachelor from Natchez to Vicksburg. I have enough matchmakers in my life, thank you very much!"

It was Sue's turn to laugh. "I know Aunt Helene's chief goal in life these days is to marry you off as soon as possible to a good man with a steady job and a decent income. I'll try to rein in my own Cupid impulses."

Removing the scrunchie from the ponytail that had only partially reined in her hair, Chantal returned to their previous topic. "So, have the cops made a ruling on the guy's death? Was it suicide, murder or what?"

"No, we haven't," a voice from the front door replied. "Mind if I come in for a minute? I was told Sue Atherton might be here."

The cousins exchanged surprised glances and Sue silently mouthed, *It's him!* Chantal uncurled from the sofa and walked to the front door. "Please, come in," she said as she held the screen door open. "I don't know if you remember me from the other day, Deputy Thibodaux. I'm Chantal Atherton, and you already know my cousin Sue."

The deputy removed his hat as he entered the house and offered her his hand. "Of course I remember you, Miss Atherton. No need to be so formal; my friends call me Marc." He smiled as he spoke, and his deep blue eyes seemed to light up with the gesture.

"Marc it is, then. And please call me Chantal." She smiled in return, while an unaccustomed flutter started in the pit of her stomach. As she half-turned to wave him into the cottage, she caught a glimpse of her reflection in the mirror above the console table. Her eyes sparkled and her cheeks were bright pink.

Letting Marc pass into the living room, she followed with downcast eyes. *That mahogany hair, and those blue eyes – so handsome! No, Chantal, don't go there. Remember Kansas?*

Oblivious to the turmoil trailing behind him, Marc joined Sue on the sofa and explained he wanted to stop by and update her on the case.

Chantal wandered into the kitchen and fixed another glass of tea, taking advantage of the cold air from the refrigerator to cool her cheeks and regain her composure. Back in the living room, she set the tea on a coaster on the coffee table and picked up her own glass as she moved to the closest armchair. Marc glanced her way and thanked her for the drink, and there was that butterfly-inducing smile again. Chantal sat, thankful the chair was right behind her; she literally felt weak in the knees.

Turning back to Sue, Marc asked, "Did you notice anything near the body that our people might have overlooked – a wallet, Medic Alert bracelet, anything? We didn't find any identification on him, and he isn't in the system – no fingerprint match in the NCIC database or the others we checked, no dental records matching the imprint and x-rays of his teeth our medical examiner made. It's like he didn't exist."

Sue searched her memory of the day and shrugged. "Sorry. Wish I could help, but after falling over the body and losing my breakfast in the kudzu, I didn't investigate any further." She glanced at Chantal and went on, "I didn't even pick up the vine I dropped, let alone poke around to see what else might be lying nearby. In fact, I think I lost a good pair of vine cutters in there. I haven't seen them since, and I didn't have the heart to go look for them."

"Oh, you mean these?" Marc pulled a pair of vine cutters, enclosed in a clear zip bag, out of the pocket of his shirt. "Once we tested them for evidence and confirmed they had no connection to the body, I realized they might be yours. That was the other reason I wanted to check in with you; I figured you might be missing them."

"You sweet man!" Sue exclaimed as she took the cutters from him. "They're my best pair and I hated the thought I might have lost them, but I couldn't go back there..." She swallowed and shook her head.

"Trust me, I understand," Marc said. "It's hard enough on us law enforcement people to deal with such things. I know it had to have been a major shock to you. Don't let it stop you from harvesting, though; I've seen your work, and it's really good. Bought a basket for my mother at the Kudzu Fest, in fact." He grinned. "Besides, if you don't help keep the stuff under control, it might take over the whole town!"

Sue breathed a shaky laugh. "Thanks again. Hey, do you want to meet Chantal and me for lunch tomorrow at Taco Loco? Say, around noon?"

"I'd love to. I've been meaning to go there ever since I moved to Atherton." Marc stood. "I need to get back on patrol now. No need to get up – I'll let myself out. It was good to see you again, Sue. Chantal, it was a real pleasure seeing you again too. I'm looking forward to our lunch tomorrow." Tipping his hat, he grinned as he left.

"My, my, my," Sue quipped in an extra thick drawl as she watched her cousin watch Marc leave, "I do declare, Chantal, I think you are sweet on our new deputy!"

"Oh, hush!" Chantal threw a throw pillow at Sue. "I am no such thing!"

But those bright pink cheeks told a different story and they both knew it.

CHAPTER 4

So, he's handsome; so what? Get a grip, Chantal! With a resolute toss of her head, Chantal tried to dismiss the notion she might be attracted to Marcus Thibodaux. Grabbing her cell phone and purse off the console table, she left for work at the bank founded by her great-grandfather and currently operated by her father.

Midtown Bank was literally in the middle of town; hence the name. The Atherton men may not have been an imaginative bunch when it came to business names, but they were very good at managing finances, and the bank had survived through the lean years and thrived in the more prosperous ones.

The bank job wasn't her ideal choice for a career move, but it meant she could try to keep an eye on her father's health while maintaining a flexible work schedule. She worked 7:30 a.m. to 5:30 p.m. Mondays through Thursdays with an hour off for lunch. On Fridays, she went to the office from 8 to noon then took off for the weekend. She generally spent evenings in either the Atherton estate's main house or the jewelry studio in the back bedroom of her cottage. Her life was simple, but she was content with it – at least, she had been until yesterday...

Shaking her head at her own silliness, Chantal walked faster as she completed the short trek from the Atherton estate to the bank. She used the back entrance, not to avoid her coworkers, but because it was the fastest way to get to her desk, since her father's office suite was behind the vault. She dropped her purse in the lower right drawer of her desk, started her computer, then headed into the break room, where she used the new one-cup brewer to make a cup of French vanilla flavored mild roast.

While the brewer decanted, she pulled liquid coffee creamer, also French vanilla, out of the refrigerator and poured a generous portion of creamer and a packet of stevia into the mug. Cup in hand, she strolled back to her office, humming and blowing on her coffee before that all-important first sip of the day.

"Good morning, Chantal," chirped Kelli, a young new teller who always sounded as though she never had a bad day in her life. "You seem more cheerful than usual. Anything new in your life?"

Chantal paused, half smiled as she glanced into her cup and then at Kelli. "Maybe..."

Kelli giggled. "Mysterious..." She walked into the break room and put her salad in the refrigerator. "Last day of training; after today I go on staff full time."

Chantal wished her a good day, then finished the short walk back to her office without encountering anyone else. The bank didn't open until 9, but several new tellers were finishing an orientation week that required them to be there at 8.

Kelli's friendly question upset Chantal a little, though she did her best to conceal her reaction. She wasn't looking for a man in her life, so why was this guy she had just met taking over her every waking thought? Was it those cornflower blue eyes that lit up when he smiled or the smooth voice that made something in her go "mmmm" as though she had eaten a Ghirardelli double chocolate chunk brownie...

Enough already, Chantal! It's out of the question, so stop it! She sighed and keyed in her computer's password.

A quick glance at her Inbox confirmed the morning would fly by; her father had left her several items to tackle. Fridays were typically slow for telephone calls, since Martin usually was either on the golf course, out of town on business, or in the community generating goodwill for the bank through his civic involvements. In this small town named after the bank owner's founding great-great-grandfather, folks knew Martin Atherton would not be at his desk on a Friday morning, so the only interruptions Chantal ever had on the last day of her work week were from out-of-town callers who weren't familiar with his schedule.

This meant she would be able to tackle the spreadsheets, letters and database update without the distractions that typically came with answering the telephone. And since she was alone, she could listen to some music without bothering her father, who preferred silence in the workplace. She clicked open her preferred media player and started the first song on one of the jazz CDs she'd ripped into the computer, then minimized the player and opened the first spreadsheet.

Four hours and two cups of coffee later, Chantal was finished for the day. She put the documents she'd completed into her father's Inbox, turned off her computer, tidied up and locked the back office, then walked through the front of the bank, waving goodbye to her coworkers. The staff – and most of the customers – returned her wave as she left to meet Sue and Marc for lunch at Taco Loco, a block away from the bank.

Reaching the restaurant first, she ordered a glass of sweet tea at the counter, then sat at the booth she preferred for its unobstructed view of Main Street. People-watching while she sipped her tea and waited for Sue and Marc to arrive, Chantal nodded in greeting to a young couple and older man who entered and sat at an adjacent booth. Luis's niece Anamaria stopped at Chantal's table with the three menus she had requested, then moved to the next booth and offered the occupants a set of menus and took their drink orders. Anamaria, a 20-year-old student at the local community college, had a ready smile and sunny disposition that endeared her to the restaurant's customers.

As Anamaria returned to the kitchen with the other diners' orders, Chantal heard the older man at the next table comment, "I think she was flirting with me. Do you think she was?" The woman replied, "Down, boy. She's too young for you."

Chantal tried to suppress a giggle but couldn't stop herself. As she regained her composure, Sue entered the restaurant, followed a moment later by Marc. If she hadn't seen them walk up from opposite directions, she would think they had arrived together. For a moment, she felt a twinge of what she could only call jealousy toward Sue, which irked her. It seemed her heart was determined to feel something for Marc regardless of her head's advice. Problem was, last time she let herself fall for a guy, it ended very badly for her. *Yeah, but Marc's a cop. He would never...*

She stopped the thought before it translated into an expression she'd have to explain away or lie about, and instead smiled and waved at Sue and Marc as they spotted her. Another wave brought Anamaria over to take their drink orders; she returned a few minutes later with two glasses of sweet tea and an order of homemade queso blanco dip and warm tortilla chips, then left to give them a little more time to decide what they wanted to eat.

Chantal decided to order the carnitas naranjadas, a dish made with diced pork tenderloin marinated in a sweet and spicy orange sauce and then roasted. Sue asked for her favorite, paella, and Marc ordered a plate of steak fajitas. All three dove into the chips and queso and started talking about their days almost simultaneously. Chantal laughed and said, "Okay, Sue, you first."

"Not much to tell, really," Sue mumbled around a mouthful of food. Swallowing, she continued, "I went kudzu harvesting this morning – no, not *that* patch, Marc –then spent the rest of the morning processing the new vines and storing them. I have a couple of basket orders to fill, but between processing vines and visiting with Attie Mae, my morning pretty well flew by."

"How is Aunt Attie? I haven't seen her in a while."

"Feisty as ever, Chantal. She told me you better get your heinie out there and say hi to her soon, too."

Chantal laughed. "Yeah, I can bet she did. She'll probably ply me with tomato relish or some such when I do go out there, and grill me for every last little detail of my ... life." She had been about to say "my love life," but caught herself in time to avoid the slip. Sue noticed the tiny pause, though, and smirked as she raised her eyebrows and sipped her tea. Chantal momentarily glared at Sue in silent reply. Marc, who was reaching for another tortilla chip, seemed to miss the exchange between the cousins.

"So, Marc," Sue asked, turning to the deputy sitting across from the women, "how has your day been so far? Oh, I'm sorry," she added with a giggle as he pointed to his chewing mouth, "by all means, finish that off first."

Marc grinned as he chased the chip/queso combo down with a bit of tea. "Actually, there has been a development on the case." He sat up straighter in the booth and put on a serious face. Chantal and Sue glanced at each other, puzzled, then began to chuckle as Marc did a fairly good impression of his boss, Sheriff Tom Aikers. "After a thorough and ex-hau-stive investigation of the facts and evidence, as well as a com-plete autopsy of the victim, we have de-ter-mined that the man in question was a homeless transient who died of a drug o-verdose." Marc had the man's "press conference" speech patterns down pat, right down to his annoying habit of drawing words out with random pauses.

"So," he continued in his normal voice, "case closed. The guy was an unfortunate victim of his own heroin addiction, apparently. There were needle tracks all up and down both arms, including one new enough to have been caused by his last hit – the one that must have killed him."

Sue breathed a sigh. "I feel so badly for him, but at least now I don't have to be looking over my shoulder every time I go out to harvest vines, wondering when the poor man's killer will come after me because I found him."

Chantal gave Sue a quick one-armed hug across the shoulders. "I know it's been nerve-wracking, cous, but it's over now."

Sue toyed with her straw for a moment as she stared into space in the general direction of the chips basket, then looked up with a small smile. "Yes, it is. Life moves on, and I have the Fall Festival at the county fairground to get ready for. I'm thinking about doubling my booth size this year – wanna come in on it with me, Chantal?"

Chantal hesitated, but only for a moment. "Why not? I've been making jewelry at a fairly good pace since I got back into town, and those kudzu leaf pendants you made for me have really worked out well. I'm sure I can get together enough inventory to share the booth with you. Do I need to apply, too, or will I be covered on your application? I know you already turned it in and got accepted."

Sue looked sheepish. "I took a chance you'd accept my offer and went on and put both of our names and items for sale on the application. You owe me $25."

"You!" Chantal swiped at Sue playfully and chuckled. "I'll get lunch today, okay?"

"Oh no, you won't," Marc rumbled from the other side of the booth. "It's not often I get to treat two beautiful women to a meal. Neither one of you is paying."

"Okay!" Sue and Chantal accepted in unison. Sue added, "We're not about to turn down an offer like that!"

Anamaria arrived with their orders on a large serving tray. Without asking what was whose, she placed each one's order in front of them, gave them all a big smile and said she'd be right back with more sweet tea. A few moments later, she freshened up all three glasses, placed the pitcher on the table and returned to the kitchen.

"I like her," Chantal remarked. "Luis has done a great job with this place and with training his people to give excellent service."

"True," agreed Sue as she blew on a forkful of paella. "Who would ever have thought Loco Louie would end up owning a restaurant and cornering the local market on such comida rica, hmmm?"

"Showoff!" Chantal teased, then added to Marc, "Sue was the second best student in our Spanish class in high school. Luis was best, of course, but it would have been weird for him not to be, since he and his family are Latino."

"Where are they from originally?" Marc asked as he constructed his first fajita and took a bite. His eyes lit up as he discovered how good "Loco Louie" was at cooking Mexican food.

"We're not sure," Chantal answered, scooping up a piece of

pork and some rice. "Luis never told us what country his grandparents came from, but his family has been in the area for three generations now. Luis is the first in his family to go to college; he earned a bachelor's degree in restaurant management before coming back to Atherton and opening Taco Loco. His family is very proud of his achievements." She took her first bite of carnitas naranjadas and smiled, pleased at her excellent meal choice.

"As they should be," Marc commented. "I was first in my family to earn a degree, too. It's no small feat these days, what with the cost of going to college and all. Luis and his family have every right to be proud." He smiled. "I have a friend back in Louisiana, Tijean, who was in the same situation. He went to college and got a bachelor's in business, then took his education back home and put everything he had into a charter boat business, specializing in saltwater fishing trips in the Gulf. He was going gangbusters until Katrina hit. Lost his house, all the family vehicles and his dog, but he managed to save his boat and tackle, so now he's rebuilding the business. He told me if it weren't for his business degree, he would have had no idea how to go about getting up and running again."

Chantal and Sue nodded in grim silence, not knowing what to say. They both knew people who had suffered to varying degrees from the impact of the 2005 hurricane, but no one they knew had had to rebuild their entire lives with nothing but a boat and a few fishing poles as tools. In Atherton, people had roof damage and some fallen trees and had gone without electricity for the better part a week following the storm, like almost everyone else in southwest and central Mississippi had, but no one in the area had lost property, vehicles or family members.

Marc saw their somber expressions and shrugged. "Whatcha gonna do? Storms blow through; life goes on. You salvage what you can, replace what you need, and keep going. Don't be sad, mes cheres," he said, lapsing into Cajun French momentarily, "we're a strong bunch down on the bayou. We know hurricanes are part of life in south Louisiana, and we deal with what we have to when we have to. It's kind of like Mardi Gras – as a cop, I've definitely seen the bad side of it, but the season brings a lot of fun and beauty too. You gotta deal with the one if you want to enjoy the other."

Chantal smiled softly. *I'd like to see his Louisiana sometime...*

The rest of the meal passed in small talk between bites. Anamaria kept the tea fresh and brought them each a serving of tres leches cake on the house; Luis insisted, she said. Although all three said they couldn't possibly eat anything else, after one bite they changed their minds and devoured the rich cake made with three milks – regular, evaporated and sweetened condensed – mmming and oohing after the first couple of bites. Realizing they were all making the same noises, they laughed and finished off their desserts without further vocalizations.

To end the meal, Anamaria served them each a small cup of light, sweet coffee – café con leche, she explained as she told them it also was compliments of the chef. Chantal smiled and thanked Anamaria in Spanish, then switched back to English and asked her if she could prevail upon her uncle to come out of the kitchen and say hello. Anamaria shook her head and answered, "He said you would ask me this, and he wanted me to tell you he regrets he cannot visit at the moment; he has a catering job at the country club to prepare for tonight. An engagement party with a Mexican fiesta theme. Perhaps next time?"

Chantal nodded and thanked Anamaria again for the excellent service she had provided them. Marc took the ticket as Ana put it on the table and handed her a $50 bill. "Keep the change, young lady. You earned it, and your uncle should be very proud of you."

"No, señor," Ana replied as she blushed a deep crimson. "I cannot take such a large tip."

Marc insisted with his patented smile, and Ana's defenses crumbled. She thanked him repeatedly, then practically ran to the cash register to complete the transaction and show her tip to Luis. "We better scoot," Marc said with a laugh. "Loco Louie might come out here and try to make me take my tip back!"

CHAPTER 5

"Now what's gotten into that girl?" Helene muttered as she replaced the phone receiver in its cradle. She turned to Chantal, who was texting Sue as she walked through the front parlor on her way to check the mail station in her mother's home office. "Chantal, do you have any idea why Brigitte would want to come by and take all her belongings home?"

Chantal stopped in mid-text and stared. "Well, Mother, it is her stuff. I'm surprised she hasn't come for it before now."

"You don't understand, dear. Brigitte has always said she didn't want certain items at the duplex because she didn't want to risk having them stolen – her better jewelry and the pieces she inherited from Grandmother Atherton, for instance – and she didn't have room for some of her larger art pieces and furniture. That was why I didn't mind keeping those things here in her former suite."

"I have no idea, then. Maybe she simply changed her mind – it is Brigitte we're talking about, after all."

Helene shrugged her right shoulder. "Perhaps. I suppose we can ask her when she comes by this afternoon."

Chantal paused, deciding what to share with her mother about the conversation with her sister the previous week. She didn't want to alarm Helene by telling her about the phone call she'd overheard a portion of – after all, she only heard a little bit of Brigitte's side and it could have meant anything – but she thought her mother should know about Brigitte's growing involvement with CUP.

"Mother, did I tell you I met with Brigitte Friday before last?" When Helene shook her head, Chantal continued, "I'm sorry; I thought I had. Anyway, she told me she hasn't been able to come over lately because she's very involved in a new organization she joined when she left First Baptist. The group is called Christians United for Peace."

Helene nodded. "I have heard of CUP; Terri Bridges at the country club mentioned something about them meeting at the old drive-in outside town. She said her son Jim is attending their meetings and seems much more focused on the spiritual areas of his life than he ever has been before. She said he can't stop talking about God, and about the group's leader, Joseph – what's his name, again? – oh yes, Joseph Zacharias. Wasn't he the young man who came to First Baptist as the new youth pastor and then left six months later claiming God told him to start 'a new work' in Atherton?"

"He's the one. Anyway, Brigitte is attending all the services – once on Wednesday, twice on Sunday, prayer meetings on Tuesday and hosting a small group meeting at the duplex on Thursdays. She said that was why she hadn't been by to see us."

"It's admirable she's throwing herself into this new thing so wholeheartedly," Helene replied, "but it still leaves Mondays, Fridays and Saturdays open, by my count, so her excuse doesn't wash."

Chantal chuckled. "I told her almost exactly the same thing. Maybe when she comes by to pick up her stuff, you can persuade her to stay for dinner tonight. It's Saturday, so she should be free, unless some other church event has suddenly popped up."

Helene smiled. "I think I'll go tell Rosalie to cook a little extra of everything in case she decides to stay. Thank you, dear, for updating me about Brigitte's situation. It still doesn't explain why she wants to take all her belongings out of the house, but at least I know she's busy and not mad at us about something."

CHAPTER 6

"Knock, knock. Is anyone home?" Brigitte called out as she entered the house. "Mother, I'm here to pick up my belongings. Mother?"

"Up here, dear, in your old suite," Helene's reply came from the second floor. "Chantal and I were getting some of your things ready to go in your car. Please come up."

Brigitte strolled up the stairs, eager to collect her things and leave but dreading the confrontation she expected. Reaching the second floor, she walked to the end of the hall where her former suite was located. As suites go, it wasn't very big –a normal-sized bedroom flanked by a small sitting room and even smaller half bathroom – but her mother insisted since it included all of the requisite rooms for a suite, it be called by its proper name.

As she entered the sitting room, Brigitte was taken back to her teenage years. Her mother hadn't changed the room one bit, and Brigitte suspected the same held true for the rest of the suite. Overwhelmed by nostalgia, she sat on the French provincial love seat and picked up a stuffed floppy-eared bunny she had carried everywhere for a couple of years during childhood. *I always hated the décor in here*, she mused, *but I loved this rabbit.*

She hugged the bunny as her mother and sister entered the room. Her mother rushed to embrace her, but Brigitte remained seated, so Helene had to settle for giving her daughter an awkward half-hug before stepping back. Chantal leaned on the doorway leading into the bedroom and watched the scene unfold between mother and daughter, wondering if her sister's agitation would manifest again as it had at Fuzzy Logic.

"Hi, honey. I'm so pleased you stopped by. Would you like a beverage or a snack?" Helene watched for any little indication Brigitte was going to relax and visit for a while, but she refused her mother's offer and wouldn't meet her eyes.

Gazing at the floor between them, she said, "Sorry, Mother, but I have other plans for the evening. For now, I'm going to take some of my smaller items. I'll be back with a truck and a couple of guys to move the heavier things tomorrow after church."

Helene sat down on the love seat and touched Brigitte on the shoulder. "Sweetheart, what's going on? Why are you so determined to push us out of your life? Have we hurt you or offended you in some way? Please, I want to understand." Brigitte stiffened and Helene removed her hand, noticing that Brigitte was shaking slightly. She looked at Chantal, lost as to how to reach her younger daughter, but all Chantal could do was shake her head and shrug.

"No, Mother," Brigitte finally answered, a tremor in her voice. "I'm simply going a different direction with my life than the rest of the family, and I don't want to be derailed from following the vision God has for me. I need some time and space to pursue this new thing, and I want..." She trailed off, uncertain how to continue. What she wanted to say would certainly cause a scene. Taking a deep breath, she decided to say it anyway. "I know what I'm doing, and it's what's best for me. Could you please respect my decisions?"

Helene stood up and turned away from Brigitte, looking again to Chantal for help. Chantal took her mother's place on the love seat and stared at Brigitte until her sister raised her head. The siblings locked gazes for a few moments, but Brigitte broke eye contact again and stared out the sitting room window, jaw tense and posture rigid.

It was Chantal's turn to take a deep cleansing breath, because what she really wanted to do was deck her little sister. This girl needed some discipline, and Christian or no, Chantal was becoming more and more willing to lay hands on the child – and not in a "let me pray for you, my sister" kind of way.

"Brigitte," she said when she had calmed down enough to speak without biting off her words, "I don't know what gave you the idea we wouldn't respect your decisions about your own life, but you need to drop the victim act. We're not trying to run or ruin your life; we just want you to drop into our lives occasionally."

Brigitte nodded, still staring out the window. It was as though she were agreeing with Chantal only because she knew it was expected of her, not because she actually believed her sister. Chantal looked at her mother and shrugged, then glared at the back of Brigitte's head.

"Mother, I'm sorry to do this to you, but I think I'll make other arrangements for supper tonight. Suddenly I feel I'm not going to be very good company. Sis, if you need my help getting any of this down to the car, text me. I'll be in the cottage."

Chantal turned and left the suite, her pace increasing to a near-run as she descended the stairs and burst out the back door. She ran laps around the walking path in the yard until she wore herself out trying to work off her anger instead of hitting someone or something. Finally, she slowed down and walked to her cottage, making an effort not to slam the door as she entered. Pulling a mixed berry wine cooler out of the fridge, she twisted off the top with as much force as she could muster and flung the cap in the general direction of the trash can. It ricocheted off the wall above the can and skittered to a halt in the middle of the kitchen floor. Ignoring it, Chantal flung herself into an armchair, put her feet on the ottoman and flipped open her cell phone.

Pressing 5 on her speed dial, she waited impatiently while the phone rang once, twice, three times before being answered. "Sue, it's your favorite cousin. Can you come by in a little while? I have some major venting to do. I'll order pizza..."

CHAPTER 7

"But Chantal, Brigitte's always been a bit on the flighty side," Sue protested around a bite of Hawaiian pizza. She chased it down with a sip of Coke. "What's so different this time?"

Chantal shook her head. "It *is* different, Sue. It's like she's trying to disown all of us or something. She keeps talking about God's vision for her life and how she can't let anyone or anything derail her from pursuing it. For goodness' sake, all we were doing was inviting her to dinner!" She bit into her pizza so hard her teeth clicked together audibly.

Sue jumped and reached into her jeans pocket. " 'Scuse me, cous; my phone's blowin' up." Sliding it open, she grinned. "It's Marc. He's wondering if we want to get together with him and a friend for – get this – pizza!" She laughed. "Should I invite them over?"

Chantal grimaced; she wanted to spend some girl time with Sue venting about Brigitte's odd behavior and trying to figure out what, if anything, could be done. Thinking about it for a minute, she realized a little objective input from a legal perspective might be what she needed, so she shrugged and nodded. "Sure. Ask him to pick up a couple of larges, though; we don't have enough here for four people. If he's taking requests, I'd like bacon cheeseburger." Sue pressed relayed the message; a few moments later the phone buzzed again and Sue confirmed the guys would be over as soon as they could pick up the pizzas.

"So," Chantal asked, "who's this friend Marc is bringing with him?"

"Idk – sorry, I mean I don't know." Sue replied with a giggle. "I had texting on the brain. Maybe his partner John – you know, the other deputy we met that day?"

"Could be. I guess we'll find out soon enough." Chantal hopped up and pulled more Styrofoam plates and napkins out of the pantry. "I hope they either like Coke or bring their own drinks, though; I sure don't see Marc Thibodaux as a wine cooler type of guy."

Sue laughed, nearly spitting out a bite of pineapple. "Don't say stuff like that while I'm chewin', girl!"

Chantal closed the pizza box and handed Sue a napkin. "Sorry. Let's finish off what we have on our plates and wait 'til they get here for the rest, okay?" Sue nodded and Chantal sat back down. "So, what about this situation with my flighty little sister? I'm baffled, and I don't know if we're overreacting or if it's something we should be worried about. Any ideas?"

Sue finished off the crust of her first piece of pizza. "Sorry, chica, I got nothin'. I think you should keep an eye on her for the time being. She's probably trying to establish a little independence, her own identity apart from the formidable Helene Atherton. No offense, cous, but Aunt Helene has a knack for trying to – shall we say, 'arrange' – the lives of everyone within her sphere of influence. I mean, look at your situation – sure you're here in the cottage instead of the main house, but she had this place built to coax you home. She knew you'd never agree to move back into the family manor, so she contracted the construction of this snug little abode. And here you are."

"True, Mom always has been kind of Martha-esque. Case in point: When I talk about her, it's 'Mom,' but when I talk to her, it's always 'Mother.' She'd have a major hissy fit if I were to be so informal as to call her 'Mom' to her face." Chantal sighed. "Sometimes I wish she were Helen Smith Atherton, not Helene, queen of Atherton."

"You see? If you feel that way, imagine how Brigitte feels."

"Yeah, I probably am overreacting..." Chantal trailed off and stood when the doorbell rang.

Moments later, Sue heard Marc in the entry saying in an exaggerated country drawl, "Evenin', ma'am. Did someone here order our special de-luxe ginormous pan pizza with everything on it? 'Cuz it's what my boss tole me ta bring, and if I cain't deliver it, I gotta eat the whole thang..." followed by laughter as Chantal backed into the living room. Marc and a tall, trim blond man with sparkling medium green eyes followed. Both were dressed in uniforms from Pied Piper, the local pizza joint.

Sue gasped and cracked up. "Sheriff's department pay is that crummy, Marc? You had to resort to moonlighting as a pizza delivery guy?"

Marc replied with a straight face, "No, we're undercover."

"Really?" Chantal chimed in, not believing him for a moment but playing along to see where he was going with it.

"Sure thing. We're investigating a rash of thefts, and Pied Piper agreed to let us pose as employees."

Chantal stared at the two men until they started laughing. "Okay, busted," Marc said. "I know the owner, and he agreed to let me borrow these uniforms and his own car so I could pull this prank."

Sue shook her head. "Get in here with that pizza, Marc. Is this who I think it is with you?"

Chantal made room on the kitchen counter for the pizzas, which were indeed huge and loaded down with the bacon cheeseburger toppings she'd requested, and handed the guys each a plate. "Dig in, y'all," she invited. "We still have some Hawaiian left from our original order. Help yourselves."

Marc spoke up. "We will, but do you mind if we bless it first? I'm assuming you've already given thanks, but since we just got here..."

Chantal glanced at Sue, sheepish at their oversight and also puzzled, since Marc made no such suggestion at their meal the previous day. Sue, equally confused, shrugged. "Please do," Chantal told Marc as she bowed her head. The others followed suit as Marc began.

"Father God, I want to thank You for the food we're about to receive. I ask You to bless it to our nourishment and bless us to Your service. Thank You for the fellowship we're sharing and for the friends You've given me in this new town. In Jesus' Name I pray, Amen."

The other three echoed his Amen, then there was a general rush for the pizza boxes. As Chantal offered Marc a slice of Hawaiian pizza, she said, "Marc, I hope I'm not putting you on the spot, but Sue and I are curious about something. Why the blessing for tonight's meal and not one for yesterday?"

Marc glanced at his companion as he explained, "I'm kind of new to the whole Christian life, and I don't always remember stuff like thanking the Lord for a meal before I dive into it. I had a reminder at lunch today that we should always be grateful and never ashamed to show our gratitude, especially in public."

Chantal nodded. "I understand. I grew up going to church and Sunday School, and I must admit I forget to say grace more often than not."

Only after they were all seated in the living room did Marc realize he hadn't answered Sue's question. "My partner John Borden here is the reason I remembered to bless the pizza. Y'all met him the other day out at the kudzu patch. John, Sue and Chantal are cousins and heiresses to the fortunes of Atherton. John is a recent transplant from Tupelo."

"Marc!" Sue exclaimed. "Don't you be telling such stories! About the only thing I'm an heiress to is the cottage I'm already living in and every kudzu patch within a 50-mile radius." John looked confused, but before Sue could elaborate, Chantal spoke up.

"Yeah," she echoed Sue. "I may be an Atherton, but it doesn't mean I'm an heiress to anything either, my friend. Unless you count being the daughter of Helene Atherton, reigning drama queen of the county, as an inheritance..."

"Oh? Surely Miss Helene isn't so bad," John said. "I've met her at an event or two, and she always seems so gracious and poised."

Chantal nodded. "It's all part of the persona she's built for herself. Her very name is an illustration of what I mean. When she was in high school she took a French class where the students had to choose a French name to be called by the teacher and their classmates for the whole year. My mom's birth name was Helen, so she chose Helene – and kept it. After high school she had it legally changed. Then, when my sister and I were born, she saddled us with French names, too. This despite the fact she's never been to France and has, as far as we know, no French blood in her family tree whatsoever."

John shook his head, disbelief in his expression.

"No, really, that's only the appetizer. There's more, and it's all public knowledge..." By the time Chantal finished defending her mother's claim to the town's drama queen title, Sue and Marc were also shaking their heads and all three of them were laughing. Of course, Sue already knew all the stories, but Chantal's delivery and her imitation of her mother's mannerisms were flawless.

As she wound down, Marc quipped, "So Chantal, tell us how you really feel..."

She sighed. "Truth is, I love my mom, but sometimes her personality is a bit... much."

"Maybe that's Brigitte's problem, too," Sue commented. "Could be why she's acting so defensive lately."

"Who's Brigitte?" Marc asked.

"My younger sister, the other Atherton girl stuck with a French name. Lately she's been acting really standoffish, but today she came by the house to get some of her things, stuff she hasn't cared about at all until now. When Mom asked why she was trying to push us away, she said something about needing time and space to pursue the new vision God has for her life, then she practically bit Mom's head off and said, and I quote here, 'Could you please respect my decisions?' All we wanted her to do was stay for dinner!"

She looked around the room. Sue and John looked sympathetic, but Marc seemed genuinely upset. "Marc? Your hands are trembling. Are you okay?"

He glanced down, took a deep breath and looked back up at Chantal. "I hope I'm wrong, but it sounds to me like your sister may be involved in a cult."

Chantal stared at him and thought about the last couple of interactions she'd had with her sister. Certain things suddenly made sense: Brigitte's agitation at the café and her phone conversation as she was leaving there, her behavior earlier in the day when she came to pick up her belongings, even her wanting to take her stuff – probably to sell it and give the money to the cult, Chantal now realized. Everything indicated someone had some kind of hold on her. Still, why was Marc reacting like that?

"Okay, it might explain some things, but it doesn't tell me why you were shaking," she pointed out. "Back to my question: are you okay?"

Marc stood, collected everyone's plates and threw them away. Retrieving a Coke from the refrigerator, he took a long drink and walked back into the living room. Chantal watched him and waited for an answer.

"No one else has heard this, not even John," he finally said. "I came here to get away from my hometown, New Era, Louisiana. I moved back there after Katrina to help the family get on its feet, but then my older brother Jake died. He was in a doomsday cult whose members committed mass suicide a year or so ago. I couldn't handle how depressed the family was afterward, so I took the first job I could snag." He sat heavily in the armchair he'd been occupying before. "I guess that's why I was trembling. I'd hate for anyone else to go through what we have, and your description of Brigitte's behavior is frighteningly similar to what Jake's was as the cult secured its stranglehold on him."

Chantal reached across the coffee table and touched Marc on the arm. "I'm sorry I brought up such bad memories for you."

"It's not your fault, Chantal," he replied softly, battling the lump in his throat. "I hope – no, I pray – I'm wrong about Brigitte."

CHAPTER 8

That night, Chantal had several nightmares about Brigitte being pulled into a cult. The dreams all ended with the cult members committing mass suicide like Heaven's Gate in California in 1997, or engaging in a gunfight with federal agents like the followers of David Koresh did in Waco in 1993. She woke up drenched in sweat and screaming her sister's name.

Sunday was uneventful – she went to church, returned home and spent the day making jewelry, watching old movies and doing laundry. Sunday night, though, was a repeat of the previous one, leaving Chantal frazzled and sleep deprived.

Dragging herself out of bed and into the kitchen Monday morning, she microwaved the last two pieces of Saturday's pizza and had them with a Coke for breakfast. Not the most nutritious way to start the day, she knew, but she didn't feel like cooking. Between the bad dreams and Marc's story of his brother's suicide, she was scared for her sister.

As she sat at her dining table with her leftover Hawaiian pizza and carbonated caffeine, she determined to look into the background of Joseph Zacharias. If he was indeed building a cult, she wanted some concrete data to give Marc. Since CUP was meeting outside town, the group's activities would fall under the sheriff's jurisdiction, rather than the police department's.

With a positive course of action in mind, Chantal felt better. She may not be able to get Brigitte to stop her involvement in

CUP right away, but at least she could gather some information to present to her sister and, if necessary, the sheriff's department and the deputy she found herself growing fond of despite her best efforts to the contrary. His vulnerability Saturday evening as he talked about his brother only made him more attractive to her.

Okay, stop that train of thought right now, Chantal chided herself as she washed her plate and rinsed out the weekend's Coke cans to put in the recycling bin. *No more romances for you, remember?*

Ten minutes later she was showered, dressed and leaving for work. She had tucked a small notepad, left over from her reporter days, into her purse. Later on she might need her digital camera, but for now her information gathering would be on paper only.

She locked her cottage door and detoured to the back door of the main house, where she put her trash into the rollaway can and dropped the Coke cans into the blue bin destined for the curb after Rosalie finished making breakfast for Martin and Helene. Rosalie Terrence, the family's longtime housekeeper, insisted she be the one to take out the trash and recycling, although Chantal had offered repeatedly to help out. Chantal had finally given up on the idea after three months and yielded to Rosalie's wishes.

Having a few extra minutes before she had to be at the bank, Chantal walked over to Fuzzy Logic and bought a medium mochaccino instead of waiting to have her usual cup of flavored coffee from the office machine. As she doubled back to the bank, she passed a young man on the corner dressed in a Christians

United for Peace t-shirt and jeans that looked like they'd been distressed from wear rather than being sold that way. Appearing to be in his late teens to early 20s, he had longish black hair and tired blue eyes and was so skinny Chantal wondered if he'd eaten lately.

He was handing out leaflets, so she took one, thinking it might be a good place to start her research. Putting it into her purse, she smiled at him and continued on her way.

At the bank, she placed the leaflet and notebook on her desk. As she did so, she noticed there were several items in her Inbox, so she put the research plans aside for later. The morning passed quickly as she typed letters, updated spreadsheets and fielded phone calls before meeting with her father and catching him up on the little that had transpired during his absence the previous Friday.

Sitting in Martin Atherton's mahogany and leather office with its walls decorated by pictures of bank milestones and personal events in his life – hunting trophies, golf tournament wins and the like – Chantal decided since she seldom had time alone with her father, this might be the only opportunity to bring up her concerns about Brigitte. "Father," she began, "I wanted to talk to you about something that's bothering me. Do you have a few minutes to spare?"

Martin glanced at his calendar then his watch and replied, "Actually, I'm speaking at the Rotary Club in about 15 minutes, so I need to leave now. Why don't you join your mother and me for dinner this evening? Perhaps we can talk then."

"Fine with me, but I'd like to talk with you alone before I bring Mother into this conversation. Can we have a little time in your study after dinner?"

Martin looked puzzled but he assented. "I'll see you at 6 sharp, dear." He stood and took his hat from the top of the hat rack. "I won't be back in the office this afternoon. After Rotary Club, I have meetings with potential corporate clients. I will be home for dinner, though, so we'll talk then."

Saying goodbye without waiting for Chantal's reply, he left through the front of the bank. He often did that on his way to lunch, both to maintain his image as a friendly neighborhood bank president and to gauge the traffic volume of the bank and the busyness of its staff. The tellers and account managers were used to his sudden appearances, so they simply carried on as usual, acknowledging him with smiles and waves.

Chantal locked her father's office and followed him out of the bank for lunch at Kudzu Café, a local diner with daily specials and generous desserts. Sally Jennings, owner and head cook, was serving a traveling businessman at the counter when Chantal entered and sat at her usual corner table. Monday was red beans and rice day, but Chantal was in the mood for something lighter, so when Sally's daughter Lisa came to take her order, she asked for the Chicken Waldorf Salad and a glass of sweet mint tea. Lisa returned a few moments later with Chantal's drink and told her the salad would be out shortly. Chantal thanked Lisa, sipped her tea and observed the diner's activity level.

It was a typical Monday crowd – city and county government employees, business staffers on their lunch break, and a few travelers like the businessman at the counter. As Chantal was being served her order, she saw Sue walk in and waved her over to the table.

"Hi, Sue. Anything special going on today, or are you stopping in for lunch?"

"Stopping in to eat and to see if Sally needs any new inventory in the gift shop," Sue said as she sat. The "gift shop" was an antique china hutch tucked into the corner of the diner near the cash register. Sally converted it into a display where she showcased Sue's baskets and handmade stationery year round and her kudzu jelly when it was in season. She invited Chantal to include some of her jewelry, but Chantal had yet to make a decision.

Sue waved to Lisa, who brought her a glass of sweet tea and asked if she wanted the special or something else. "I'm in the mood for a BLT, hold the T, on wheat with light mayo and sweet potato fries on the side. Can I get that?"

"Sure thing! Coming right up."

"Guess Saturday's pizza fest flung a craving for bacon on you, huh?" Chantal grinned. "I'm going semi-healthy today. I ate leftover pizza for breakfast and I'm having dinner with the parents tonight. There's no telling what calorie-laden concoction Rosalie will serve. So for lunch, it's salad."

After Sue's sandwich and fries arrived, the two paused for a silent blessing of the meal before digging in; their dinner with Marc and John had made them aware of their shortcomings in the "thanking the Lord for this food" department.

"You know, I've been uneasy since Marc told us about his brother," Chantal said. "I've had nightmares two nights running about Brigitte being in a cult and ending up dead."

Sue shook her head. "I sure hope she's not tangled up in anything like that. I've read horror stories about families trying to get their children back to normalcy after being in a cult. It's a long, hard process and it doesn't always work."

"I'm going to try and talk to Dad after dinner about my suspicions," Chantal replied. "I hope he listens and doesn't dismiss my concerns out of hand."

"Your dad? No way!" Sue exclaimed. "It's not as though you spent your whole childhood trying to get his attention while he was busy with bank and community projects."

"Not at all. And it's not as if he thought our problems were petty dramas and Mom's business to handle."

"Sure, and Aunt Helene was never too busy with her own community involvements to give you and Brigitte some of her time. And heaven forbid anyone accuse her of paying attention to you girls merely to enhance her reputation or the family's image in the community."

Chantal shook her head. "I know we're joking about it, but the truth is, Rosalie mothered us more than Mother did." She sighed. "I did my best to win their approval, but I don't think they ever noticed. When I finally figured that out, I was in college. That's when I decided to follow my heart and switch from business to journalism. I wasn't going to follow my dad's career path. So much for that..."

"I know. And you were happy traveling and writing for the magazines and papers. But you've always been the dutiful older daughter. I knew you'd be back before long when Uncle Martin started having health problems." Sue ate a fry. "At least you didn't go Brigitte's route and rebel to get their attention. Breaking curfew, sneaking out of the house at night to hang out at the river with her friends, spray-painting graffiti on the town water tower? It's a miracle she got away with so much."

"Not really. Every time she got caught, the officer brought her home and Mom and Dad handed out some punishment that was too mild to be effective. That was about the extent of things. Nothing we did ever brought more than mild approval or disapproval. That's why we eventually went our own ways. We quit trying to either please or hurt our parents." Chantal picked at her salad until Sue shook her out of her reverie.

"Look alive, girl; we're about to have company," she whispered, then raised her voice. "Hi, guys! Come join us – we haven't gotten too far into lunch yet."

Chantal looked up to see Marc and John heading for their table. She shot a quick glare at Sue, who grinned like the Cheshire cat in *Alice in Wonderland* and moved to the chair to

Chantal's left so the guys could sit across from the cousins.

Marc and John removed their hats and hung them on the nearby coat rack before taking the vacant seats, Marc next to Chantal and John next to Sue. Lisa saw the men sit down and bustled over to take their orders – two sweet teas and two cheeseburgers with everything. Marc ordered sweet potato fries, while John asked for regular. The deputies insisted the women continue eating instead of waiting on their food to arrive.

Sue told the guys they were discussing the conversation the four of them had Saturday evening about Brigitte and cults. Chantal piped in, "I'm really worried, Marc. I can't help but think you may be right about my sister. What can we do?" She didn't mention she was starting her own investigation; she strongly suspected he might try to discourage her.

Marc touched her hand. "If you think this CUP group might be more than simply a new church, we can look into it. For now, we'll need to keep it informal and on our own time, since there's no charge against anyone, but we'll be glad to check it out, right, John?"

John nodded. "I once worked a case in Tupelo where a dead calf was found on a church doorstep the day after Halloween. I was called in to investigate, and we discovered there was a satanic cult operating on the outskirts of town. I'm not sure it's satanism in this case, but it is possible we're dealing with a cult. Even so, unless we have evidence of illegal activity, we can't begin a formal department investigation – but we can do some research on our

56   *Chantal's Call*

off time."

Chantal sighed her relief. "Thanks, y'all. I feel better knowing you think this is worth checking out and I'm not merely feeling paranoid because of some pizza-induced nightmares." She removed her purse from the back of her chair. "Hate to eat and run, but my break is almost up. Talk to you later, Sue. Marc, John, keep me posted, okay? Thanks again, guys."

CHAPTER 9

When Chantal returned to the bank, she had nothing other than the mail to occupy her time, and the telephone was unusually quiet for a Monday, so after processing the small stack of letters and birthday cards addressed to her father, she started her investigating CUP and Joseph Zacharias. The usual search engine queries – Google, Altavista, Yahoo and Ask Jeeves – yielded no results for Christians United for Peace. When she ran the same search for Joseph Zacharias, she again came up empty.

Not sure what to do next, Chantal decided to call First Baptist and see if she could get any background information on Zacharias before she did anything else. She called the church office, but the phone rang six times and went to voice mail. Uncertain how to word her message, she hung up without leaving one. If she were still working as a reporter, she wouldn't have hesitated to identify herself, state her request for information and leave a contact number. Since she couldn't claim reporter status, she didn't know what to say without either lying or raising suspicions she didn't want to stir up yet.

Drumming her fingers on the desk, she considered options. As a private citizen, she didn't have many. Sighing, she looked at the CUP flyer. *I may have to attend a few meetings if I want to find out anything.*

She closed her eyes and shook her head, dismissing the idea. When she opened her eyes again, her glance fell on the small pile of birthday cards on the corner of her desk. *Oops. Dad's birthday is in two weeks and I haven't gotten him anything yet. Can't go giftless to his 65th; Mom would pitch a fit.*

She went back to Google and searched for baseball-themed gifts. Her father was a Braves fan and she considered a number of Atlanta items, from caps to jerseys and hoodies, but her dad already had several caps and he wasn't the kind of guy to wear team logo shirts.

However, he did have a penchant for novelty gifts, as long as they weren't too tacky, so she Googled "novelty gifts" and checked out a site called "What on Earth?" that came up in the search results. They offered the perfect item, a pepper grinder housed inside a fake baseball bat made out of beech wood. It came in two sizes; she chose the larger one, almost 29 inches long.

Completing the order, she grinned mischievously. *He's gonna love it,* she thought as she pictured him showing it off to his buddies when they cooked out. She selected USPS Priority Mail and entered her private mailbox as the shipping address so her father wouldn't inadvertently see his present ahead of time.

Chantal turned her attention back to the investigation. She decided to call Ryan Jennings, son of the Kudzu Café's owner and managing editor of the *Atherton Gazette*. The local paper was published three times a week and featured mostly local interest stories, although the occasional national headline made its way to the front page – things like presidential election results and NFL drafts of former local high school gridiron heroes.

Ryan was another high school classmate who left to earn his degree and some work experience before returning home, and he was the only other journalist to come out of their graduating class. Unlike Chantal, Ryan had been involved in journalism almost from the time he could write. His father was managing editor before him, and he spent two years of high school editing the school paper and most of his summers since eighth grade interning at the *Gazette*.

Chantal hummed along with the hold music while she waited for Ryan to pick up; the song was something country, which she didn't normally listen to, but she recognized it vaguely. Since the paper used a local radio station for its hold sounds, she heard a car dealer's commercial and an anti-drug public service announcement before Ryan finally answered.

"Hey, Chantal! What's kickin'?" They had dated him briefly in high school; she remembered him as a lanky teenager with sandy brown hair and inquisitive hazel eyes. His appearance hadn't changed much since, and she could picture him on the phone, leaning back in his chair, feet up on the desk, sporting his trademark grin.

Ryan always had been easygoing – unusual in a newspaper editor, but it worked for him. In his reporter days, that laidback demeanor disarmed his interview subjects – a fact he used to great advantage as he first put the interviewee at ease before hitting with the hard questions.

"Nothing much, Ry. How about with you?" Chantal leaned

back and propped her feet on the open desk drawer. Knowing she was in for several minutes of small talk, she got comfortable.

After the requisite catching up and "how come we don't go out any more" chitchat, Ryan asked, "Now I know you didn't call to rehash old times, so what's really going on?"

Chantal hesitated, not sure how to start. Finally she asked a question. "Are you open to hiring a freelancer?"

It was Ryan's turn to pause. He knew Chantal worked at her father's bank; why would she need to moonlight?

Sensing his reluctance, Chantal decided to level with him and hope he didn't take her suspicions and assign one of his reporters to the story. She explained what was going on with her sister and told him she wanted to investigate Joseph Zacharias, but she needed the paper's backing so she could start asking questions without running into brick walls and possible legal problems.

"Why not?" he finally said. "If there's a story I can publish from it, I'll pay you for it. You can tell anyone you need to you're working on a story for the *Gazette,* and if they call to verify, I'll back you up."

"Thanks a load, Ryan! This will make things a little easier. Gotta go now, but I'll keep you posted." Chantal hung up and called First Baptist again. This time, the secretary answered. "Good afternoon," Chantal greeted her. "Is Pastor Barton in?"

CHAPTER 10

Chantal browsed the bookshelves in her father's study after dinner while waiting for him to join her. Like his office at the bank, the study was filled with mahogany and leather furniture, mementos of his Army travels, and pictures and plaques of high points in his life.

The books were mostly inherited from his father. Martin was not much of a reader, so most were classics previous generations enjoyed, but he kept more for show than anything else. Chantal pulled down a leather-bound copy of Jane Austen's *Pride and Prejudice* to take back to the cottage and reread. She knew her dad wouldn't miss it; when she was a teen, she had the book in her room for over a year and he never noticed it was gone.

After ten minutes he still had not joined her, so Chantal sat in one of the overstuffed armchairs, propped her feet on the ottoman and started reading. About 50 pages later she looked up and realized she still was alone, so she bookmarked her place and carried the book out into the parlor. No one was in sight, but she heard dishes clinking in the kitchen, so she walked in to see if Rosalie knew where her father was.

"Miss Chantal! What are you doing in here?"

"I was in the study waiting for Father to meet me after dinner for a conversation. I started reading and lost track of time, but he should have joined me by now. Do you know what might be keeping him?"

"That man!" she exclaimed. "I'll bet he completely forgot he was supposed to be talking with you, child. Remember that telephone call he took during dessert? Well, he lit out of here right after you went into the study. Now here it is an hour and a half later, he's still not home and he's gone and left you hanging in there."

Chantal shook her head. "Typical. Guess I'll try to talk to him tomorrow. If you see him, please tell him how long I waited."

"Sure will, honey. You have a good night, okay?"

"Thanks, Rosie. You do the same. I'll see you later." Chantal left through the kitchen door, shoulders slumped. Rosalie scowled as she attacked the dishes with the anger she would like to direct at her employer, but didn't dare. She may have been with the family long enough to be like a surrogate mother to Chantal and Brigitte, but she was still the housekeeper, and she knew it.

CHAPTER 11

"My sister, how are you this fine evening?" Joseph greeted Brigitte as she pulled into the parking lot of the defunct drive-in theater CUP used for its meetings.

"I'm well, Brother Joseph. I pray you are too." Brigitte parked her Volvo and stepped out to give their leader a proper greeting.

"My cup overfloweth," Joseph replied as he embraced and kissed her on the cheek. He held the embrace a few seconds longer than Brigitte would have, but she didn't protest. Finally he stepped back and she answered, "As does mine." She gave a slight bow and moved back toward her car.

"I have an offering, Brother. Shall I give it now?" Brigitte popped the trunk on her car.

"Please do, my sister. Do you need any assistance?" Joseph moved toward Brigitte, but she had already removed a small box from the Volvo's trunk and closed it.

Turning to him, she said, "These are a few earthly possessions I think we should sell for the work of the ministry. Please do with them what you will." The box held jewelry, figurines and other items Brigitte had taken after her conversation with Helene and Chantal.

They were all family heirlooms and quite valuable; Joseph could see at a glance the box contained at least one Lalique vase, small bronze sculptures by renowned Art Nouveau and Art Deco sculptors Icart and Chiparus, and good jewelry spanning several decades of styles. Some of it was undeniably costume, but even those pieces were clearly on the higher end of the collectible jewelry price scale. If the pieces were all authentic – and from Joseph's knowledge of the Atherton family, he would expect them to be – there was a small fortune in the box.

Looking somberly at Brigitte, he asked, "My sister, are you certain you are ready to part with these worldly goods?"

Brigitte gazed at him with trusting eyes. "Of course I am, Brother Joseph. Did our Lord not tell the rich young ruler to sell all he had and follow Him? If that is His command, how can I withhold anything?"

"My sister, you are truly a blessing to the Lord's work here. I will turn these items over to our finance minister for processing." Joseph put the box in the trunk of his car and turned to Brigitte. "We have some excellent news to share. We'll be announcing it first here tonight to the prayer warriors, then to the general congregation tomorrow."

"What is it, Brother?" Brigitte asked.

"Patience, my sister. You will hear soon enough."

Brigitte turned back to her car to retrieve her CUP robe and pull it over her clothes. She locked her purse in the trunk and pocketed the car keys, then walked over to the concession stand turned storage shed to pull out the chairs and set up for the prayer meeting. Joseph took his leave, holding up his cell phone to indicate he had a call to take.

Walking to the wooded area at the edge of the drive in, Joseph slid his phone open. "Yes?" he inquired in a smooth tenor.

"Brother Joseph, I thought you might want to know Brigitte's behavior has raised the suspicions of her sister Chantal," a female voice on the other end of the call informed him. "She called earlier to speak to Pastor Barton. When I put the call through, before I hung up I heard her tell him she was working on a story about Christians United for Peace."

"I thought she worked for her father at his bank."

"She does, but she used to be a newspaper reporter. Perhaps she is doing some freelance work for the *Gazette* and her story has nothing to do with Brigitte's membership in our organization, but it seems too coincidental, don't you agree?"

"Yes, I do. Thank you for the information, my sister. I will keep an eye on this situation. Nothing may come of it, but if the Lord reveals to me His work may be threatened by this nonbeliever, I will take the appropriate measures, you may rest assured. When the enemy comes in like a flood..."

"...the Lord will raise up a banner against him," his caller finished the scripture verse. "Amen, my brother. So let it be done." Joseph slid his phone shut and walked back into the clearing, gazing at Brigitte while considering his course of action.

Brigitte, oblivious to Joseph's observation, laughed as she worked with another CUP member to arrange the chairs. "Praise the Lord!" she exclaimed as she finished. "My cup overfloweth, and I am indeed blessed."

CHAPTER 12

Chantal reread her notes from Monday's conversation with Pastor Thomas Barton. He didn't have much to say about Joseph Zacharias, except that he had come to First Baptist the previous summer as the new youth pastor, stayed six months then left the church to "start a new work of the Lord." Chantal already knew all this, so she pressed for details from Zacharias's past.

Pastor Barton said Zacharias applied for the youth pastor job fresh out of seminary somewhere out west and was accepted unanimously by the church counsel after they observed him working with the youth for a month of Sundays. It was his first job, to Pastor Barton's knowledge, and he thought Zacharias would be a great youth leader; he had the natural charisma of a leader and his high energy level meshed well with the borderline hyperactivity of the tweens and teens to whom he was expected to minister.

When Chantal followed up with a request for the name of the seminary from which Zacharias graduated, Barton said he didn't have the name in front of him and would have to get back to her on it. He then excused himself, saying he had a counseling appointment and would call her Wednesday.

Hanging up the phone, Chantal had the distinct impression her pastor was dodging her questions. But why?

So now Wednesday was half gone and she still hadn't heard from him. She was considering attending church in the evening to gauge how he reacted to her presence. She hadn't attended a midweek service since returning home, so he might be somewhat surprised, but if he exhibited an unusual amount of nervousness or evasiveness, it would verify something was up and she needed to pursue it.

To add to her frustration, her father had been out of the office most of the day Tuesday and Wednesday, and had made no effort to get together with her or explain why he left her sitting in his study Monday night. He had done it most of her life – running off to meetings, events, poker night, whatever, without any notice whatsoever to his family – and Helene seemed to be resigned to it, but Chantal was upset with him. He wouldn't put up with it if someone stood him up for a scheduled meeting, so why did he think he could do it to his own daughter?

Sighing, she decided to take a quick coffee break before her thoughts took her down a dark and angry path where she didn't want to go. As she stood, her phone rang.

"Figures," she muttered as she sat, picked up the phone and summoned her warmest telephone voice. "Good afternoon, Midtown Bank. How may I direct your call?"

"May I speak to Chantal Atherton, please?" responded a nervous male voice.

"This is she. How may I help you?"

"Chantal, it's Pastor Barton. I'm sorry to have taken so long to call you back, but I needed to get some information before we resumed our conversation." From the background noises, Chantal figured he must be calling from his cell phone. "Would it be all right if I stopped by the bank to speak with you? I'm out running errands downtown now and I can be there in about two minutes."

"Sure. I'll let the front desk know you're coming in to see me, and they'll buzz you back. See you shortly, Pastor." Hanging up, Chantal walked out front and stopped at the desk of Jennifer Carson, the new receptionist, and let her know admit the Pastor when he arrived.

Back in the break room, she refilled the coffee maker's water decanter and brewed a cup of spiced Mayan chocolate coffee, a new blend she had ordered a couple of weeks earlier from the brewer manufacturer's website. As the smooth, decadent combination of coffee, cocoa and cinnamon landed on her taste buds, Chantal smiled.

She made it back to her desk as a knock sounded on the office door. "Come in," she called out. Pastor Barton entered with a file folder in his hand and accepted her invitation to have a seat. He declined her offer of coffee, but accepted a Coke.

"I can't stay long," he said, taking the soda. "I have to get ready for church tonight. I did want to drop this file off though, and I needed to find the documents before I could copy them. I wanted to make sure I gave you correct and complete information." He passed the file to her over her desk. Chantal opened it, finding inside a copy of Joseph Zacharias's résumé and seminary diploma.

"Thank you, Pastor, but couldn't you get in trouble for giving this to me?" Chantal asked. "If this came out of his personnel file..."

"I assure you the originals from which I made those copies did not come from his personnel file," he replied. "It's amazing what you can obtain when you know where to look."

Chantal raised an eyebrow, but refrained from pushing the matter. Obviously her apparently squeaky clean spiritual leader had a few fact-finding skills it would be best not to question too closely.

"I won't keep you too long, Pastor," she said as she flipped through the papers in the file. "Is there anything you want to add to the information in here?"

"Actually, I want to ask you something," he answered, prompting her to look up and meet his gaze. "Why are you pursuing this? And don't tell me it's for a story you're freelancing for the *Gazette*; I know that's only your cover. Oh, I'm sure Ryan agreed to back you up; those old high school crushes come in handy sometimes, don't they? He may even pay you for a story if there is one worth publishing. But there's something else going on here, isn't there?"

"Pastor Barton, I can't go into details right now because I don't have any concrete information other than what you've brought me, but let me ask you this: Have you noticed how many of our church's younger members have left to join this CUP organization?" When he nodded, she continued, "Have you spoken to any of them since they left?"

He looked down at his hands, then brought his eyes back up to hers. The look in them was haunted as he said, "Yes, and I feel I've failed them all."

CHAPTER 13

When Chantal went to church that night, she noticed a difference in Pastor Barton's preaching – there was a repentant sound to his voice, but at the same time she sensed a fire that had been lacking before.

He put aside his ongoing study of the Book of Psalms to preach another message. "I realize this change is last minute," he told the small midweek congregation. "However, I very strongly feel this message is timely and necessary."

Opening his Bible, he turned to Luke 11:35 and read, "Therefore take heed that the light which is in you is not darkness." Looking up at the congregation, he explained: "This verse is part of a passage about letting what is in you shine out. You see, some Pharisees had just accused Jesus of casting out demons in the name of Beelzebub, which was a name for Satan. Jesus was explaining you can't cast out devils in the name of the devil, and it is from his explanation we have the truism 'A house divided against itself cannot stand.'

"After this passage, he goes on to talk about the eye being the lamp of the body; he says if the eye is good, the body is filled with light, but if the eye is bad, the body is filled with darkness. Then he cautions his followers to take heed that the light in them is not darkness.

"What does all this mean? Well, later in Luke, in chapter 21, verse 18, to be precise, Jesus cautions his followers again, saying:

'Watch out that you are not deceived. For many will come in my name, claiming, "I am he," and, "The time is near." Do not follow them.' He's warning them to be discerning about the teachers they allow to lead them, as there will be many false teachers and prophets in the end times."

He turned several pages and said, "Later in the New Testament, in the epistles, there is a reference in Paul's second letter to Timothy about morally bankrupt men who would lead others astray in the end times. In Second Timothy, chapter 3, verses 12 through 17, Paul admonishes Timothy to continue in the faith he has learned from his mother, grandmother and Paul himself rather than listen to these false teachers. He reminds Timothy that true followers of Christ can expect to suffer persecution for their faith, but they should persevere. Listen to this: 'In fact, everyone who wants to live a godly life in Christ Jesus will be persecuted, while evil men and imposters will go from bad to worse, deceiving and being deceived. But as for you, continue in what you have learned and have become convinced of, because you know those from whom you learned it, and how from infancy you have known the holy Scriptures, which are able to make you wise for salvation through faith in Christ Jesus. All Scripture is God breathed and is useful for teaching, rebuking, correcting and training in righteousness, so that the man of God may be thoroughly equipped for every good work.'

"As Paul admonished Timothy, my friends, I now admonish all of you – and myself as well – to continue in what we have learned and become convinced of so we may be thoroughly equipped for every good work. As we go forth tonight, let's give this message to anyone God opens the door for us to share it with, especially those whom we have not seen here in a while. They may be the ones most in need of these words from God's Word. Have a blessed evening, and may God's peace go with you."

CHAPTER 14

Friday afternoon, Chantal reclined in her favorite chair, sipping a cup of vanilla rooibos tea and thinking about Pastor Barton's Wednesday message as she prepared to turn in for the evening. She felt sure their conversation earlier that day had prompted his choice of topics for the sermon.

As she mulled everything over yet again, Chantal put her empty coffee mug in the sink and ran a little hot water in it; she would wash it in the morning with the breakfast dishes. Although Pastor Barton's message had continued to work its way into her thoughts over the last two days, for now she wanted to forget about the whole Brigitte drama and crawl into bed. She intended to relax with a little *Pride and Prejudice* before falling asleep. On the way through the living room, she picked up the baseball bat pepper grinder she had ordered for her father's birthday and put it just inside her bedroom door so she'd remember to wrap it the next day. It had arrived at the post office that afternoon, and she was pleased the real product measured up to the promises of its online description.

Lying down on her side with the book propped up on a pillow next to her, Chantal soon rediscovered something she had forgotten about Jane Austen's writing – those long sentences of hers were like driving on the interstate. After a while she found herself nodding off from the literary version of highway hypnosis. She managed to stay awake for ten minutes before succumbing...

A noise – small, slight, but out of place – woke Chantal with a start. She lay in bed trying to determine the source of the sound and quickly concluded an intruder might be in the cottage. Her cell phone was charging on the desk in her office, leaving her without a way to call for help.

As soon as this is over, I'm moving that charger in here, she thought as she moved silently out of bed, slipped on her house shoes and went to the bedroom door. She grabbed the pepper grinder on her way into the dark living room. It may not have been a real bat, but it looked like one and had enough heft to work as a weapon. Recalling a summer of girls' softball league from her teen years, she choked up with both hands and prepared to swing if necessary.

The living room was clear, so Chantal stopped and listened again. It sounded like the noise was coming from her office. Gripping the pepper grinder even more tightly, she walked across the living room to the office door, which was slightly ajar. A flashlight beam played across her desk and the wall behind it. She pushed the door further open with the grinder, then brought the bat into position as she entered the room and flipped on the light switch with her elbow.

Startled by the noise and sudden light, a masked intruder whirled away from her desk, which he was in the middle of ransacking, and flew at her. Chantal swung with all the force she could muster. The intruder tried to block her swing with his large heavy-duty flashlight, but he didn't get his arm up quickly enough and the bat connected with the side of his head instead. The beech wood housing and the pepper grinder inside both broke, spewing beech shards, peppercorns and ground pepper all over the room. Chantal sneezed twice as she dodged to her left and ran for the phone while the intruder sprawled in the office doorway, dazed and bleeding through his mask from the impact and sneezing from the pepper in the air.

Chantal punched 911 into her phone and held it in her left hand as she walked back over to the intruder. While she waited for the dispatcher to take her information and send the police, she brandished the broken bat in her right hand and said, "Don't even think about moving, buddy! The cops are on the way and I'm ticked off enough to put a few of these splinters into some very uncomfortable places on your person, got it?"

The intruder nodded and pulled himself into a sitting position on the floor with his legs bent, feet flat and arms crossed on top of his knees. He laid his head on his forearms and stayed that way, sneezing on his knees, until the police department's four night patrol officers arrived a few minutes later. When they knocked on the cottage door, Chantal called out, "Come on in, y'all. We're in the living room," as if she were entertaining a guest instead of holding a burglar at bay.

Timothy Andrews, the first officer through the door, stopped short in the living room as he took in the scene – Chantal Atherton at the edge of her living room in penguin-dotted red pajamas and fuzzy pink slippers, holding what appeared to be a broken baseball bat in one hand and her cell phone in the other, still open from her 911 call, and standing guard over a sneezing and obviously cowed would-be thief. Fighting to keep a straight face as he took out a notepad and pen, he asked, "Can you tell us what happened, Miss Atherton?"

While a second officer got on his cell phone and called the two-member forensics team to the scene, the other officers walked between Chantal and the intruder, pulled him to his feet and cuffed him. One of them removed his mask and Chantal exclaimed, "Jim Bridges! What the heck are you doing breaking into my house?"

Jim scowled and turned to the officer who unmasked him. "I ain't saying a thing without my attorney."

The officer shrugged and led Jim away, reciting his Miranda rights as they walked. Chantal watched them leave then turned to Officer Andrews. "Sorry, Tim. Seeing who it was under the mask rattled me even more than having him break into my house did. His mother and mine are friends from the country club. Miss Terri is going to be mortified when she gets a call to come bail her son out of jail..."

Timothy grinned and replied, "She may not be traumatized so much as annoyed. This won't be the first time she's had to escort her child home from our fine detention facility – but you didn't hear it from me." Chantal raised an eyebrow and gave him a lopsided smile, and Tim cleared his throat and resumed a professional demeanor. "Now, what happened here?"

Chantal closed her eyes momentarily to order her thoughts, then said, "Why don't we have a seat and I'll tell you about it?" She walked over to the nearest armchair and plopped into it, dropping the pepper grinder and closing her cell phone. She rubbed a hand over her face, suddenly aware of how drained she felt now that the adrenaline rush was gone.

"Chantal?" Tim prompted again. "I don't want to push you, but I do need to get back to the station and file a report." He turned to the forensics team, who had just entered, and pointed out the main item of evidence. "What is this thing?" the petite auburn-haired female office asked. "It looks like a bat, but there's pepper all up in here."

"Yeah," Chantal replied wearily. "It was a present for my father..." She went on to recount the entire incident. Finally Tim waved for her to stop and burst into guffaws.

"I'm sorry, Chantal," he gasped. "I know I should be more professional, but this is too much. I know no one in the history of this police department has ever had to file a report on a burglar being stopped in the commission of a crime by a pepper grinder, of all things." The other officers had stopped cataloguing evidence as the tale progressed, too entertained to work.

"Maybe in the morning I'll find the humor in all this, Tim," she replied in a quiet voice that instantly stopped everyone's laughter, "but at the moment I have a lot of unanswered questions - namely, why did he break in to start with? - as well as a ransacked office and a broken front door – and I'm out a birthday gift for my dad."

CHAPTER 15

"I still have no idea why Jim Bridges broke into my house, Sue," Chantal commented as she stirred her coffee. "Nothing was missing from my desk or anywhere else, and Jim didn't have anything of mine on him when he was booked. Other than the insurance deductible I had to pay to repair the door and the money I spent to replace Dad's birthday present, I didn't really lose anything except a night's sleep."

"And your sense of security," Sue responded. Chantal nodded; she couldn't argue. Her new door had three different locks on it, and she was thinking about having an alarm system installed.

The cousins had met for breakfast at Kudzu Café before embarking on another vine harvesting session. After the break-in, Chantal decided a little physical labor away from the house might be therapeutic and invited herself to join Sue out by the river. Now they were polishing off the last of their pancakes and bacon before heading out to the same kudzu patch they'd visited a couple of weeks earlier.

"Why that particular patch, Sue?" Chantal pushed her empty plate away and swallowed the last of her coffee.

Sue shrugged. "I need some vine pulling therapy too, and I figured why not go back to where my trauma started and face it down once and for all."

"Makes sense." Chantal stood and pulled $20 from her jeans

pocket to cover their meal and the tip. "Let's hit it." She dropped the money on the table and they waved goodbye to Sally as they headed out to Sue's truck.

When they arrived at the vine patch, Sue nodded toward the spot where she found the body. "Check it out – the kudzu's already covered it." She shook her head. "Let's get going." She jumped out of the truck, fished two buckets out of the truck bed and handed one to Chantal. "Remember what I showed you last time?"

Chantal nodded and followed Sue into the patch. They worked at a slow, steady pace, drifting apart as they followed the vines. An hour into the harvesting, Sue's cell phone rang.

"I think I'm back where you were that day," Chantal said without preamble. "I found something." When she heard no reply, she added, "Sue? Did you hear me?"

Sue's brow furrowed as she tried to make sense of the comment, then she remembered Chantal had wandered north as they parted company while she had meandered south, so Chantal's vine following must have led her back to the spot where Sue found the dead man.

"Yeah – forgot I had company out here for a minute. You found something? Why do you think it has anything to do with the guy I stumbled over?"

"A hunch. My bucket is full, so I'm heading back to the truck. Meet me there?"

"Sure thing; I'll be right there." Hoisting the bucket full of vines, she started walking northeast until she spotted the red pickup, then cut across the short distance to reach it.

Chantal arrived first and was stowing her bucket as Sue walked up. "Want to see what I found?" Chantal stripped off her gloves and fished a grimy necklace with a broken chain out of her pocket. "Recognize the pendant?"

Sue's eyes widened and she nodded. The pendant was a smaller silver version of the logo on every CUP t-shirt she had seen around town in the last several months.

"Got it!" she exclaimed as she slid open her cell phone and retrieved the photo she had taken of the body. "I knew he seemed familiar, but I couldn't place him. Now I remember..."

Chantal waited, but Sue seemed to be lost in thought. "And?"

"Sorry. I was trying to recall where I put the photos from the Kudzu Fest. I don't think I've printed any yet, but I have my camera with me. Care to make a Walgreen's run?"

CHAPTER 16

"You did what? I'll be right there. I can't wait to hear this." Marc dropped the phone back into its cradle on his desk at the sheriff's department and grabbed his jacket. "C'mon, John. You're not gonna believe what Sue and Chantal have been up to now."

Marc told the dispatcher they were going into the field to investigate a new lead in the apparent suicide case from earlier in the month. John's eyebrows went up, but he didn't comment until they got to their squad car.

"We're doing what? I thought that case was closed."

"So did I," Marc replied, "but Sue and Chantal have been out in the kudzu again this morning and they found something that might reopen it."

They found the cousins sitting in Sue's truck on the edge of the area where she had discovered the body.

John went to the driver's side, while Marc circled the pickup and leaned on the passenger side door. "So, what's this about y'all finding something out here?"

Chantal grinned and held up the broken necklace. "Your folks must have missed this when they were canvassing the scene. It was on the ground under a tangle of kudzu."

Marc took the dirt-crusted necklace from her and looked at it. "And why do you think it has anything to do with the body Sue fell over?"

"This," Sue said, reaching across Chantal to pass Marc a picture. After finding the pendant, the women had gone to Walgreen's, printed a batch of photos from that summer's Kudzu Fest and returned to the patch before calling Marc.

Marc studied the photo before confirming Sue's suspicions. "Yeah, he's our guy, all right, and the CUP t-shirt he's wearing does indicate he was most likely a member of the group."

"So do the flyers he's handing out in this photo," Sue pointed out as she passed him a second picture.

Marc agreed. "Okay, so we have photographic evidence of his likely involvement in CUP, and this pendant is obviously modeled from the t-shirt logo. It is possible the necklace simply came off his neck when he fell into the kudzu."

"Not likely, unless it snagged on a really tough vine," Chantal spoke up. "Look again at the chain. It's been broken by force. See how this link is stretched?" She took the necklace from him and held up the section in question. "That indicates it was jerked off the wearer's neck. The chain should have left a mark. Did the dead guy have any long, thin friction marks on the back or side of his neck?" She put the necklace back in Marc's hand and rested her hand over his for a moment before realizing what she was doing and pulling back.

"Not as far as I can see," Sue said. She was studying her cell phone again. "Of course, he's lying on his back in this shot, and my resolution is not great on this thing..."

"Do you mind?" John asked with his hand extended. Sue

handed the phone over to him with a grin. "Girl, you are something else!" he exclaimed as he saw what she had been examining. "I can't believe you took a picture of the corpse!"

"What?" Marc rounded the front of the truck and joined John in staring at the tiny photo. "Sue, what on earth would make you do something like that in the first place?"

"He wasn't too badly decomposed and he looked familiar. After I recovered from the initial shock of falling on him, I took a closer look but knew I didn't have much time before y'all got here. So, I thought if I took a picture and looked at it, something would jog in my memory. Between the photo and the pendant Chantal found, I remembered I saw the guy at the Kudzu Fest. And since I always take shots at the shows and fairs where I vend so I can post them to my website, I happened to have a couple of pictures of him from that weekend." She handed John a duplicate set of the Kudzu Fest photos.

John returned the phone to Sue with an admiring look in his eyes. "You two ought to join the sheriff's department. We could use more people with your detective skills. Right, Marc?"

"Sure enough. We need all the help we can get over there."

"So," Chantal said, "do you think this will convince the sheriff to reopen the investigation into your John Doe's death? I mean, what if he was killed because something he knew could expose Joseph Zacharias as the con man – or worse – he most likely is?"

The deputies exchanged looks and Marc answered, "I think

that might do it, Chantal."

CHAPTER 17

Brigitte turned in a slow circle, surveying the farm, its two outbuildings and the land on which it all sat. She smiled, picturing the ministry that would grow out of this place – a church, school, dormitories, offices, a publishing house, gardens, a small store...

She daydreamed about CUP's future as she walked to the farmhouse, where Joseph and several of the elders had gathered to discuss renovations. Before she reached the front door, Joseph emerged with four other men.

"Good afternoon, my sister!" Joseph quickly moved in for a hug and kiss on her cheek. Brigitte blushed and looked down as he stepped back. She wasn't sure what to think of these minor shows of affection. She hadn't seen him greet the other women that way, but then again, it wasn't as if she witnessed every interaction he had with the members of CUP. *And besides, the Bible does tell us to greet one another with a holy kiss*, she thought, dismissing her concern as an overactive imagination.

"Good afternoon, my brothers," she returned the greeting to the group rather than to Joseph alone. "How go the renovation plans?" She hadn't yet seen the insides of the three buildings, but judging from the outsides, they would need some work before being fit to inhabit.

"We have been in prayer," Joseph told her, "and we are in agreement the Lord wishes us to take possession of our Canaan immediately and carry out its transformation as we live in this new Promised Land, as the children of Israel did with their Canaan." He turned to the other men, who quickly nodded in accord. "At tonight's service, we will issue the call from the Lord for our people, His people, to come out from among the world and separate themselves unto Him in this place. This will be our last meeting at the drive-in. This weekend, we will cross over into our New Canaan."

Brigitte looked around the group. They all seemed excited about the prospect of CUP moving its base of operations onto the farm. She was too, and yet she had a slight feeling of unease she couldn't explain. She ventured a question. "Will we be using the farmhouse or one of the other buildings for church services and prayer meetings?"

"My sister, everything will take place on this land. All meetings will be moved here. We have more than enough room in the main building for church services, classrooms and anything else we may need to do."

"So, no more small group meetings in our homes?"

He laughed. "My dear sister, this is your home now. You will have no further need to live in that squalid little house. We will all live here, in community, as the Lord intended."

The duplex where she currently lived was anything but squalid. Her father had the place custom built; it was spacious and properly maintained by the handyman and gardener who took care of her parents' house. It was also nicely designed and furnished on the inside, thanks to her mother. Helene would have Joseph's head on a pike for insulting the place.

Brigitte kept the thought to herself, however, and simply said, "Brother Joseph, I'll be more than pleased to join the CUP community here for meetings and church services for the time being, but I must honor my lease, which doesn't expire for another two months. Besides, if we are going to live in community, I assume we would be bringing only essential possessions, so I'll need a little time to sell my furnishings. The money will go to the Lord's work through CUP, of course."

Joseph hesitated before answering, and it seemed to Brigitte that he struggled to maintain a calm demeanor. Finally he smiled and said, "My dear sister, your joyful spirit and positive attitude are a balm to all of us, and your continual presence will be a true blessing to the community. However, I understand the desire to bid farewell to your former life. In fact, I can imagine many of our members will need to do the same.

"My brothers," he continued, turning to the men behind him, "I believe the Lord has used our sister to speak wisdom to us in this situation. We will announce at tonight's meeting that anyone who wishes to join us here immediately may do so, but those who need some time to unburden themselves of possessions and obligations which would hinder their growth and participation in the Lord's work here will have until December 1 to join us in New Canaan. If they have not crossed their own Jordan River into this Promised Land by then, we will know they were never truly Christians United for Peace and they will not share in the Lord's inheritance here with us."

He turned back to Brigitte to see her reaction. She smiled brightly and nodded. "As our Lord's servant says, so let it be done," she said with a bow. "And now, if I may take my leave, my brothers, I need to begin making arrangements to sell some things."

Joseph smiled and stepped forward to embrace her again, but Brigitte had already stepped back and turned toward her car. She walked as quickly as possible without looking like she was running away, but it was exactly what she wanted to do.

She unlocked the car with the remote before she reached it and slid behind the steering wheel with a sigh. She wanted to believe that what Joseph and the elders proposed was right for all of them, but a nagging doubt haunted her thoughts. *Lord, is this really what You want? If it is, please give me a sign.*

As she looked up, a flock of doves flew over the farmhouse. *Thank You, Lord!* The birds were quickly gone, but for Brigitte, their appearance was sign enough. Doves were a symbol of peace and of the Holy Spirit. What further proof did she need?

CHAPTER 18

Chantal rose from the floor cushion where she'd been sitting for the past 15 minutes and dashed to answer the insistent ringing of the doorbell. Well, not exactly dashed – her left foot had fallen asleep from the weight of her right leg resting on it in the cross-legged position she'd occupied. Still, she managed a fairly fast limp as her foot tingled its way awake.

Stepping back to let Sue pass, she chuckled. "Bring the whole workshop, did you?"

Sue laughed and dumped her double armload of supplies on the floor by the coffee table. "No, only a couple of projects I wanted to work on today." She helped herself to a glass of sweet tea before settling opposite Chantal at the table.

It was a craft day for the cousins. Sue was trying a new basket design, and Chantal was incorporating kudzu pendants into necklaces and bracelets. Sue made the focal pieces by gluing freshly picked baby kudzu leaves to translucent capiz shell pendants and pouring clear resin over the top. The preserved leaves took on a lacy appearance during the process, and the thinness of the shell backing allowed light to show through, creating an ethereal effect. Sue hadn't been making them long; for now, Chantal had exclusive rights to use them in her jewelry.

"You know," Sue teased, "if you don't start selling some of this stuff soon, I may go into the jewelry biz myself. I want my pendants to be seen and worn, not worked up into some pretty thing that's only going to collect dust in my cousin's cottage."

Chantal studied the necklace she was making and tried to decide what accent bead to string next. "Actually, I talked to Sally earlier today and accepted her offer to sell some of my items through the Café gift shop. I need to finish one or two pieces, card and price them all, and figure out how I'm going to display the collection."

Pairing a small faceted lemon chrysoprase bead with a slightly larger smooth amethyst, she fashioned a sterling silver bail and hung one of the kudzu pendants on it. She slid the finished pendant onto the necklace, then quickly finished stringing beads in a mirror image of the pattern she'd created on the other side of the pendant. Before she attached the clasp, she held the necklace up to look at the design and check the length.

Satisfied with her finished creation, Chantal added the clasp, then made a pair of dangle earrings to complete the set. She'd used crystal beads and gemstones in shades of green, yellow and purple to evoke the colors of spring growth and kudzu blossoms. The lacy leaf captured in the pendant was the perfect complement to the delicate beads.

"Done," she said, more to herself than Sue, but her cousin glanced up from the pile of vines she was attempting to turn into a basket and smiled.

"I like it a lot, Chantal, and I suspect it won't stay in the china hutch long. Now, if I can figure this dadgum thing out..."

"What are you trying to do?" Chantal asked, her curiosity in

Sue's project piqued now that her own was done.

"I thought I'd try weaving a triangular basket instead of the usual roundish, squarish or melon-shaped one, but I'm not entirely sure how to go about it. If I were weaving a reed basket, I could use a ready-made slotted triangular base. Since I'm working with vines, though, I don't have the luxury. I may have to rig up a framework of my own if I can't find another solution."

She shrugged and scribbled on a green tinted legal pad, sketching out ideas and then striking through them, her increasing frustration evident in the growing volume of her sighs. After several minutes of fruitless pondering and note taking, she dropped her pencil on the note pad and picked up her tea. "To creativity," she toasted wryly as she lifted her glass. Chantal grinned and clinked tea glasses with Sue.

As Chantal put the glass to her lips, her cell phone vibrated on the coffee table. After two vibrations it stopped, signifying a text message instead of a call, so she took a long drink of her tea before setting the glass down. Flipping open her phone, she read the message and told Sue it was from Marc. He and John wanted to take them to lunch at Taco Loco. "You up for it?"

"It sure beats sitting here obsessing over something that may be a geometrical impossibility," Sue replied, standing and taking her empty tea glass to the kitchen for a refill. "How soon can they be here?"

Chantal keyed in the question and sent it. Moments later she chuckled. "They're out front now. They were just waiting to see if we were interested."

"Sure of themselves, aren't they?" Sue set her glass in the sink instead of refilling it. "Come on, unfold yourself from the floor, cous."

Chantal put on her new necklace and earrings. "Might as well road test them." Sue grinned and followed Chantal out, locking the cottage door.

"I was thinking, Sue," Chantal commented as they walked toward the front of the main house to meet the guys, "if you put three holes on the bottom of some of the kudzu pendants, it would give me more versatility with the designs. Think the capiz shells could handle being drilled so much?"

"I don't know; they're pretty delicate, even with the resin strengthening them. I'll give it a try, though. At most, I'll be out a shell or two if it doesn't work." She smiled at John and Marc as she exited the front gate. "Hi, y'all! Your invitation couldn't have come at a better time. I was getting fed up with my project and needed a break."

Marc held the gate open for Chantal, who smiled her thanks as she passed through. "My project went a little better, thank goodness," she remarked.

"Is what you're wearing it?" Marc asked. When Chantal nodded, he said, "I like it – reminds me of Mardi Gras. The colors are close, although the yellow bead isn't gold, so it's not quite the same. Still, that's what I thought of when I first saw it. There's a – I don't know, a joyfulness, maybe? – in the design."

Chantal blushed and thanked him for the compliment. "I'm going to start selling some of my pieces at the Kudzu Café. Sally will showcase them for me in the china hutch and sell them for a small commission. I hope they'll attract buyers..."

"Oh, I'm sure they will, if they're all as pretty as what you have on," Marc assured her, which caused her to blush even more. "If you need any help getting the pieces ready to sell, I'm free to card and price this afternoon..."

Sue, walking with John in front of Chantal and Marc, glanced back and smiled. John gave her a gentle nudge with his elbow and grinned. "So," he said, "what's good at Taco Loco?"

"You mean you haven't eaten there yet? My favorite is the paella, but everything I've tried is good. I guess it depends on whether you like chicken, beef, pork or seafood."

John nodded. "I'm in the mood for something different. Wonder if they have any dishes featuring rabbit or catfish?" He opened the restaurant door and held it for the rest of the group.

"Hola, Luis!" Sue called out as she entered. "My friend here is in the mood for something a little wild today – got anything with rabbit or catfish?" The few diners already eating looked Sue's way with expressions ranging from amusement to queasiness; apparently some of them didn't enjoy the thought of bunny being served there. Luis waved at the foursome through the kitchen's pass-through window. Moments later, he entered the dining room, wiping his hands on a kitchen towel hanging out of his apron pocket.

"Bienvenidos a todos," he greeted the group. "Good to see you again. For Sue's amigo I will prepare a special dish. I have both rabbit and catfish. Which would you prefer?"

"Hmm. I had a dish in Venezuela years ago – it was made with rabbit, battered and fried, then cooked in a beer-based sauce with braised root vegetables – carrots, onions, potatoes – or maybe it was yuca. Can you make something like it?"

Luis thought for a moment. "If you are not in a hurry, I think I can create something similar, yes."

"That's what I'd like, then. Muchas gracias," John said.

"Muy bien. If you will all make yourselves comfortable, I'll have Anamaria out in a moment to take the rest of your orders."

True to his word, Luis sent Anamaria out to their booth immediately after telling her what John had ordered so she could put it on the ticket. She finished writing it as she arrived at the booth. She greeted everyone and asked for their orders with a teasing word of warning: "Now, Tío Luis can cook only one special per party."

Sue grinned. "Has he taken the catfish tacos off the menu yet?"

"No, they're still there. Fried or grilled?"

"How about half and half? Or is that too *especial*?"

Giggling, Anamaria shook her head. "We can do both. Señorita Chantal, are you having the carnitas naranjadas again today?"

Chantal shook her head and looked at Marc, who nodded.

"Not today. Marc and I want to share the Fajitas for Two, and we'd like the mixed combo, por favor."

"Claro que si," Ana replied with a smile. "Would you like a pitcher of tea, or do you want individual drinks?" The group agreed to the tea and Anamaria left to give her uncle the ticket. She returned with the tea pitcher, four glasses of ice, a large basket of tortilla chips with a carafe of salsa and four small bowls for individual portions. "If you need anything else, let me know. I'll have your orders out in a little while."

Chantal and Marc reached for the tea pitcher at the same time, but Marc was a tiny bit faster, so he poured for the group. Meanwhile, Sue doled out portions of salsa for everyone. "Mmm," John hummed approvingly as he took his first bite, "this is the best salsa I think I've ever had north of the border. Homemade?"

Sue nodded. "So are the chips. Pretty much all the food here is, other than stuff like the cheese, of course – and that may be, too, for all I know. Luis and his family grow their own vegetables and buy what they don't grow from local farmers as much as possible. Same with the meats, fish and seafood – they buy local first, then regional, like Gulf Coast shrimp, oysters, crabs and crawfish. It's one of the reasons I like the paella here so much – it's mostly local and all as fresh as you can get without growing or harvesting the ingredients yourself."

While Sue and John discussed the merits of Taco Loco's salsa and the owner's preference for local ingredients, Chantal and

Marc were holding their own conversation on the window side of the booth. After small talk about work and life in general, Marc cleared his throat and tried to sound casual as he told Chantal he had to leave town for a few days.

"Oh? What's going on?"

"It's a family matter over in New Era I need to attend to; my grandmother is going into the hospital tomorrow afternoon for what the doctors are calling minor surgery, and my parents want me to come see her before the operation. I probably won't be gone more than a day or two, but my parents think it's best for me to come home now in case something happens, so I'm taking a week of personal time in case I need to stay longer."

"When do you leave?"

"In the morning." Chantal gave Marc a puzzled look, so he explained, "Grandma's not at the hospital yet, and I need to tie up a few loose ends around here before I head out. Besides, I don't want to go back on my offer to help you out with the jewelry pricing."

"Now, don't use me as an excuse to procrastinate," Chantal chided half-jokingly. "I don't want your family to blame me if you don't get there in time."

"They haven't even met you yet," Marc replied with a grin. "I doubt they'd blame you for my decisions."

Chantal blinked as she laughed nervously. *We've never even been on a date, and he's implying he wants me to meet his family? I don't know about this...*

"...have the cards and tags?"

Chantal realized he had asked her something. "Sorry, Marc. My brain wandered off for a minute there. Yes, I have the supplies for carding and pricing the jewelry. We can work on it after we're done here, if you still want to help."

"Definitely. Do you have a DVD player? We can stop by the video store on the way back to your place and pick up something to watch while we work."

"I do indeed. It would help pass the time, and I have plenty of movie snackage too." Chantal jumped partway out of her seat as her phone buzzed in her left hip pocket. "Sue, can you scoot out? My phone's blowin' up and I don't want to be rude..."

Answering the phone as she went, Chantal walked outside and over to the small park next to the restaurant. "Hello?... Oh, hi, Mother... Actually, I was at lunch with friends..."

"I'm so sorry to disturb you, dear," Helene replied without one bit of remorse in her voice, "but I had to talk to someone about your sister's latest behavior, and your father is out of pocket again today."

Chantal sat on a stone bench, shooing away an overly friendly pigeon. "What did Brigitte say now?"

"It's more what she is doing. She sold everything she owns and is moving out of the duplex on Friday." A deep sigh followed this pronouncement.

Chantal echoed her mother's sigh. "How did you find out about it?"

"She called us to break her lease – said she was moving in with roommates to save on expenses. We weren't happy about it, but we knew better than to argue with her."

"Of course. It wouldn't have done anything except push her farther away. But what about her selling everything? Surely she didn't tell you she was going to do that?"

"Indeed not," Helene answered. "She called the *Gazette* to place an ad to sell her furniture, and Crystal – Gwen's daughter, you know, Gwen from the country club? – anyway, Crystal called Gwen, and she called me. To have to hear about it that way was simply mortifying."

Chantal cleared her throat. "Mother, maybe you're jumping to conclusions. Maybe she's selling the furniture because her roommates have enough already. Have you spoken to Brigitte?"

"Of course, dear, it's the first thing I did after I hung up on – I mean, with – Gwen." Chantal chuckled silently at her mother's slip; she knew Helene would never consciously admit to being so abrupt as to hang up on a telemarketer, let alone a close friend. She turned her attention back to her mother's story and heard "...finally admitted to me she was indeed selling all her earthly goods to give the money to that CUP group."

"But if she's selling everything and moving out of the duplex, where is she going to live? Where do these roommates she mentioned live? It's not as if we're overrun with apartment complexes in Atherton..."

Helene choked back a sob as she answered, "That's the worst

of it, dear; she's moving into some run-down farmhouse out in the county with the other members of that group. I can't believe it – never has an Atherton woman done something so completely contrary to who we are." Chantal could picture her mother putting her hand over her heart. Typical – Helene Atherton, when confronted with the reality of her youngest child possibly being sucked into a cult, could only think of what such news would do to the family's good name.

Chantal felt her blood pressure rising. Her lips pursed and her jaw tightened as she fought to maintain composure and not blast her mother for being so maternally deficient. Finally, when she didn't speak for a couple of minutes, her mother said, "Honey, are you there? Did the call drop? Hello?"

"I'm still here, Mother, but I do need to rejoin my friends. I promise you, though, I'll find out what I can and get back to you about this as soon as possible, okay? I'll talk to you later. Love you." She hung up before her mother had a chance to drag the conversation out, then to calm down, she did a quick lap around the quarter-mile walking path encircling the small park before going back to Taco Loco.

Pasting on a smile as she rejoined her party, Chantal saw lunch had arrived. "I hope I didn't keep y'all waiting too long. Mom needed to talk for a few minutes, but I'm all yours now. Marc, would you do the honors?"

Marc smiled and bowed his head; the others followed suit. "Father God, we thank You for this time to share a meal and fellowship. We ask You to please bless what we already ate, what we're about to eat and the hands that prepared and served it." After a pause, he added, "And Father, we also ask You to keep those we love in the palm of Your hand and keep a hedge of protection around them no force can break through to do harm to them. In Jesus' Name we pray, Amen." He opened his eyes to find Chantal staring at him. "Are you okay?"

"Why did you pray the last part?" she whispered.

He shrugged and reached for her hand. "I felt led to. Why?"

A tear slipped down her cheek as she related her phone conversation. Marc and John exchanged looks of concern and Sue slipped an arm around her shoulder in a brief hug.

When Chantal finished, Marc took her hand and looked into her eyes. "I promise you, we will do whatever we can, as law enforcement officers and your friends, to rescue your sister, if she needs to be rescued – and it sounds like she might, before this is all over."

Then he smiled and added, "But rest easy – God obviously wanted you to know He's keeping His eye on her; that's the only explanation I have for why I prayed about something other than the food. Speaking of which, are you going to be okay to eat this here?"

Chantal gave him a lopsided grin and wiped her cheek with her free hand. "I'm not that distraught. Let me at those fajitas!"

With a laugh, Marc let go of her hand and picked up a tortilla. "Chicken or beef, cher?"

CHAPTER 19

Chantal and Marc were enjoying a moonlit stroll along the banks of the Mississippi, walking with their arms around each other in the chilly evening air, when Chantal's phone started buzzing. She flipped it open and said hello, but the phone kept buzzing...

Grumbling as she slapped at the snooze bar of her alarm clock, Chantal tried to recapture the dream, but the sunrise through her curtains flooded out the images.

Passing through the living room, she snagged the two bowls left on the coffee table the previous afternoon. One had a few unpopped kernels of popcorn left in it, and the other was decorated with three sunflower seeds clinging to its sides and a lone blue candy-covered chocolate piece in the bottom Marc and she somehow missed. Absentmindedly popping the chocolate into her mouth, Chantal emptied the bowls into the kitchen garbage can and quickly washed them before starting breakfast.

While her microwave breakfast sandwich cooked, she wandered back into the living room and returned the two rented videos – *Sahara* and *Bruce Almighty* – to their DVD cases, then picked up the empty tea glasses. Breakfast dinged as she was filling one of the freshly washed tumblers with milk, so she plated her sandwich on a small orange Fiesta ware dish and took breakfast into the living room so she could eat while she got her jewelry to take to Kudzu Café during lunch.

The earrings were carded and ready to be hung on the small rack she intended to put in the china hutch at the Café, but the necklaces and bracelets still needed to be boxed. Marc had offered to help her with that too, but after carding earrings and tagging everything, they both needed a break from sitting on the floor and inhaling marker fumes, so they stopped working and watched the two DVDs they rented on the way back from Taco Loco.

Sue and John stopped by long enough for Sue to retrieve her basket supplies, then begged off from the work/movie session, saying they each had other plans. Whether those plans were together or separately was never made clear, but Chantal suspected they'd opted to catch a movie at the theater in Natchez.

Whatever the reason for their desertion, Sue and John left Chantal and Marc to themselves. Recalling the previous day's activities, Chantal smiled; she enjoyed spending time with Marc. Their tastes in movies, music, books and food were similar – they even had the same favorite movie viewing snacks, kettle corn and trail mix. The afternoon had been a welcome break from all the sister/mama drama in Chantal's life, and she was sorry Marc felt it necessary to call it an evening around 7:30 after they shared a small cheeseburger pizza from Pied Piper.

"Sorry to leave, cher," Marc had said as Chantal walked with him to the front door, "but I need to pack for the trip to Mom and Dad's. I know it's only three hours or so down the road, but since I might be gone for a week, I need to throw a few things in my backpack." He pulled her to himself in a one-armed hug. She let him draw her in and put her arms around his waist. They stayed like that for a minute, her leaning on him as he leaned against the doorframe with his left arm tucked behind him.

"I'll be praying for you and your family, Chantal," he murmured into her hair. "Remember, I'm only a text away, and if you need me to come back for any reason, just call." He dropped a kiss on the top of her head and she looked up at him and nodded. He dropped his head and grazed her lips with his, lingering a moment before pulling away. Pushing away from the doorframe, he straightened and removed his arm from her waist.

"Good night, boo," he said in a husky voice as he backed down the step and onto the sidewalk. Turning away, he walked up the path to the back of the main house, then turned and looked back. Chantal was leaning against the doorframe as she watched him leave. She gave him a soft smile and a small wave. Smiling back, he turned the corner and disappeared from her sight. She sighed as she closed and locked the door...

I hope he doesn't stay gone too long, she thought as she finished boxing the jewelry, ate her now-cold breakfast, took the bin full of jewelry to the entry table and sat it next to her keys and the two DVDs.

She finished getting ready for work with time to spare, so she decided to return the videos and take the jewelry to the Café right away instead of waiting until lunch. Sally had already cleared two shelves in the china hutch for her, so all she had to do was go set up the display.

Ten minutes later, the videos had been dropped in the store's return slot, the jewelry display was set up and Chantal was headed to the bank, having stopped at Fuzzy Logic for a mocha latte on the way. As she reached the bank, her hip buzzed. She pulled her phone out and read the text:

Mornin boo. Headin out now. Text ya when I get there. :-)

Chantal replied that she'd be praying for his grandmother and family. She was still smiling and looking at her phone as she hit the Send button; she didn't see her father striding down the hall toward the restroom. He slowed down, but she didn't and walked right into him. "Oh, sorry, Father! Good thing I have a lid on this latte."

Martin gave her a tight smile. "What had you so preoccupied, dear?"

"A text from a friend who's leaving for a few days to visit family." She wasn't ready to talk to her parents about Marc. She wasn't even sure what to call their relationship yet, let alone explain it to her mother and father.

Martin gave her a knowing look but only said, "I hope he enjoys the visit."

Chantal spun and watched him walk away. *I didn't say it was a 'he', Dad, so what do you know already, and how do you know it?*

She laughed softly, reminded that living in Atherton had distinct disadvantages when it came to privacy – especially if you happened to be an Atherton. She and Marc had been seen publicly together on more than one occasion. A comment from one of the tellers or a remark from a golfing buddy would be enough to inform Martin his daughter was seeing someone. *Heck, he could have glanced out his bedroom window around 7:40 last night...* Chantal's thoughts trailed off as she smiled at the memory and reached for the first item in her Inbox.

It was a letter from her father to someone whose name she didn't recognize, at an address in Natchez. Placing the rough draft on her type stand, she opened her lower left drawer and pulled out a sheet of her father's personal letterhead, since the sticky note on the letter indicated it was personal and not bank related.

The letter was brief and cryptic, simply thanking the gentleman to whom it was addressed for his prompt and discreet handling of "a very delicate matter." Chantal's curiosity was piqued, so she saved the document to her computer's Miscellaneous file before printing it.

Two hours and a second cup of coffee later, Chantal had cleared her box, taken several phone calls on Martin's behalf and scheduled three lunch meetings for later in the week. She picked up the pile of letters and documents. Knocking on the doorframe, she walked into his office, set the pile in front of him, and took a seat in the chair opposite his desk, notebook and pen ready for any notes he might want to give her. He asked if she would mind brewing a cup of decaf while he looked through the pile, and she left to crank up the brewer.

In the couple of minutes she was away, he read and signed

the mystery letter, sealed it in its envelope and put a stamp on it. When she returned, he glanced up from a spreadsheet, thanked her for the coffee, and went back to what he was doing. Chantal sat and waited.

Five minutes later he had dealt with all the papers she'd put on his desk. He looked up to find her still sitting there. "Did you need something, dear?" he asked.

"I was waiting to see if you needed anything," she replied.

"No, thank you. You've taken care of everything with your typical efficiency, which I greatly appreciate." He paused, cleared his throat and continued, "I recall we were supposed to have a talk after dinner a couple of weeks back and I ended up having to leave for a last-minute meeting. I'm sorry I left you sitting in the study like that; it didn't even occur to me you were in there waiting for me."

"I'd forgotten all about it, Father. No big deal."

"Why did you want to talk with me?"

She decided the direct approach would be best. "I'm concerned about Brigitte and this group she's gotten involved with, Christians United for Peace. Saturday of last week, she came home to retrieve a few belongings, and I got the feeling she planned to sell them. Some of the items were family heirlooms, and I hate to think they might be sold to help finance a cult."

"A cult?"

"I believe so, yes. Just yesterday, I received a call from Mother about Brigitte selling all her furnishings and moving out of the duplex and into a farmhouse out in the county with other CUP members."

He shrugged. "Your mother has kept me apprised of your sister's activities, dear. I'm not happy about her selling off her possessions, of course, and I certainly don't condone her choice to break the lease two months early and move out of the duplex, but she is an adult and capable of making her own decisions.

"If it turns out this organization she's involved with is indeed a cult and she becomes unable to govern her own affairs soundly, then we are prepared to step in and do whatever is necessary to help her. However, we won't do that without her invitation and permission, any more than we would have forced you to come back here against your will."

Chantal's eyes grew wider with each sentence. "I can't believe you're so detached about all this! And as for the last part, you apparently don't know how much Mother pressured me to return here, take this job and move into the cottage."

"Pressured you, yes. Forced you? No, my dear, she didn't force you to do anything. If you'd continued to say no, she would have eventually given up asking. However, she knew that being a good daughter, you wouldn't stay away from home when we needed you." He patted his chest and raised his eyebrows.

Chantal huffed, but she knew he was right. They had played to her sense of family duty and she had succumbed. As things were turning out, it was probably for the best; she might be the only one concerned enough about Brigitte to take action. And of course, she might not have met Marc if she hadn't come back...

A familiar-feeling smile stole across her face, and she nodded. "I concede your point. And much as I disliked the idea at the time, I'm glad now to be home. I missed small-town life more than I realized."

"I'm pleased we resolved that." Martin stood. "I know you're worried about your little sister, but trust me; I'm keeping a closer eye on the situation than you think."

In a rare display of affection, he rounded the desk and gave his daughter a brief hug. "I have to head out now; I have a bank board meeting in half an hour, then the Kiwanis Club and another meeting at the country club. I'll most likely be out all afternoon. If there are any emergencies, leave a message on my voice mail and I'll check it between meetings."

"I'll hold down the fort." She returned to her desk and picked up her cell phone as it buzzed with another message from Marc:

Made it home. I'll text again after I see Big Mama.

K :-), she replied, then followed up with a message to Sue asking if they could get together for lunch at Beaux Thais, the Cajun/Asian fusion restaurant at the end of Main Street. Sue replied she'd meet Chantal there at noon. As she closed her cell phone, the land line on her desk rang. "Good morning, Midtown Bank. How may I direct your call?"

* * *

Walking the five blocks to the restaurant, she mentally listed everything she wanted to discuss with Sue – her father's mysterious letter, his reaction to her comments about Brigitte and CUP, the outcome of the previous afternoon's video session with Marc...

When she arrived at Beaux Thais, she saw Sue already seated near the back of the restaurant, away from the windows. "Hey, girl. Why the seclusion?"

"Figured we might not want all of Main Street in on our conversation," Sue replied with a glance toward the front windows. Chantal followed her gaze and noticed that a member of CUP was outside the restaurant distributing leaflets.

"Good call." Taking a quick glance at the menu, she decided on the Chicken Satay Salad with Coconut Lime Dressing and mint tea. Arriving a couple of minutes before Chantal, Sue had already placed her order for the shrimp etouffée.

Sue sipped her tea. "So, spill. What's up?"

Chantal recounted her morning at the bank. "I'm not sure what to make of it all. Dad sounds like he's more aware of the situation than I thought, and maybe he is. Who knows?"

"What about the letter you mentioned? You gonna check the name and address?"

"As soon as I get back to the office." She accepted her tea from the waitress and thanked her, then told Sue, "Also, Pastor Barton gave me a folder of information about Joseph Zacharias, but I haven't had time to dig into it yet. Dad's out of the office all afternoon, so unless the phone rings off the hook, I intend to do some research."

"Sounds like a plan. Let me know if you need another Googler on the job." Sue grinned.

"Will do. So, what have you been up to today?"

Sue described her ongoing attempts to weave a triangular basket without using a starter base; so far, the vines weren't cooperating. "I may have to haul out the power tools and make a base of some sort before it's all over, but I'll either lick this problem or come up with some other design I like better."

"I know you will. I took my stuff to Sally this morning and set it up before work. Told her I'd check in at the end of the week unless I heard from her before then."

"Excellent! So, how did the carding and pricing session go after John and I left?" Chantal blushed and looked down at the table. "That good? Details, cous – I want details!"

The waitress arrived with their meals, so Chantal took a minute to bless the food and gather her thoughts before she responded.

"I think we can safely call yesterday Marc's and my first date. And as first dates go, it was probably the best one I've ever had." She took a bite of salad and hummed her approval of the chicken satay and the salad dressing as she chewed. She went in for another bite, but Sue intercepted Chantal's fork with her own.

"Don't leave me hanging! Why was it so wonderful? I mean, other than the obvious fact you were on a date with a hot cop?"

Chantal burst out laughing and clapped a hand over her

mouth. "Boy, you don't mince words, do you? Yeah, sure, he's hot – no argument there. But that really had very little to do with it. Truth is, the date was good because I felt so comfortable with him."

She told Sue everything that happened, ending with the brief kiss on the front porch. She smiled softly. "I felt safe there, leaning against the doorframe with him. He's not at all like – "

"Like?"

Chantal shook her head. "The last relationship I had, back in Kansas – it really messed me up on several levels. But this is different. It's natural, like we've been together our whole lives. I can't imagine Marc ever hurting me, at least not on purpose. Last night is a prime example. It would have been easy for us – for me, at least – to give in to the moment, but he was a complete gentleman about it."

She sighed and looked at Sue. "I know the feelings you have at the beginning of a dating relationship aren't love so much as infatuation, but I gotta tell you – whatever it is, I'm in the deep end of the pool here, despite my best intentions to stay out of the water."

Sue grinned and took a sip of her tea. "It's good you recognize your feelings for what they are, but don't dismiss the possibility they might be the real deal."

Chantal shook her head. "I know, but while this whole situation with Brigitte is unresolved, I don't think I can trust my feelings." Sue gave her a puzzled look and she said, "I can't help but wonder if my response to Marc is because of his concern for my sister and our family. What if the only reason I'm feeling this way is because – "

"Because Marc's on a case that might have an impact on all of you, because he's compassionate and understands what you're going through since he lost his brother to a cult, and because – let's face it – he is oh so easy on the eyes?" Sue chuckled. "Look, girl – every bit of that might be true, but so what? Just because y'all met in unusual circumstances, it doesn't mean something real can't come out of it."

Chantal looked doubtful, and Sue sighed. "Do me a favor, will you? Don't shut down on Marc – and yourself – because you're not sure where things will go. Give it some time and see what develops, okay? It might not go anywhere, but who knows? This could be – "

"Don't you dare throw some old movie cliché at me about the start of 'a beautiful friendship,' or something equally lame," Chantal interrupted with a laugh. She held up her right hand. "Okay, I promise; I'll give whatever this is a chance. Satisfied?"

Sue speared a shrimp with her fork and grinned. "That'll do – for now."

CHAPTER 20

As the sun climbed into a cloudless Friday sky, Brigitte packed the last of her clothes. After filling two suitcases and a shoulder tote, she ended up putting the rest of her wardrobe Inboxes from the local U-Haul.

She looked around the barren bedroom and sighed, then smiled. She couldn't believe her parents agreed to let her to break the duplex lease on such short notice, but they apparently believed her story about moving in with some roommates elsewhere in the area.

She was equally amazed by the sale of her belongings. Her ad in the Natchez paper attracted an auction broker who offered an impressive sum for everything from the dishes to the furniture. He said he'd give Goodwill anything he couldn't auction off or sell online. That pleased Brigitte; not only would her possessions help fund CUP's ministry, but some of the items might benefit another worthy organization.

She had offered to donate several things to CUP for use at the farmhouse, but Joseph said he'd already purchased the needed items. He explained it would be best for everyone moving into the farmhouse to make a clean start, so he bought white bed linens, towels and dishes, undecorated flatware and plain drinking glasses. Brigitte could see the logic; if she were using things from her former life every day, she might be tempted to abandon the path she felt God leading her down with the ministry...

Carrying the last box to the Volvo, she turned and took one more look at her home for the last five years. She swallowed and blinked back a tear. *Is this truly Your will, Lord? If it is, please give me Your peace about this, because I can't shake the doubt. This feels wrong.*

Turning her back on the house, she put the box in her car and drove away in a cloud of gravel and dust.

Heading toward the farmhouse, she cranked up the radio to drown the voice in her head telling her to go back to the duplex, call her parents and tell them she had changed her mind.

It's too late! I've sold all I have and the money is already in CUP's coffers; I've broken the lease with my parents and they say they have a tenant lined up to move in; and I've made the commitment to join the community at the farmhouse. I can't back out now...

She sang along with the radio, drummed her fingers on the steering wheel, counted cows as she passed pastures – anything to keep from thinking about what she was doing.

Brigitte pulled up to CUP's new headquarters building and hopped out of the Volvo. She grabbed her purse and the largest suitcase and took them inside, returned to the car and brought the rest of her bags. She left the boxes in the car until she knew what room she'd be staying in so she wouldn't have to move her clothes around several times.

"Ah, Sister Brigitte. Welcome to New Canaan!" Joseph emerged from the kitchen and rushed to embrace her. Brigitte returned his hug and asked where she should put her clothes.

"Come with me." He grabbed the smaller suitcase and led her up a flight of stairs, leaving her to haul the larger suitcase up to the second floor. "We have sleeping rooms set up for the men and women – separate accommodations, of course; we must not harbor even the appearance of evil. You'll find a footlocker at the end of your bed for your clothing and toiletries. Anything that doesn't fit in your locker will go into a communal closet room, to be shared among the community's members as needed."

Brigitte stopped in the middle of the hallway as Joseph continued walking. At the door to the women's sleeping room, he turned to invite her in and saw that she seemed dazed.

"My sister, surely you didn't intend to keep all these wonderful clothes to yourself? Remember, part of our covenant with each other is to share all we have, as the church of Christ did in the Book of Acts. Living here will not require an extensive wardrobe, and whatever surplus you have must be given to the common good. You do know that, don't you?" He took the rest of her luggage and walked back to the sleeping room.

"But Brother Joseph, what about my job? I have to maintain a certain wardrobe for work. I can't go to a lawyer's office dressed in jeans and CUP logo tees, not even on casual Friday. I'll be reprimanded the first time I walk through the door dressed like that."

Joseph stopped at a bed halfway into the room and put Brigitte's bag on it. He parked the larger suitcase next to the bed, retrieved the smaller one from the doorway and set it next to the larger one.

He placed his hands on Brigitte's shoulders. "My sister, I have plans for you. I need an office assistant and I want you to be that person. With your administrative and legal background, you can be of invaluable service to the ministry. I didn't intend to announce my plans this way, but here we are. Would you please consider resigning from the law firm and running the office for me?" He gave her shoulders a gentle squeeze and looked deep into her eyes.

Without intending to, Brigitte responded to his persuasion. "Of course, Brother Joseph. I would be honored to serve the ministry in such a vital way." She hesitated. "Of course, I must do things properly and give my two weeks' notice at the law firm..."

"Absolutely! I would expect nothing less from a woman of integrity. You have no idea how much you have pleased me – and our Lord – by your decision today, Sister Brigitte."

He gave her a lingering hug before stepping back. "I'll leave you to get settled. If there is anything else you need to bring in, please let me know and I'll have one of the brothers come assist you. You're the first of our sisters to arrive, but I expect the others to arrive later today and tomorrow." He gave her his charismatic preacher's smile and left.

Brigitte sat on the bed she'd been assigned and put her head in her hands. She felt like she'd been thrown into the Mississippi

River with no warning. Should she cry out for rescue, keep treading water, or give up and succumb to the water's pull? *I'm so tired...*

She kicked off her shoes and lay down on the unmade bed. Unloading the car and unpacking could wait.

Some time later, she felt herself being shaken awake. As her eyes focused, she saw Melissa Saunders, a former classmate from high school and a member of CUP who had joined the ministry a month or so earlier.

"Hi! I didn't want to wake you, but Brother Joseph asked me to. He said you should finish unpacking and get your bed made so you can go to the office and meet with him about your duties. He gave me some linens for both our beds; I put yours over there."

Brigitte looked at the foot of her bed and saw a neatly folded pile of sheets, blanket and flat pillow – all white – perched atop her footlocker. She also noticed the boxes from her car were now on the floor around her locker. She didn't remember leaving the car unlocked...

Shaking her head to clear the last sleepy thoughts, she thanked Melissa, made up the bed and put away her clothes and toiletries. What didn't fit in the locker went back into the suitcases and under her bed. She would deal with what to keep and what to donate later.

She stowed her purse in the locker, but since it had no lock, she put her bankcard and driver's license in one pocket of her jeans and her car keys in the other. She made a mental note to go into town later and buy a combination lock. She might be living among Christian brothers and sisters, but she wasn't going to leave her purse unguarded. In fact, she decided she would point out that oversight to Joseph when they met.

Locating the bathroom at the end of the sleeping room, she took a quick look in the mirror and fluffed her hair before leaving to meet with Joseph. She took the stairs to the first floor, found out where the office was located and set off at a brisk pace toward the small building she'd driven past on her way to the farmhouse.

She entered and heard Joseph in the inner office. Realizing he was on the telephone, she looked around what she assumed was her office. The room was sparsely furnished: a computer desk, laptop and combination printer/scanner/fax machine, a copier and two filing cabinets.

The stark white walls were unadorned other than a banner on the wall behind the desk. The banner was off-white with gold braided trim and CUP's logo – a golden goblet, engraved with a Celtic trinity knot, superimposed over a circle. Beneath the logo, the ministry's motto, taken from Psalm 23:5 – "My cup runneth over."

Gazing at the banner, Brigitte wondered: *Why do we use that verse? What does it have to do with peace or unity? It's more of a play on our name than anything else...*

The door to the inner office opened. Joseph saw Brigitte and smiled. He put an arm around her shoulders and guided her to the chair at the computer desk.

"Welcome to your new office," he said. "Right now there's not much telephone work, but it will increase as we extend the scope of our outreach. For the time being, most of the assistance I'll need is with correspondence, research for messages and meetings, record keeping, that kind of thing.

"I'll also need you to work with Brother Justin on the website launch. He has a real talent for site design and writing code, but I want you to collaborate with him on site content."

Brigitte nodded as he continued to list her duties. From what he was saying, it sounded like a typical administrative assistant job. Brigitte figured it couldn't be any more demanding than working for three lawyers.

Their meeting only took about five minutes. Joseph ended by saying until Brigitte was finished at the law office, he would only need her help with minimal office matters that could be done in half an hour or so either at the beginning or end of her day; it was her choice. Brigitte told him she'd be glad to tackle anything needing to be done when she returned each day.

"Very good, my sister. If there is nothing else we need to discuss, I have other matters to attend to, and I'm sure you would like to arrange the desk to your liking," Joseph said as he turned to walk back into the inner office.

"Actually, Brother Joseph, there is a matter concerning our sleeping quarters."

"Oh?" Joseph returned to stand by Brigitte's desk. She sensed a tenseness in his body language and suddenly felt intimidated; it felt as though he were looming over her.

"Never mind," she said, deciding not to mention the need for locks on the footlockers. She decided she'd go get one and tell him about it later. "After I'm done here, I have a few errands to run in town. I'm low on certain toiletries, and I promised my sister I'd meet her for coffee this afternoon. I should be back within two hours."

Joseph was silent long enough for Brigitte to begin feeling uncomfortable before he said, "Very well, my sister. I look forward to your return." Walking back to his office, he turned and added, "While you're in town, why don't you pass out some flyers? I'd appreciate it if you could spare a few minutes to do a little ministry outreach while you are out and about."

Brigitte flushed and nodded. *Maybe it's my imagination, but that sure felt like a rebuke.*

Joseph beamed at her. "Many thanks, Sister Brigitte. Your devotion blesses me and pleases our Lord."

She smiled, feeling relieved and thinking she was being overly sensitive because of the day's events. Turning to the computer, she booted it up and took a few minutes to become familiar with the operating system and hard drive contents. It was a typical laptop with the same programs she used at work, so she wouldn't have any trouble.

She took inventory of the office supplies on her desk and in the storage cabinet around the corner. She added sticky notes to her mental shopping list, then knocked on Joseph's door and told him she was leaving to run her errands. Occupied with something he was writing, he nodded without looking up and said, "Don't forget to take some flyers with you, sister. They're in the top drawer of the filing cabinet."

Brigitte found the flyers and took a handful, then ran back to the farmhouse to grab her purse. Jumping into the Volvo, she headed into town, calling Chantal as she drove. "Hi, sis. Want to meet for coffee at Fuzzy Logic?"

"Sounds good, Brigitte. Sue's with me. Is it all right if she comes along?"

Not really. "Sure thing, Chantal. It's been a while since I've seen her; we can catch up. See y'all in ten?"

Chantal agreed and hung up. Brigitte gripped the steering wheel and confessed her regret to the Lord about telling Brother Joseph the coffee date was already planned. She debated whether or not to tell Joseph when she returned, but decided it had been a harmless prevarication, an excuse to get back into town so she could buy the padlock. There was no need to burden him over something so minor...

Humming along with a pop song on the radio, she cruised into town and parked in front of Fuzzy Logic. While she waited for Chantal and Sue to arrive, she handed out the flyers to every passerby she encountered. Everyone took the flyers politely but no one stopped to talk about the ministry, which suited Brigitte just fine.

Satisfied she had fulfilled her obligation, she entered the

coffee shop and ordered a large cinnamon latte, then sat in one of the comfortable arm chairs in the back corner. A few minutes later she spotted Chantal and Sue. Before joining Brigitte, they stopped at the counter to place their orders –iced mocha latte for Chantal and a fruit smoothie with honey for Sue.

The women embraced and Chantal noticed Brigitte held the hug longer than expected. They separated and sat as the barista arrived with their orders.

"You okay, sis? I'm glad you wanted to get together, but you've been kind of keeping your distance lately."

Brigitte sighed. "I don't know, y'all. I'm having second thoughts about moving out to the farmhouse. You do know about that, don't you?" When Chantal nodded, Brigitte said, "Yeah, I figured Mother would tell you the second we hung up yesterday. I was so gung-ho for the idea at first, but now I'm thinking I should have stayed in the duplex."

You bet you should have stayed, and you shouldn't have sold your stuff. Chantal left the thought unspoken and instead asked, "Why do you say that?"

Brigitte swirled her latte. Chantal glanced at Sue, but no one spoke.

Finally, Brigitte shrugged. "Maybe I'm nervous about moving into a house with a bunch of other people, but I felt so uncomfortable there today. We don't have separate bedrooms, for one thing." Seeing the surprised looks on Chantal and Sue's faces, she added, "What I mean is, the women have one room and the men have another, but there are only two sleeping rooms, like we're camping at a lodge or something. And that's not all..."

Chantal struggled to stay calm as she sensed her sister's mounting tension. "What else?"

"Brother Joseph asked me to leave my job and work in the ministry office. I insisted I needed to give two weeks' notice at the law firm if I do it, and he agreed, but he sounded like he didn't really mean it. And there was no mention of a paycheck with this new position. Granted, I don't really have any bills to pay since I'm out of the duplex, but still..."

Chantal swallowed. What she was hearing alarmed her, but she didn't want to drive her sister away right as she was making an effort to communicate. She looked at Sue for help, but Sue shrugged and shook her head.

Brigitte looked at both of them, waiting for a response. Finally she exclaimed, "What? Aren't either of you going to put your two cents' worth in here? I expected one or both of you to tell me I should get my stuff and leave there as soon as humanly possible..."

Chantal cleared her throat. "Brigitte, of course I want you to do what's best for you, and I never was in favor of what you've done, but as Dad reminded me, you're capable of making your own decisions. Let me ask you one thing: Do you think Joseph Zacharias is a true prophet of God, teaching the real Word of Christ?"

"Absolutely! I haven't heard one thing in his teaching that

would make me think otherwise," Brigitte declared. "It's not his beliefs I'm wondering about; it's whether or not communal living is right for me." She shook her head. "I guess I'm a little uneasy about making such a big change in my lifestyle, but I'll be okay after I adjust."

"What about your job? Have you made a decision yet?" Sue asked.

Brigitte nodded. "I'm going to take the ministry job. I'll talk to Joseph about pay when I go back. Right now I need to buy a few toiletries and some sticky notes; we don't have any at the office." She picked up her latte and purse. "Thanks for letting me vent, girls. I'll keep you both in my prayers; please keep me in yours. See you later!" She walked away rapidly, not giving Sue and Chantal a chance to hug her goodbye.

Sue waited until Brigitte left before rounding on Chantal. "Why didn't you tell her what you really think? I can't believe you let her get away!"

"I didn't hear you raising any big objections either! Besides, you saw how she was when she left; I don't think we could have said anything to make her see the truth. She thinks Joseph Zacharias is the best thing since sliced bread. Until her eyes are open to who he really is, she'll follow him anywhere he says go."

The women lapsed into silence as they finished their drinks. Sue knew Chantal was right, and neither knew of any way the situation could possibly end well for Brigitte. As they walked back to the cottage, Chantal prayed, *Lord, show me what to do now.*

CHAPTER 21

Sunday morning dawned gray and drizzly, an apt backdrop to Chantal's mood as she rose and dressed for church. Since her meeting with Brigitte on Friday, she had been in a blue funk. Her father's birthday dinner Saturday was subdued. Martin was pleased with his gifts - the pepper grinder from Chantal and a custom-made driver his wife ordered to replace the club he'd pitched into a water hazard during a bad round of golf a month earlier. Still, Brigitte's absence deflated the celebration; Martin and Helene retired to their suite immediately after the birthday cake was served.

As for Chantal, she hadn't been able to concentrate enough to make any new jewelry to replace what Sally sold that week at Kudzu Café. Even knowing Marc was due back in town early Sunday afternoon didn't lift her spirits.

She spent Saturday moping around the cottage, fighting restlessness by dusting and rearranging knickknacks and pulling weeds in the flower garden. She went to the main house only for a couple of hours for the birthday dinner, then turned in for the night with *Emma*, hoping a dose of Jane Austen would dispel her gloominess. It didn't.

Hoping to combat her dreary mood, Chantal chose a fuchsia dress, a pair of chandelier earrings she had made to go with it, and semi-dressy navy flats – pretty, but sturdy enough to walk a few blocks in. She swept her hair up into a loose chignon, geared up –

Bible, purse, short trench coat and umbrella – and headed for church.

Arriving a few minutes before 9, she found the women's classroom and took a seat in the back. As class members began arriving, they greeted each other and chatted, catching up on the week's activities. Almost everyone stopped to welcome Chantal and express the hope she would join them again next week. She smiled and said thanks about fifteen times before the teacher, who happened to be Sally Jennings, entered and started the lesson.

After a prayer, she directed the class to open their Bibles. "Let's start in verse 20 of Second Peter, chapter 1. I'm reading out of the New International Version, so my wording may be slightly different from yours, but the ideas are the same."

She read II Peter 1, verses 20 and 21: "Above all, you must understand that no prophecy of Scripture came about by the prophet's own interpretation. For prophecy never had its origin in the will of man, but men spoke from God as they were carried along by the Holy Spirit." Looking up, she asked, "Now, what was Peter saying here?"

A young woman in the front row offered, "Was he saying the Bible isn't simply some manmade book dreamed up by the authors, but that it was given by God to the men who wrote the different books?"

"Exactly. Of course, the scriptures we know as the Bible weren't called the Bible back then, but you're essentially correct. Good answer, Lisa." She smiled at the young woman, then added with a look around the classroom, "Of course, I'm not at all biased, even if she is my daughter."

The class laughed and nodded, and Sally continued, " Now, let's move on to chapter 2, verses 1 through 3." She read: "But there were also false prophets among the people, just as there will be false teachers among you. They will secretly introduce destructive heresies, even denying the sovereign Lord who bought them – bringing swift destruction on themselves. Many will follow their shameful ways and will bring the way of truth into disrepute. In their greed these teachers will exploit you with stories they have made up. Their condemnation has long been hanging over them, and their destruction has not been sleeping."

Sally paused and surveyed the class. "Seems fairly straightforward, doesn't it? False teachers, motivated by greed, will try to lead as many people as possible astray from the true gospel of Christ. What do you think Peter meant here by greed?"

The class members looked at each other and then at Sally, but no one answered. "I know," she said with a chuckle, "sounds like a trick question, doesn't it? The answer seems so obvious. We think of a hunger for money when we think of greed, and that certainly can factor into the equation – look at all the televangelists who've been investigated and even arrested in the last couple of decades because of financial wrongdoings.

"However, this greed goes deeper than merely wanting to separate people from their money. The word used here is 'pleonexia,' a Greek word translated as 'covetousness' in the King

James Version of the Bible. It comes from a root word whose first definition is 'one eager to have more, especially what belongs to others.' So we can see the greed, or covetousness, being spoken of here isn't necessarily about money, but about taking away from God and His kingdom that which belongs to Him, namely His people."

Chantal raised her hand and Sally nodded for her to speak. "But how can a person take someone away from God? I mean, He's all powerful, so how – "

"Excellent question, Chantal. I'm glad you joined us today." Sally looked back down at her Bible. "Notice what the verse we read says? 'They will secretly introduce destructive heresies … and will bring the way of truth into disrepute.' In other words, they sow doubt among the believers as to whether what the Bible says – what God says in His Word – is true, and so they lead them astray. They may even use verses from the Bible, but they'll twist those verses to suit their false doctrines."

Some of the class nodded, while others still looked confused. Sally said, "Let's look at some background in the Old Testament to broaden our understanding a little. Let's go back to the beginning in Genesis chapter 2, verses 16 and 17, where God told man he could eat of any tree in the garden, but not to eat of the tree of the knowledge of good and evil or he would surely die. Now, we know how the story goes from there, right? A certain serpent paid Eve a visit at some point after she was created, and made a mess of things.

"Before I go further with the account, I want to point out that the story of Eve's creation occurs after the admonition from God not to eat of the tree of the knowledge of good and evil. God warned the man not to eat of the tree and then a few verses later we're told He created the woman. Since the Bible doesn't tell me otherwise, it's possible she got her warning about the tree from the man and not directly from God."

Sally paused and then asked, "Has anyone here ever played Post Office? You may also know it as Telephone. It's the game where one person whispers something in the next person's ear, and that person whispers it to the next person, and so on until the message gets back to its originator. If you've ever played it, you'll remember the ending message never was the same as the beginning message. You'll see why I bring this up in a minute."

She resumed telling the story of Eve's conversation with the serpent. "So, a few verses after God told the man not to eat of a certain tree, He had the man take a nap and extracted from him the material to make a companion for him. She was called a 'woman' because she was taken from the man. The two of them were introduced, and all was well in the garden.

"Some time passed – we don't know how much – and the woman got into a conversation with the serpent. Now, I don't know about y'all, but I'd find it odd if a water moccasin started talking to me and I could understand it," Sally quipped.

The women laughed and agreed, and she continued, "Apparently, though, the man and woman were used to it, so perhaps it was the way things were before the fall of man. Anyway, the woman is having a chat with the serpent, and he starts asking questions about the trees in the garden. His first question is meant to sow doubt – "Did God really say, 'You must not eat from any tree in the garden?'" – and of course, the woman tells him no, they can eat from the trees, but not that one tree. Now, if you'll notice, she says they were told not to eat from or even touch the tree, or they would die. Did God tell the man not to touch the tree?"

Heads started shaking as the women looked back at Genesis 2:17 and realized there was nothing said about touching the tree. Sally asked, "Why do you suppose the woman would think such a thing? Is it possible God's original warning got embellished a bit in the retelling? This is what makes me think the man, not God, told the woman about the tree. I could be wrong, but it seems to me if God had told them not to touch the tree, it would have been mentioned in His original warning to the man.

"So, back to the story. Here we have the woman talking to the serpent, who has already cast a seed of doubt by questioning God's command. The fact that the woman doesn't have the command straight in her mind doesn't help matters. So, his answer to her continues the process he's already started. He says, 'You won't die if you eat the fruit. God knows if you eat it, your eyes will be opened and you'll be like God, knowing the difference between good and evil.'

"Get it, y'all? He called God a liar and accused Him of

holding out on the man and woman. The truth is, though, God was protecting them from experiencing the pain of evil and the temptations of the sensual pleasures of this world. Since the serpent needed them to be vulnerable to these things in order to make his plan work, he twisted God's words to sow doubt into their minds and tempt them to eat the forbidden fruit."

Chantal said, "So, you're telling us the false teachers Peter talks about are behaving like this serpent, making up stories and twisting God's words to lead people astray from His truth?" Sally nodded. Chantal asked, "So that means even though we're dealing with people – the false teachers, I mean – we're not really dealing with people at all, are we?"

Sally pointed to Chantal and said, "Bingo! Let's go back to the New Testament, to Ephesians 6:12." When everyone had finished flipping pages, she read, "For our struggle is not against flesh and blood, but against the rulers, against the authorities, against the powers of this dark world and against the spiritual forces of evil in the heavenly realms."

Looking up again, she asked rhetorically, "And who would these rulers, these spiritual forces, be? Satan and his fallen angel followers, right? So, even though you may be faced with a live human being who is trying to deceive you with false teachings, that person is being influenced, perhaps even possessed, by a demon assigned by Satan to wreak as much havoc as it can among God's people."

Sally took the class to Ephesians 2 and read the first ten

verses. "You'll see here we were all under the influence of this world and the ruler of the kingdom of the air – that would be Satan, whose name means 'Adversary' – until we accepted the free gift of salvation.

"God gave us this gift because He loves us, His creation. The gift works because of God's grace and the obedience of His Son Jesus – who is fully God and fully man – to go to the cross on our behalf as a sinless sacrifice. When we accept his atoning death and resurrection, our salvation is secured. It's not because of any works we may do; those are a demonstration of our salvation, not a means to earning it. This is the truth; anything else, no matter how good it sounds or how comforting or exciting it feels, is a lie meant to lead us astray."

"Sally, I have a question," one of the women said. "I'm glad you brought us this lesson today; it's useful information and we can all apply it to our lives. But we've been going through the book of James for the last few classes. Why did you deviate from the planned lesson?"

Startled, Chantal stared at Sally and waited for her answer. Sally hesitated a few seconds before replying. "The only way I can really explain it is that when I was preparing the lesson earlier in the week, I felt like God wanted me to talk about this today instead. Someone here, perhaps several people, are either dealing with this issue right now or know someone they care about who is dealing with it." The wall clock chimed and Sally said, "We have five minutes before church starts. Let's close with a prayer.

"Lord God, I thank You for this very valuable lesson. Please show us through Your Holy Spirit how to use this information so we and those we cherish may come into the light of Your love and the path of Your truth through our Lord Jesus Christ, Your Son. For it is in his name we pray this. Amen."

As the class disbanded and the women headed for the sanctuary, Chantal remained seated with her head bowed. *So, Lord, now that I know what I'm up against, what do I do about it?*

CHAPTER 22

Brigitte fidgeted with the envelope she held for several moments before leaving her desk and knocking softly on the door of her employer and uncle, Lawrence Atherton.

The founder and senior partner of Atherton, Barnes and Compton, Lawrence was the oldest of the three brothers who had inherited the mantle of civic and business leadership from their family's previous generation. Brigitte's father Martin was the middle brother, while Sue's late father Nathan was the youngest.

The three brothers, as expected, had taken up professions approved of by their parents. Martin took over the bank when their father died; Lawrence started as a solo attorney and built his practice into a thriving three-lawyer firm; and Nathan became a doctor. He had once been the only general practitioner in town, but in his early 50s he took on a younger partner, to whom he sold the practice when he retired at 55. Two years ago, he died in a small plane crash as he was heading into the Amazon. He had been working with a team of physicians to provide medical care for indigenous populations who didn't have the money or means to go to a doctor or hospital.

Of the three brothers, only Lawrence had remained unmarried and childless; he poured all his time and energy into building the law firm and seemed to have no desire for a wife and family. The senior Athertons, who passed away while the girls were still children, were acutely disappointed none of their sons had produced a male heir to carry on the family name. Unless Chantal, Brigitte or Sue had a male child and insisted on giving him her last name, only the town itself and Lawrence's law firm would carry the Atherton name after this generation.

As Brigitte waited for her uncle to invite her in, she reflected that she, her sister and cousin certainly hadn't felt compelled to carry on the family traditions. None of them had become (or married) a doctor, banker or lawyer, although Brigitte had been considering a career in law, which was why she took the job at her uncle's firm. Now, though, it seemed her career was going a different direction...

Hearing no answer, she knocked again, a little louder this time.

"Enter." Lawrence Atherton's commanding voice never failed to intimidate his paralegal niece. Gulping, Brigitte pushed the door open and walked up to her uncle's desk. She extended the letter and he reached for it reflexively. She waited silently while he slit the envelope with his gold-plated opener and read her resignation letter.

Lawrence eyed her somewhat sternly. "Does this have something to do with that CUP group you joined?"

Brigitte's eyes widened. She hadn't said much about CUP around the office, not out of embarrassment or fear but simply because it hadn't come up in conversation. Neither had she mentioned it in the letter; she merely said she had accepted an opportunity with a nonprofit organization she felt could benefit from her legal and administrative background. She was truly surprised her uncle even knew about CUP, let alone knew she was a member.

"I take it that's a yes," Lawrence remarked. "Brigitte, sit down for a minute."

She sat, so accustomed to taking direction from him as her employer she didn't even hesitate. Lawrence studied her for several moments as she fidgeted under his steady gaze. Finally unable to stand the silent staring, Brigitte said, "Did you want to say something to me, Uncle Lawrence? I really need to get back to my desk..."

"Why are you doing this, Brigitte? I know it's not about money; I pay you more than any nonprofit possibly could. Are you unhappy here?"

Brigitte shook her head. "No, Uncle Lawrence, I'm not unhappy at all. I just think I can be of more use at CUP's headquarters. Joseph needs a capable administrative assistant to help with the website, the office and the bookkeeping, and he said I was his first choice."

Lawrence leaned back in his leather chair and folded his hands over his stomach. "I see. And will this nonprofit organization be paying enough to cover your expenses?" Seeing Brigitte bristle, he added, "I don't mean to pry, but you are my niece, after all, and I am concerned about you."

Brigitte pursed her lips, then nodded. "I understand your concern, really I do. But I'll be fine. I'm moving in with friends and we'll all be sharing expenses."

"Moving in with friends? Don't you mean moving into a commune? Oh yes, my dear," he said in reaction to her look of shock and surprise, "I know about the farmhouse and land Mr. Zacharias purchased for CUP's use."

Brigitte stood, rigid with suppressed anger. "Uncle Lawrence, I do not need your permission, any more than I need Father's and Mother's, to do what I believe God wants me to do. Now, whether you accept my resignation or not, I will be leaving in two weeks. I would strongly suggest you go ahead and hire my replacement so I can show her what she needs to know to be an effective assistant to you and your partners." She turned on her heel and marched out of his office, almost slamming his door on the way back to her desk.

* * *

The next two weeks passed in a blur for Brigitte. Her uncle wasted no time in calling a temporary staffing agency and having someone sent out to take her position. She spent the rest of her days at the firm showing the new paralegal where files were kept both on the computer and in the cabinets, where the law firm's library was and how it was organized, and all the other things pertaining to the firm's daily operations. She had already put together a binder of important information, which the partners had dubbed "Brigitte's Bible," and on her last day at the office she passed it along to her successor.

"Now remember, Deanna," she said as they left at the end of the day and Brigitte handed over her keys, "my cell phone number and new office number are inside the front cover of the binder. If you have questions or can't locate something and need my help, give me a call."

Deanna nodded and took the keys. She gave Brigitte a quick hug. "It's been good working with you. You've been a great teacher. I wish you success with the new job." She gave Brigitte a parting wave before getting into her dark metallic blue subcompact and leaving the parking lot. Brigitte watched her leave, then turned back and looked at the office building one last time. *I sure hope this was the right move.* She walked to her car, wiping away a tear.

As she was about to step into the Volvo, her cell phone vibrated in her purse. Reaching in to grab it, she flipped it open before the call could go to voice mail. "Hello?" She could hear the tremor in her voice and hoped her caller didn't notice it.

"Sister Brigitte? Are you well?"

Brigitte took a deep breath before replying. "Yes, Brother Joseph. I'm fine. I just got a little emotional about leaving my job. I've been here for so long, and it's hard to leave, especially since I was working for family..."

"I understand completely, my sister. Transitions are seldom easy, especially when you feel those you love don't understand why you're making the change. That's why I called; I sensed you needed a word of encouragement. I feel the Lord wants me to tell you he is pleased with your courage and obedience to move forward and he has great blessings in store for you as you move into your Promised Land."

Brigitte hesitated, then asked, "Don't you mean CUP's Promised Land, Brother Joseph?"

She could tell he was smiling as he replied, "No, my sister, I mean your Promised Land. Of course this new chapter in CUP's history is an important time for all of us, but I'm sensing the Lord has a special blessing and an important role for you in that history. I don't want to overwhelm you on such a difficult day; we can discuss all this later. I wanted to let you know your commitment to the Lord's work has pleased him – and me – very much."

"Thank you, Brother Joseph," Brigitte answered, feeling better. "I'm heading back to New Canaan now. Is there anything we need in town I can pick up on my way through? I have to cash my final paycheck..."

"No, my dear, there's nothing we need at the moment except your presence. We'll see you shortly. I must go now as there are matters requiring my attention here." Before she could say goodbye she heard the click of a broken connection. She closed her phone and dropped it into her purse, then sat in her car for a few more moments before leaving the law firm parking lot for the last time.

As she drove, she mulled over what Joseph said. She and the other CUP members were accustomed to his declarations from the Lord, but she wondered what this special blessing and important role could possibly be. All she had done so far was host a small group meeting, faithfully attend services and participate in outreaches, and agree to take responsibility for the daily administration of the ministry office. In her opinion, none of that merited any special reward; it was what anyone else would have done, had they been called upon instead of her.

Perhaps it was because she was one of the first to move to New Canaan and because she agreed to give up her job in the outside world in order to serve the ministry full time. Whatever the meaning of this latest word from the Lord, Brigitte appreciated the encouragement from Brother Joseph; it came in time to squelch the latest attack of doubt to besiege her.

She tuned the car radio to the local Christian station as she drove to Regions Bank, then turned the radio down as she entered the drive-through and cashed her paycheck. She was fortunate to find an open lane with no cars ahead of her; the entire transaction took less than three minutes, and she headed back out of town with barely a glance in her rearview mirror. She turned the radio back up as she pointed the Volvo toward New Canaan and sang her way out to the farmhouse, feeling a peace she had been missing in recent days.

CHAPTER 23

"I need a break." Chantal unfolded her legs and stood. She and Sue were once again on the floor in Chantal's living room, where they had almost completely covered the coffee table with jewelry and basket supplies and finished pieces. The county's Fall Festival was less than two weeks away, and the cousins were using every spare minute to increase their inventories for the event, which was slated to run from October 31 through November 2.

"Could you snag me a Coke, please?" Sue asked without looking up from the triangle basket she was making. She had finally stopped trying to weave the bottom of it and instead used her power tools fashion a wood base that held the spokes of the basket. She was more than halfway finished weaving vines through the spokes and didn't want to stop for such trivial matters as getting a drink or restoring the feeling to her numb legs.

"Sure thing, cous. I'm in need of some bubble water myself. I like how your basket is coming out. The alternating stripes of the vines, with some stripped and others with their bark still on, look good."

"Thanks." Sue moved her head from the left side to the right to stretch her neck and relieve some of the tension in her shoulders. She rolled her shoulders backward, then alternated raising them in one-shoulder shrugs. Glancing at the necklaces and earrings on Chantal's side of the coffee table, she said, "Cool stuff, girl. We may have to work out an exchange – one of my baskets for one of your necklace and earring sets, maybe."

Chantal grinned. "Sounds good to me." She handed Sue a Coke, popped the top on her own can, and took a long drink. "Mmm, that hits the spot."

She stretched her free arm up and winced as her shoulder protested the movement. "My body can't take being stuck in one position for so long. I need to take a breather and work out some of the kinks in my muscles and the cramps in my hands. How long have we been at this anyway?" She glanced at the clock on her microwave. "No wonder I'm so stiff! We started at, what, 1 p.m. or so? It's 5 now, and this is the first time I've gotten off the floor since we sat down!" She shook her head.

Sue laughed. "Yep, that's what happens when you get in a creative zone. You lose track of time, and you ignore the aches and pains because you want to do one more thing..."

Chantal chuckled. "Don't I know. It's why I don't start on jewelry projects before work or church. There's no way I'd get there on time if I did. Hey, you want a pizza?"

"Nah, I'm about pizza'd out. I am getting hungry, though. I guess we should think about getting some food into us sometime in the next hour or so..."

An insistent knock interrupted the cousins' conversation. Chantal gave Sue an "I don't know who it could be" look and shrugged as she went to answer the door. Seconds later, she backed into the living room laughing, followed by Marc and John hauling a large picnic basket and cooler. Marc had a blue gingham picnic blanket folded over his left shoulder.

"Hi, guys!" Sue greeted them. "I realize y'all aren't psychic, but if I didn't know better, I'd swear you were reading our minds! We were talking about taking a supper break."

"We could say we have the room bugged," John said, "but there's no way we could have fried this chicken that fast. No, we figured you'd be so busy getting ready for the festival you wouldn't take time to cook, and since Luis is catering a party, Taco Loco is closed."

"That's why we decided to exercise our own culinary skills and make supper for y'all," Marc added. "Do you want to go to the park for a picnic, or have it right here?"

"You guys are too much!" Chantal exclaimed. "You cooked for us?"

"Yes, indeed. So, where shall we spread out this feast, here or in the great outdoors?"

"Tell you what, why don't we compromise? Let's eat outside, but not at the park. We can have our picnic right here. There's a grassy spot beside the cottage where we can spread it all out, and I can turn my stereo on for some dinner music. When Mother had the place built, she made sure the sound system included outdoor speakers hidden in some fake rocks in the garden for such occasions as this."

Marc looked at John, who nodded. "Sounds good. We'll take this outside and start setting up while you select some music. I'm in the mood for modern jazz, but I'm sure whatever you pick will be great." Marc leaned forward and gave Chantal a light kiss on the lips, then the guys exited with the cooler and picnic basket. After a few moments, Sue and Chantal could hear them setting up near the garden's koi pond and fountain.

Chantal sighed and smiled. "Those two sure take good care of us, don't they, Sue?" She moved to the stereo and adjusted the settings so the music would transmit through the outdoor speakers, then she pulled up her mp3 player's Mississippi Music playlist, a mix of country, blues and jazz by Magnolia State artists. Setting the player to shuffle the playlist, she pressed the Start button and turned to look at Sue, who hadn't replied. "Cous, are you okay? Things are good with you and John, aren't they? You didn't answer me..."

Sue glanced up, nodding as her eyes focused and she noticed the concern on Chantal's face. "Sure thing; everything's fine with John and me. I zoned out again, trying to decide how to finish off the top edge of this basket..."

Chantal laughed and held out her hand to help Sue stand. "Forget the basket for a few minutes, will ya? We have two handsome men waiting outside with food they cooked especially for us. You can go back to obsessing over your art later."

Sue chuckled. "Deal. Speaking of the guys and supper, have you had any of Marc's cooking yet?" She and Chantal moved toward the front door.

"Nope. This will be the first time."

"Same with John and me," Sue replied. "I hope they can actually cook. I mean, I'll be polite regardless, but ..."

Chantal bit her lip. "Ooh, I didn't think of that. Here's hoping..." She held up her right hand and crossed her fingers.

Sue snickered and gave Chantal a playful shove out the door. "You said it," she replied in a stage whisper, then raised her voice and said, "Get out of my way, girl! I want some chicken..."

* * *

"Oh, my goodness! I haven't had chicken this good in a long time," Chantal exclaimed as she bit into her second piece.

"I haven't had chicken this good ever," Sue remarked. "What's the secret? It's so moist, but not greasy."

Marc grinned. "Buttermilk. You let the chicken marinate in it for at least half an hour, then you dredge the pieces in seasoned flour. Dunk them in buttermilk again and then dredge them in the flour a second time. That gives the chicken an extra crispy coating. Of course, you have to get the oil to the right temperature, too, or the chicken ends up raw inside, tough outside, or some combination of the two."

"What seasonings do you put in the flour?" John asked as he reached for a drumstick. "I really like the balance of the savory and spicy flavors."

"Sorry, it's an old family recipe, and I've been sworn to secrecy. Big Mama said if I told it to anyone other than my wife and children, she'd have my hide, even if she had to come back from the grave to do it."

"By all means, let's not risk the wrath of Big Mama," John laughed. "Maybe one of these days you'll be willing to part with the recipe, though..." He glanced at Chantal and raised his eyebrows, then bit into the drumstick to hide his grin as Marc shot him a "shut up" look.

Chantal and Sue, sitting next to one another at adjoining sides of the picnic blanket, had gone back to discussing the upcoming festival. Neither one showed any indication of having heard John's comment. Marc gave John another warning glance and exhaled deeply, relieved to have avoided what could have been an embarrassing moment. The truth was, he was starting to have such thoughts about Chantal, but they'd only known each other a few weeks, and he was concerned maybe his heart was running away with his common sense...

"Earth to Marc? Where'd you go?" Chantal waved her hand in front of Marc to get his attention. "Do you want any chicken or anything, or are you ready to break out the dessert?"

Marc cleared his throat, hoping his voice wouldn't betray the emotion behind his thoughts, and said, "Dessert sounds good to me, but I didn't make any. Sorry about that."

"No problem, hon," Chantal replied. "I have a chocolate peanut butter pie in the fridge. I bought it from Kudzu Café for dinner at the main house last night, but Mother told me she and Father had a prior engagement and wouldn't be able to make our usual Saturday meal." She stood and stretched. "Sue, can you help me put away the leftovers? I assume you'd prefer me to put them in my fridge than in the ice chest, Marc."

"Definitely," Marc said. "The cole slaw and potato salad both have mayo in them, so they should be refrigerated. Y'all need any help?"

"No. You and John can take care of the picnic garbage, and we'll take the food in and bring dessert out in a minute, okay?" Chantal picked up the platter of chicken and bowl of cole slaw, while Sue snagged the potato salad and cornbread muffins. As they headed back into the cottage, the guys started picking up paper plates and plasticware.

Inside the cottage, Sue covered the dishes while Chantal pulled out the pie and started fitting the leftovers into the refrigerator. Sue laughed softly. "Good job, Chantal."

"What?" Chantal said, looking back at Sue. "It's not a major act of genius to put food in the fridge..."

"No, I'm talking about that award-winning act you put on out there like you were oblivious to what was going on. You know what I mean."

Chantal turned to stare at Sue. "What on earth are you babbling about?"

"Oh come on. You're not gonna stand there and try to make me believe you actually didn't hear the whole recipe conversation the guys were having, are you?"

Chantal shook her head. "I have no clue what you're talking about, Sue."

Sue's eyes widened. "Really? Well, let me tell you..."

* * *

Chantal was flushed as she delivered the pie to the picnic blanket. She put the pie and a server down in the middle of the blanket, straightened and said, "Excuse me a minute. I want to walk off a little of that excellent meal before I get into the pie. Y'all go on and help yourselves, though..." She turned and walked into the garden without waiting for a response.

Marc raised an eyebrow at John, then stood and excused himself. Heading down the path after Chantal, he caught up with her near the hedgerow maze at the back of the garden. "Chantal, are you okay?"

"Have a lot on my mind is all," she said, avoiding his gaze. She started to walk into the maze, but Marc caught her by the elbow and gently turned her back toward him. Cupping her chin in his hand, he turned her face up so he could look into her eyes.

He searched her expression for a clue to her suddenly subdued behavior. The flush still on her cheeks, and the way she tilted her face to look past him, told Marc more than Chantal might have wanted. He sighed and said, "Oh. Guess you did hear that dumb remark of John's, after all. I didn't think you did; you sure didn't act like you heard him..."

Chantal continued to look past Marc's shoulder for a few moments, then brought her gaze back to him. "Actually, I didn't hear it. Sue caught the whole exchange, looks and all, and she told me while we were putting the food away." She took a deep breath and continued, "Why did John's comment upset you, Marc? Surely you plan on marrying someone someday..."

"Of course I do," Marc answered. "It's just what John implied when he said it..." He sighed and cleared his throat. "Chantal, I care for you very much. The thing is, we've only known each other a little over five weeks –"

Chantal stopped him with a touch of her finger to his lips. "We need to take our time to get to know each other, right? Besides, until this situation with Brigitte is resolved, and until my father is given the go-ahead from the doctor to resume his normal schedule and activity level, I can't give anyone my full attention, and that wouldn't be fair to either of us."

Marc rested his hands on her shoulders. "Then we're in agreement? We'll take things slowly, see what develops?"

She rose up on her tiptoes and gave him a light kiss. "Agreed."

He hugged her, and she slipped her arms around his waist, leaned into him and lay her head on his chest. He rested his cheek on the top of her head and smiled in the deepening twilight. They stood that way for several minutes, enjoying each other's presence as they watched the cloud-enhanced sunset change from orange and mauve to purple and indigo.

Finally, Chantal pulled back a little and looked up at Marc. She started to ask if he wanted to walk the maze with her, but she didn't have time before Marc pulled her closer and kissed her, a long tender kiss that quickly became more urgent for both of them. Marc broke the kiss with a shudder.

"I think we better head back to the picnic," he murmured. "Otherwise our agreement about taking things slowly might not last long."

Her nod was shaky as she stepped out of his embrace. "Yeah, that was some kiss." She blew out a ragged breath. "We might want to stay out of dark corners, huh?"

Marc threw his head back and laughed. Taking Chantal's hand, he turned back toward the well-lit side yard where Sue and John were making short work of the pie. "Hey," he called out, "did y'all save any dessert for us?"

CHAPTER 24

The next two weeks sped by as Chantal and Sue prepared for the Fall Festival. Chantal spent most of her off-work time either on the floor in her living room or at the table in her studio, producing more jewelry in 14 days than she previously had in two months.

Until then, she had considered her jewelry work a hobby that paid for itself when friends, coworkers or family members bought a ready-made piece or commissioned a custom item. However, thanks to the modest success she was enjoying at Kudzu Café and the possibility of more sales at the county festival, Chantal was starting to think perhaps she could move beyond a hobby to an actual business. She hadn't disclosed these thoughts to anyone, not even Sue; she wanted to see how the festival went before she made any decisions.

Meanwhile, the ideas for individual pieces and sets were coming faster than she could execute them, so she bought a sketch book to get her designs down on paper before she lost track of them. She suspected her growing friendship with Marc was at least partly responsible for the boost in creativity; all the endorphins running through her system needed an outlet, and working on her jewelry let her focus that energy on something concrete.

Sue was riding a creative wave of her own, holed up in her cottage so she could produce more baskets, some handmade paper accented by pressed baby kudzu leaves and wildflowers, and a couple of wall hangings she had started but left incomplete while working on other items.

While waiting for the handmade paper to dry, she made another batch of kudzu leaf/capiz shell pendants for Chantal to use during the festival. The cousins had agreed their booth would attract more interest if they were crafting items between sales, so she had pledged to make a dozen pendants that could be sold alone or incorporated into Chantal's work.

Two nights before the festival, Chantal and Sue packed everything into wheeled plastic bins with pull handles to facilitate transport to the booth site in case they couldn't park nearby. Sue had the tables, tent and bug repellant from previous shows, so Chantal had a fairly short list of items to take: inventory, work in progress and tools; materials for packaging sales; display props, a mirror, business cards and brochures; a bank bag with $100 in small bills; a mini cooler filled with bottled water; a comfortable chair and sunscreen. Since she was pricing and packing jewelry as she finished it, she had most of the preparations complete by Wednesday night.

Thursday night, the men took the women to supper at Beaux Thais, then to look over the festival space and their booth location. The cool October air was refreshing. Chantal took a deep breath and closed her eyes for a moment, opening them to find Marc gazing at her.

"Whatcha lookin' at?" she asked with a grin tugging at the

corners of her mouth.

"You," he replied. Her gaze slid away to a maple tree in the distance. "I love how much you appreciate things like the night air or that maple you're staring at so hard." He chuckled when she cut her eyes back to him in surprise. "Yeah, I noticed how much you like the changing colors of the trees. I figure you're probably getting ideas for your jewelry."

She laughed softly. "God is the Master Designer. Why shouldn't I take a few cues from His handiwork?" She shook her head, relishing the breeze that lifted the hair off her neck. Marc held out his hand and she let him steer her toward an oak where Sue and John waited.

"This is our spot – prime real estate near the festival entrance," Sue said as she indicated a space a little over 10 feet wide by 10 feet deep. "We'll set up the tent here and put the tables along the sides and back wall. We'll have to decide the exact layout tomorrow, but I know we can come up with something that works for both of us."

"Oh, sure, Sue. I'm not concerned about it. I just hope we do well. Every fair I've been to lately has been overrun with jewelry booths, so I'm not expecting big sales."

"Don't even think that way! This festival limits how many people can sell any one kind of thing so there'll be more variety for the attendees. Besides, I've seen what the other jewelry vendors will be offering. It's good, don't get me wrong, but none of it is like yours. In addition to using kudzu leaves in several of your pieces –"

"Thanks to you," Chantal interrupted.

Sue laughed. "True, but still, what I was going to say is besides the kudzu, you make things with a distinct style and sense of color. Most of the other jewelry vendors you'll see this weekend do simple pieces anyone could make. Your work stands out. If you don't believe me, ask Sally. When I went by to check on my inventory the other day, she told me a woman from out of town bought more than half your pieces and said she planned to give you a call about making more."

Chantal's eyes widened. "What? This is news to me! I've been so busy getting ready for tomorrow, I haven't even thought about my pieces at the Café. I did get a call on my cell phone a couple of days ago, but I didn't recognize the number. I completely forgot to check my voice mail messages..."

"What are you waiting for? Do it now."

Chantal rolled her eyes and fidgeted while the voice mail recording announced she had one new message, then grew still as the message played. Blinking rapidly, she saved the message, put the phone back in her jacket pocket and cleared her throat as she looked at Sue.

"Well? Was it the lady Sally mentioned?"

"I need to check my messages more often. It was Sally's customer. She owns art galleries in Vicksburg and Memphis, and she wants to feature some of my work in a regional show. She asked me to call for a meeting at my earliest convenience."

"Awesome!" Sue grabbed Chantal in a tight hug and danced her around in a circle as Chantal laughed. "See, I told you, girl! You got skills..."

Chantal broke away and threw her hands up in the air. "Wow! I'm so amazed I don't know what to say."

Marc grinned and gave her a slightly less exuberant hug than Sue's. "I know what to say. 'Thank You, Lord' seems appropriate to me."

Chantal gazed up as she leaned into his arms. "You're right, Marc. Thank You, Lord, for this wonderful opportunity – and for the chance to celebrate with my closest friends." She sighed and smiled, then turned her head to look at Sue.

"Do you think I should pull any of my inventory and save it for my meeting with the gallery owner – I think she said her name was Amelia Starnes – or put it all in the festival?" she asked her cousin.

"Don't hold anything out," Sue advised. "If it all sells – and let's hope it does – you can always make more. Besides, she already bought several items; I'm assuming she plans to show at least some of them."

"True." Chantal nodded. "Guys, I hate to cut the evening short, but we have a busy weekend ahead, and I still have to go to work in the morning. Sue, I'll swing by the print shop and get our banner after work, then come straight to the park. You want me to pick up a sandwich or something for you on the way?"

"Don't worry about it, Chantal," John said. "Marc and I have it covered. You come on out here after work, and we'll deliver your lunch and help set up."

Chantal smiled at the guys. "Y'all spoil us, you know that? Thanks."

Marc slipped his hand in hers as they headed back toward his car. "I'm glad you let me spoil you. It's the best part of my day."

CHAPTER 25

Friday morning dawned bright and clear, with just enough cloud cover to keep the day from getting uncomfortably warm. Chantal packed everything for the festival into her car, microwaved a breakfast pocket sandwich and ate it while she walked to work, and made herself a cup of spiced Mayan chocolate coffee before plunging into the Inbox.

Phone calls were minimal and so was the workload; her father was out participating in the Festival's charity golf tournament. Shortly before noon, Chantal shut down her computer and prepared to leave. As she reached for her purse, the desk phone rang.

"Good morning, Midtown Bank." She glanced at the wall clock and hoped the call would be short. She still had to get her car from the house, pick up the booth banner and help Sue set up.

"Hi, Chantal. I haven't heard from you lately, so I thought I should check on the status of your research into the story we discussed."

"Ryan, I'm so sorry. I've been so busy the last few weeks, I've kind of let that slide. I'm sharing a booth with Sue at the Fall Fest, but after it's over I'll get right back on my research and let you know what I find out, okay?"

"No problem – I'm in no hurry for your copy. I heard about the break-in at your house and wanted to touch base with you, see how you're doing."

"I'm fine – nothing was stolen. In fact, I still don't know what the motive was. Thanks for reminding me; I'll ask Marc if he can find out something."

"Marcus Thibodaux, huh? You two seem to be hitting it off, from what my sources say."

Chantal grinned. "So you're keeping tabs on me, are you? Careful, my friend, we wouldn't want anyone to accuse you of using your position as managing editor in an unethical way, now would we?"

Ryan chuckled. "No danger there. I found out everything I know by being out and about. This place is so small if I sneeze on one end of town, someone on the other end is bound to say 'God bless you, Ryan.'"

"So true, my friend. Well, I have to get by the print shop to pick up our banner. See you at the Fest?"

"You bet. I may even buy something..."

Chantal hung up smiling. She always enjoyed her chats with Ryan, and she was glad he'd reminded her about the stalled investigation. Between dates and festival preparations, she'd barely given CUP a thought for the last two weeks.

She tidied up, locked up and headed toward the front of the bank. As she left, she called out to everyone within earshot: "Remember, the Fall Fest starts today. See y'all there!"

Thirty minutes later, she was helping Sue with the tables. Sue had predicted that the guys wouldn't arrive until after she had the tent up and anchored, and she was right. They arrived looking contrite and bearing two to-go boxes.

John handed Sue the boxes. "Sorry we're late. We had to investigate a vandalism report at the Starlite drive-in, then we got a bunch of calls out in the county, including a case of attempted cow tipping."

Marc gave Chantal two large Styrofoam cups full of sweet tea. "The culprits were some boys cutting school. They discovered they couldn't push over a cow and scattered before we arrived."

"No worries; I usually have to set up by myself anyway," Sue said. "Chantal and I handled it. Didn't you get yourselves any lunch?"

Marc answered, "We ate a couple of burritos on the way here. Y'all sit and enjoy your meal; we'll finish placing the tables."

Sue directed them where to put things between bites of chicken chimichanga. After they set up the final table and a folding corner shelf unit, John asked, "Can we do anything else before we head back out on patrol?"

Chantal nodded as she swallowed a bite of avocado from her taco salad. "If you don't mind, we still need to get our merchandise and supplies out here." She tossed Marc her car keys.

"Sure thing, boo." While the guys were bringing the bins, Sue and Chantal finished lunch and strung up their banner, white with maple red lettering in honor of the fall festival. It read,

"Kudzu Creations by Sue/Jewelry by Chantal."

Sue squinted at it for a moment, then turned to Chantal. "Not bad, but you need a more creative name for the business if you're going to be showing in fancy Memphis galleries."

"Yeah, but I froze when Mike asked me what I wanted to put on the banner. I figured we might as well keep it simple for now. That's why I did my brochures and cards at home; I can print only what I need, and when I do come up with an official name, it's easy to make changes."

They turned to watch as the guys lugged the bins to the booth. "Man, this stuff is heavier than I thought it would be," John commented. "No wonder you have such great biceps, Sue."

"Yeah, between pulling vines and schlepping the finished products to fairs and shows, I can't help but get a workout." Sue took the bin and her keys from John and kissed him on the cheek. "Thanks, babe. I'll take it from here." She started to unpack the bin and set her wares up on one side of the tent.

Marc pulled Chantal's bin to the other side, set her keys on the nearest table, then put his hands on her shoulders. "We'll drop back by after work with supper, okay, cher?" He pulled her in for a quick hug. "Gotta go; we just received a call that the boys trying to tip the cow at the Johnson ranch were seen a few minutes ago making the goats faint at the Swensen place."

CHAPTER 26

As the sun set on the Festival's first day, Sue and Chantal packed their wares and cash, secured everything in their vehicles, lowered the walls of their tent, locked it for the night and joined their dates at a picnic table within view of the bandstand, where a local country group was starting to play. The Festival had an overnight security team, but neither of the cousins wanted to risk having someone sneak under the tent walls and make off with their goods, especially since the livestock-harassing truants hadn't yet been apprehended.

When Marc and John arrived with supper, they said the group of high schoolers seemed to be on a real Halloween prank spree. John set pizza boxes on the table and gave them a summary of the day's calls. "So far, they've knocked half the speakers off their stands at the drive-in, tried to tip a cow, scared a herd of goats into fainting and falling over, spray-painted unrepeatable graffiti on the town water tower, and prank-called Pied Piper with a 20-pizza order for the retirement home."

"Fortunately, the kid working the phone at Pied Piper recognized the caller's voice," Marc added as he pulled plates, napkins and four Cokes out of the picnic basket. "He said it was one of the high school's usual troublemakers. After claiming he was having a problem with the computer, he put the guy on hold, checked with the retirement home to confirm they weren't placing the order, and then called the police department. By the time he got back to the caller, the prankster had hung up, but at least the police department has a name to work with now."

"I'm confused," Chantal commented. "If he knew who was calling and figured it was a prank, why did he check with the retirement home?"

Marc chuckled. "I asked him the same thing when I went to pick up our order. He said the prankster has grandparents in the retirement home; he thought it was possible they were hosting a pizza party and had their grandson call in an order. He figured it would be better to check than maybe lose a big order and have a bunch of 'grumpy old people' – his words, not mine – to deal with if he was wrong."

"Good thinking," Chantal conceded. "Sounds like he has a solid head on his shoulders. Who was it?"

"Sorry, can't reveal that yet. The sheriff and police departments are working it as a joint investigation since both jurisdictions are involved, and we're keeping the details to ourselves as much as we can. It's also for our tipster's safety; if the suspect finds out who turned him in, it could go from pranks to assault really fast."

Chantal nodded. "Guess we should change the subject then." She held her hands out to Sue and John, and Marc blessed the meal before they dug into the two large pizzas.

"So," John said between bites, "how did the first day go?"

"Pretty good," Sue replied. "Chantal sold half a dozen single items and a set, and I sold two baskets and a wall hanging. That's not bad for the first five hours. Tomorrow will be even better; the festival starts at 9 a.m. and we'll be open until sundown. The bands will be going all day, and there are art activities for the kids, artists' demonstrations, and a ton of food. Most of the town will be here and we'll get a lot of traffic from weekenders, too."

Chantal added, "Some of the vendors weren't here yet, so the shoppers who didn't want to wait until tomorrow bought from Sue and me today. All in all, it was a much better start to the weekend than I expected." She reached for a second slice of Hawaiian pizza. "As a matter of fact, I – " She stopped in midsentence and stared toward the bandstand.

"Chantal? Lose your train of thought?" Marc teased.

She shook her head and pointed at a gaunt figure in the shadow of the bandstand. The others turned to look and Sue gasped.

"Is that Brigitte?" she stage whispered. "What the heck happened to her?"

"I'm gonna find out." Chantal sprang up from the picnic table bench and took off at a jog toward the bandstand with the others at her heels. As the haggard young woman in an oversized white CUP t-shirt and too-big jeans spotted the foursome, she backed into the shadows, turned and ran.

"Marc, stop her!" Chantal broke into a sprint. Marc easily moved ahead to block the woman's escape. Catching up, he took hold of her arm as gently as possible and restrained her until the others arrived. She struggled to break free, but was too weak to loosen his hold.

Chantal stopped next to Marc and faced her sister, who was crying and pleading with Marc in a thin voice to let her go. He dropped her wrist as the foursome surrounded her. "Brigitte, honey, what is going on with you?" Chantal asked. "You look like you haven't eaten or slept in days!"

Brigitte stiffened and pulled herself to her full height. "I'm perfectly fine, thank you. I'm seeking God's instruction for my life now that I've joined the ministry full time, and Brother Joseph suggested I fast and pray in order to make my seeking more effectual."

Chantal stared at Brigitte, whose initial defiant glare withered under her sister's steady gaze. Her expression was desperate as she begged, "Please, Chantal, let me go. I came to the festival with a few of my brothers and sisters to pass out some flyers, and now we're expected back at New Canaan. If we're late returning, Brother Joseph and the elders will get concerned and come looking for me and my team."

Chantal sighed. "Okay, Brigitte. You win. We won't interfere with your ministry. But if you ever decide you want out of CUP, you know where we are. Meanwhile, are you sure you don't want a slice of pizza? We have plenty..."

Brigitte's face momentarily lit up, but she shook her head. "No, thank you. It's not yet time to break my fast, and when it is, I will break it properly." She stared at Marc and Chantal until they moved aside. Without another word, she walked away toward a small group of equally hungry-looking young people who had gathered nearby.

Chantal turned away and wiped tears from her cheeks. Marc drew her into his arms; Sue and John stepped in to comfort her. Chantal held onto Marc and cried freely for a minute, then took a deep breath and willed herself to stop. She drew back, thinking she was glad she didn't wear any makeup as she noticed the wet spots on Marc's uniform shirt. He looked down and grinned. "No mascara stains, huh? I'd hate to have to explain that to the sheriff..."

She smiled, but her expression sobered as she watched her sister walk unsteadily toward a van emblazoned with the CUP logo. She looked up at Marc, and there were fresh tears in her eyes. "We have to do something for her. I can't let her go on like that..."

Marc nodded and pulled her closer. "I know. We'll figure something out..." He held her, caressing her hair and shoulders until he felt the crying stop. "Ready to head back now?" She nodded into his chest. he slipped an arm around her shoulder and turned her back toward the picnic table. Sue and John followed as far as the dance pavilion, and John looked at Sue. "Wanna work off some pizza?"

Sue laughed and led him onto the dance floor, where they joined a growing group of mostly Halloween-costumed two-steppers. Chantal and Marc glanced back but continued to their table, where they discovered their pizzas had mysteriously disappeared.

Chantal's eyebrows raised. "Think it was the Halloween pranksters?"

Marc nodded with a grin. "So much for supper. Feel like dancin' a while?"

CHAPTER 27

Brigitte trembled as she sat in the van. The ministry team arrived back at New Canaan without further incident, and she reassured everyone her interaction with Chantal would not have a negative impact on their outreach efforts. When she braked in the farmhouse parking lot, the other six members piled out and went inside to give their reports.

Meanwhile, Brigitte continued to sit in the driver's seat and wait for the shaking to subside. She had been on a water-only fast for seven days, and the encounter with her sister had depleted her small energy reserves. She fiddled with the van keys still hanging in the ignition and thought about the conversation with Chantal. *Will she ever understand what I'm doing?*

A knock on the van window startled her.

"Sister Brigitte, are you well?" Joseph reached for the door handle and she unlocked it as he pulled up. He held out his hand to her. Still wobbly, she gratefully took it and stepped down from the van, barely remembering to remove the keys as she exited.

He stood looking at her, and she remembered he'd asked a question. She nodded, then blanched as a wave of vertigo washed over her. "Perhaps not as well as I thought, Brother Joseph," she answered, leaning against the van for support. "I'm not accustomed to fasting this long. I haven't even had the energy diluted fruit juice would have provided..."

She trailed off as a look of rebuke surfaced on Joseph's face.

Hoping to forestall any criticism, she continued, "Please understand, my brother – I'm not complaining or grumbling, merely stating the facts of my physical condition. My spirit is indeed willing to seek God's plan however you deem appropriate, but my flesh is not used to being so severely disciplined."

Joseph's expression cleared as he offered her his arm. "Well spoken, my sister. Allow me to support you, and we will talk of this further inside." Brigitte clung to him as they entered the farmhouse. Most of the CUP members were in the main room awaiting Brigitte's report, but Joseph stopped only long enough to tell them their sister needed a time of refreshing first.

One of the elders, noting Brigitte's obviously weakened condition, urged the group to come together and lift her up in prayer. As Brigitte and Joseph headed toward the staircase, she heard the sounds of intercession and smiled faintly in gratitude.

At the bottom of the staircase, Brigitte stumbled as she lifted her foot. Joseph caught her and kept an arm around her waist as they reached the empty second floor. He murmured scriptures as they walked down the hall, and she staggered slightly as fatigue began to overcome her. She barely noticed it when they passed the communal sleeping room and continued to the end of the hall, where Joseph's private quarters were located.

Keeping his hold on her, Joseph opened the entry door with his free hand and ushered her into a lavish, Morocco-inspired suite that bore no resemblance to the spartan room Brigitte shared with the other female CUP members. Exhausted and ravenous,

Brigitte could only think this was the first time anyone outside Brother Joseph's inner circle had entered these rooms. The expensive furnishings and rich colors barely registered.

She stumbled again just inside the door, and Joseph steered her to a chaise longue covered in dark amethyst velvet. Inviting her to recline, he went into another room and brought back a small glass of diluted black grape juice.

"My sister, I believe it is time for you to end your fast." He sat and offered her the juice glass. Not trusting herself to keep a solid grip on the cup, she left it in his hands and took a few slow sips. When she was able to take the glass, he walked back into the other room – Brigitte realized it was a kitchenette – and returned with a piece of unleavened bread and a chalice of what appeared to be more grape juice.

"Communion?" She drained the first glass and set it on the floor next to the chaise.

Joseph smiled. "Can you think of a more appropriate way to break a fast, my sister?" He sat again. Breaking the bread, he fed her a small piece and then ate one himself before putting the chalice to Brigitte's lips. She took a sip and stopped in surprise as she realized it was an excellent merlot wine. Joseph noticed her hesitation and smiled.

"This is a special occasion, sister. You are the first of our group – other than me, of course – to complete a seven-day water fast, and you are the first to share communion with me outside a regular service."

"I am indeed honored, Brother," Brigitte said. "But surely wine is a bit strong for me at this point. I would not have it said I broke my fast inappropriately..."

"How can communion be an inappropriate breaking of one's fast unto the Lord? Rest assured no one will judge your actions here tonight, my dear one. What I have approved, no one will disapprove." He moved the chalice to her lips again, and she took another sip. He smiled and took a long drink from the cup, then took her juice glass and the communion items back to the kitchenette. When he returned the third time, he carried a platter of fresh fruit, crackers, cheese and dark chocolate squares.

Brigitte looked at the platter questioningly, and Joseph scolded in a teasing tone, "Now remember, there's no need to question Brother Joseph's choices. Cast your cares on me, my dear one, for I care for you."

The small amount of communion bread Brigitte had eaten did little to slow the effects of the wine, and she giggled. Confusing Joseph's paraphrased reference from I Peter with a verse from elsewhere in the New Testament, she stammered, "Phillip- phil- philippians, right?" She reached for a chocolate-dipped strawberry. "Mmm, this is a wonderful break-fast, my brother. Thank you."

Joseph smiled in a way that, had she been sober, would have sent her running for the Volvo. However, she was tipsy from the wine and the small dose of Rohypnol Joseph slipped into her first glass of grape juice. "Are you ready to hear from the Lord, my sister?" he asked, tilting his head as he watched her consume all of the chocolate and most of the strawberries.

She stopped with a strawberry at her lips and nodded, looking like a little girl waiting for a Christmas present. Joseph did his best to take on the sober look of a prophet, but like Brigitte, he'd had little to eat that day. The communion wine, along with other naturally produced chemicals starting to race through his system, was beginning to affect him too.

He took a deep breath, stood and began to pace as he declared, "The Lord has shown me, my sister, that as He has appointed me to be His Moses to these people, so has he appointed you to be His Zipporah to me."

Through the fog permeating Brigitte's brain, she recalled Zipporah was the daughter of the Midianite priest with whom Moses stayed and whose flocks he tended. That same Zipporah became Moses' wife...

"Wife?" Brigitte blurted, dropping the strawberry onto the platter. "Are you proposing to me, Joseph?"

Joseph stopped pacing and gazed at her. "No, my dear one, I am revealing to you what the Lord has called you to here in New Canaan. He has appointed you to be my helpmate. It is not a question of my desire or yours; it is a matter of His will."

"But – but – but who is to bless this union?" she wondered. "After all, you're our leader; who else is qualified to unite us?"

Joseph held out his hand. She took it and stood, still shaky but able to move on her own now that she had some sugar in her system. "Will you trust me, my dear one?" he asked as he took both of her hands in his own.

"Of course I do, Joseph. I always have," she whispered.

"Then repeat after me..."

CHAPTER 28

The next morning, Brigitte awoke in a tangle of lavender silk sheets and confusion. She started to sit up, but her head was assaulted by throbbing pain, so she lay back on the thick down pillow behind her. She raised her left hand to rub her forehead, but stopped and stared at the platinum band adorning her ring finger. *What? When? How?* She looked around in a panic, taking in her surroundings for the first time and recognizing she wasn't in the women's room.

As her gaze settled on the chaise longue in the sitting room, she saw the tray of half-eaten fruit on the floor and a white CUP t-shirt and jeans flung across the chaise. She glanced around and spotted a trail of undergarments leading to the bed. She blushed to the roots of her hair as she looked down and realized those were her clothes all over the place.

Vague memories floated around the edges of her consciousness, and she groaned. *I'm Mrs. Brother Joseph Zacharias! Or am I? All we did was say some words to each other with no one present to witness it, and then we...*

She fell back on the pillow and closed her eyes as tears streamed. She shook her head to clear it, then winced as the pain throbbed again. Taking another look around the bedroom, she saw the antique furnishings, velvet draperies, Oriental rug and striped jewel-tone canopy over the four-poster bed. *This is not the room of a poor bachelor minister of the Lord! He had this place decorated professionally with the purpose of bringing a wife in here. And heaven help me, apparently I'm her...*

Wiping her eyes and cheeks, she wondered if the clothes scattered about were her only wardrobe option. Spotting a walk-in closet to the left of the bedroom door, she dropped out of the bed and wrapped the sheet around her toga-style in case someone happened to walk in on her.

As she walked around the foot of the bed, three things stopped her: a note on the pillow next to hers, a single calla lily with the note, and a small red spot in the middle of the sheet on the bed. Her face burned as the evidence of her spent virginity confirmed her fears, and she hung her head as she shuffled to the closet.

Inside, she found built-in drawers, shelves and rods all filled with new clothing in her size, including undergarments. A shiver ran down her spine as the implications became evident. On a short rod by itself hung a white caftan richly embroidered with ivory silk and silver metallic thread. A pair of matching slippers rested on the floor beneath it.

A note pinned to the caftan read: "For you, my beloved." Removing the caftan from the hanger, she took it into the bedroom, put it on the foot of the bed and unpinned the note from it. Retrieving her undergarments from the floor, she tossed them into the hamper in the closet before plucking a fresh set out of a drawer. Feeling a sudden need to restore some order to her life, Brigitte picked up the rest of her clothes and added them to the hamper's contents, then took the tray of food to the kitchenette.

Back in the bedroom, she climbed a small step stool so she could sit on the pillow-top mattress of the king-size bed and consider her situation. She stared at the spot on the sheet. *When I joined this group, I was just another member doing what I thought the Lord wanted. When did things change? How did I end up here...?*

No answers came to mind immediately, so she reached for the flower and read the note:

> My beloved,
>
> Your obedience to the Lord's vision for us is truly a delight to me. I know His calling upon us to be matriarch and patriarch of New Canaan will be blessed and fruitful, as our union will be. Your purity is a blessing I had not anticipated, but for which I am indeed thankful to our Lord.
>
> With all my love, I await our next meeting.
>
> Your Joseph

Brigitte reread it twice, finally remembering the proclamation Joseph had made before they exchanged vows – or rather, before she repeated the vows he had apparently composed for her. He had said she was to be Zipporah and he would be Moses to the people of CUP.

Frowning, she tried to recall the story of Moses and Zipporah.

She had been given to him in marriage by her father, the priest of Midian. When Moses went back to Egypt to lead the Israelites to the Promised Land, she went with him, but at some point he sent her back to her father. Later, her father Jethro brought her and her sons back to Moses.

The Bible didn't say anything more about her, so Brigitte wasn't sure if she stayed with Moses or went back to Midian with Jethro a second time. *Will I be sent away at some point?*

Sighing, she slid down from the bed and entered the bathroom adjoining Joseph's bedroom – her bedroom now too, she corrected herself. She stopped short at the sight of the spa-like space with its heated towel rack, marble vanity countertop, two sinks, jetted chromatherapy soaking tub and separate shower with two full-body sprayer sets. On some level she was deeply offended that the leader of CUP would have indulged in such luxuries for his personal quarters while causing the rest of the group's members to share sleeping rooms and multi-stalled bathroom and shower facilities.

However, she was so tired and achy from the previous night's unaccustomed activities that she hesitated only a moment before dropping the bed sheet and closing the door. As she did so, she noticed a plush white bathrobe hanging on a brushed nickel door hook, and she pushed the sheet into a corner with her foot. *Those sheets will have to be washed – or burned – anyway.* She turned on the faucet, emptied half a bottle of lavender and vanilla bubble bath into the tub, and slipped into the depths of the warm water.

Close to an hour later, she turned off the jets and chromatherapy lights, drained the tub, and turned off the nature sounds CD in the wall stereo above the bathroom's main light switch, then blew out the vanilla candles gracing the corners of the tub.

Standing, she shook off the last few bubbles clinging to her skin and stepped into the shower to rinse off the bubble bath residue and shampoo her hair. She meant for it to be a quick shower, no more than five minutes at most, but when the water rained down from the giant shower head above and the two full-body spray bars on opposing walls started shooting out pulsing jets, she lost all track of time in the head-to-toe aqua massage.

A persistent knock on the bathroom door pulled her out of her daydreams. Shutting off the shower, she quickly pulled on the robe and opened the door enough to peek through. Seeing it was Joseph, she blushed. "G-good morning."

He laughed lightly. "It's almost noon, my love. I just wanted to check on you. Last night was – momentous – for both of us, I believe."

She looked at her bare feet and nodded shyly. Opening the door further, she stood there, unsure whether to go out or invite him in. He drew her out into the bedroom, led her to a love seat she hadn't noticed before and sat. She joined him, noting absently she'd forgotten to wrap her hair in a towel. She hoped the robe would absorb the water...

Joseph tipped her face up so their eyes met. "My dear one,"

he said, "I know the last few hours have been life-altering for you, but rest easy. The CUP family knows of our union and that the Lord has declared us to be Father Joseph and Mother Brigitte to them now." Her eyes widened and she started to protest, but he shook his head to silence her.

She subsided and he continued, "In this new role, you are to be the Proverbs 31 woman to this household – you are to oversee the daily operations of New Canaan in addition to continuing your administrative duties in the ministry's office. The brothers and sisters are to defer to us in all things, and if our will is questioned in any area, you are to come to me. Do you understand?"

She nodded mutely, overwhelmed by what Joseph was saying. For the first time in a week, she smiled. *This feels like a promotion*, she thought. *I guess the Lord does reward diligence and obedience to His will.*

"Excellent. I know you are more than capable of succeeding in the calling our Lord has given you, my love. Otherwise, He would not have had me choose you as my bride."

He drew her into his arms and gave her a long kiss, and to her surprise, she responded with enthusiasm. All her previous misgivings seemed to have been washed away in the full-body massage of the shower in her new spa bathroom...

CHAPTER 29

Chantal had been hunched over a TV tray full of supplies and tools for about an hour. Thelma Jones, president of the VFW Ladies' Auxiliary, came by as they were setting up Saturday morning and requested a full set of jewelry – necklace, bracelet, earrings and anklet – in red, white and blue for all the patriotic holidays. While Chantal worked to finish the set before noon, Sue handled sales for both of them and fielded merchandise questions.

Chantal finished the set and stood as Thelma arrived to pick up her jewelry. She paid Chantal twice what she asked and insisted she keep the difference for her trouble, since the order was on such short notice. Knowing it would be pointless to argue, Chantal smiled and took the money. "Now, Miss Thelma, if you have any problems, you know how to get hold of me, okay? If something's too long or too short, or if something breaks, let me know and I'll take care of it."

"Honey, I know it's all perfect," Thelma said, patting Chantal's hand. "You do excellent work. I have several pieces your mama has given me for birthdays and Christmas, and I love all of them. That's why I had to have you make me some one-of-a-kind patriotic jewelry. Thanks again, hon." She surprised Chantal with a smooch on the cheek and bustled off toward the tent where the pumpkin pie bakeoff was being judged. Chantal turned to Sue and shrugged.

Sue laughed. "You might want to attend to your cheek, cous; I don't think that's your shade of lipstick." Chantal half laughed and half groaned as she picked up her handheld mirror and retrieved a moist towelette from her purse.

"You're right, Sue. It's not my color. It isn't hers, either, but I'm not about to tell her. Guess she wanted lipstick to match the pies she's going to taste..." She dabbed, then rubbed at the stubborn burnt orange lipstick until the last trace was gone. A red spot remained from the scrubbing she'd given her cheek. "Oh well, I guess it'll fade in a bit..."

She put the mirror back on the jewelry table and tossed the towelette into a paper bag she was using for trash. Wiping her hands on her jeans, she adjusted her black mock-turtleneck pullover and put on a long necklace featuring freshwater pearls in bronze, gold and burgundy, then added the matching earrings. "Think I'll go model my wares for a few minutes, Sue. I'm swinging by the food court while I'm at it; do you want anything?"

"The guys are bringing lunch, so I guess not – unless you want to grab some Cokes and a dessert of some sort."

"Okay. I'll pass by the library bake sale and see what they have." Chantal strolled off in the direction of the food court. She stopped at the silent auction being held on behalf of the children's shelter and checked on Sue's basket and her necklace and earrings set. Bidding was good on both donations, she noted with satisfaction. As she stepped away and turned to leave, she bumped into Hannah Swensen, wife of Atherton Police Chief Ted Swensen.

"Sorry, didn't mean to run you over. How is the family? Have your mother-in-law's goats recovered from yesterday?"

"They're fine – the family and the goats," Hannah chuckled. "Thanks for asking. And no need to apologize for the run-in; I was so busy admiring auction items I didn't look where I was going." She noticed the necklace Chantal wore and asked, "Did you make that? It's gorgeous!"

Chantal ducked her head and smiled. "Thanks. I did, and I made this set too," she said, indicating the donation she'd been checking. It was another seasonal ensemble with tiger's eye quartz, reddish-brown tiger iron, and dark gold freshwater pearls. Clear Swarovski bicone crystals with a copper finish added sparkle.

Hannah's eyes widened. "Beautiful! It's exactly what I need for the law officers' ball coming up in December. I know it's more of an autumn set, but it will coordinate perfectly with the gown I'm planning to wear. Tell you what – I'm going to try to win this set, but if I'm outbid, can I get you to make me something similar, maybe a cross between it and what you're wearing?"

"Sure thing! Why don't you swing by the booth sometime tomorrow after the auction results are announced, and we can work out the details if need be. Meanwhile, I'm on a quest for cookies. Do you know where the library bake sale booth is?"

Hannah grinned and pointed to a large red and white striped tent with an entrance flanked by two six-foot-tall plywood panels shaped and painted to resemble brightly colored stacked books. Chantal smacked her forehead in mock embarrassment. "Now, how in the world could I have missed it? Thanks, Hannah. See you later!"

Two stops later, she returned to her booth loaded with four soft drinks and a plate each of miniature pecan pies and homemade cookies. At the same time, Marc and John walked up with the picnic basket and a pair of folding camp chairs similar to the ones she and Sue were using.

"Hey, y'all! I got dessert and drinks. What's on the menu for lunch?" She handed Sue the plates and bag of drinks, then took the picnic basket from Marc. The guys set up their chairs while Chantal unloaded the basket onto a table Sue had cleared of merchandise. Out came four salads in covered plates, homemade balsamic vinaigrette, garlic and cheese croutons, flatware and napkins.

"We thought you might want something light since it's warm out today," Marc explained.

Chantal opened her salad and smiled at him. "Grilled chicken, Fuji apple slices, toasted walnuts, cheese crumbles and mixed greens – you hit it out of the park with this one. It's the perfect salad for a November afternoon." She sprinkled a few croutons on and drizzled the vinaigrette over the salad, then passed the containers to the others. This time John offered thanks for the meal.

"Whoo, boy, whoever marries you is gonna be one blessed woman!" Sue exclaimed after her first bite of the salad. "If everything you do in the kitchen is as good as the last couple of meals from that basket, she'll never have to cook." She glanced at Chantal, who turned bright red and started coughing.

"Walnut," she explained when she got her breath back, but John and Sue's faces told her they weren't buying the excuse. Marc looked at nothing in particular and seemed nonchalant, but the faint flush on his cheeks betrayed his reaction.

Sue cleared her throat and changed the subject. "So, did y'all ever catch the Halloween pranksters?"

John shook his head. "No, apparently the Pied Piper prank halted their activities for now. We know who the ringleader may be, but unless we actually catch the group doing something, we don't have many options at this point. We want to press vandalism charges for the drive-in damage and the water tower graffiti, but there were no eyewitnesses to either incident. We'll have to bide our time until either they pull another prank or someone slips up and admits to one or both acts."

"What about the Swensens' goats?" Chantal asked. "I bumped into Hannah and she said they're okay, so I'm guessing Ted's parents aren't looking to press charges."

Marc nodded. "Good guess. Ted said his folks are used to kids doing that, and it doesn't bother the goats enough to be worth prosecuting. The only reason they reported it was the kids did some slight damage to their fence when they climbed over. One of the split rails broke, so Ted's father thought he should call in a report in case he discovered additional damage and had to file an insurance claim. As it turns out, there's only one rail to replace, and he keeps extras on hand."

"I'm glad it wasn't anything more serious. I know how much Ted's parents depend on those goats. Without them, the farm's nothing but fence filler," Sue commented.

"True," John agreed. "I've been buying their cheese and milk ever since I got into town, and I'd miss it if they went out of business."

"Really? I wouldn't have pegged you for a goat's milk kind of guy..."

He chuckled. "Yeah, I got hooked on it years ago. It's easier on my digestive system than cow's milk. In fact, the cheese crumbles in this salad are from the Swensens' goats. Along with the apples and walnuts, it was my contribution to the meal."

"Excellent contribution," Chantal said. "I like the flavor; it's milder than I would have expected. My only previous experience with goat's cheese – at least, as far as I know – was a salad full of feta, and let me tell you, that was some fetid feta! It put me completely off even the idea of goat's cheese."

"Well, I'm glad to be able to reintroduce it to you." He put his empty salad plate back in the picnic basket. "Now, did someone mention dessert?"

"Help yourself. We have mini pecan pies and a cookie tray

full of goodies baked by the Friends of the Library." Chantal handed him the plates and picked up her salad again, then set it down abruptly and declared, "I don't believe it!" She stared off into the distance as her expression dissolved into shock.

Sue followed the direction of Chantal's gaze, and she dropped her fork onto her plate. She looked at Chantal and exclaimed, "Is that a wedding ring on her finger?"

Chantal nodded in mute amazement. Her sister, who less than fifteen hours earlier had looked like she needed a glucose IV solution and at least two days of bed rest, was walking through the park looking rested, well fed, properly clothed and unaccountably happy, given her physical and emotional state the night before.

Chantal and Sue looked at each other and without a word bolted from their chairs, leaving Marc and John to trail after them once again. This time, Brigitte stopped and smiled when she spotted them. She held her arms out and hugged Chantal and Sue when they reached her location near the swings.

"Hi, sis. Hi, cous. How are y'all this wonderful day?" She stepped back and gave them all another smile. "Deputies, how are you doing? Nothing too stress-inducing on the job lately, I hope?"

John and Marc shook their heads and assured her that aside from a few typical Halloween pranks, everything was good. Meanwhile, Sue and Chantal stood staring at her, waiting for an explanation as to the new jewelry and the sudden mood swing. She noticed their focus wandering between her eyes and the ring and back again, and she blushed.

"Remember what I said yesterday about seeking God's direction?" The four of them nodded, exchanging worried glances. " I received my answer last night. The Lord called me to join Joseph in his ministry. We are now partners in every way and leaders of the CUP family."

Chantal gulped and looked at Marc, panic evident on her face. Marc looked into her eyes and moved closer to her, and she felt herself growing calmer. Brigitte, who was explaining her new duties as co-leader of CUP to John and Sue, missed the brief exchange.

"...so now I've been given charge of both the office and the daily operations of the main house at New Canaan," Brigitte concluded. "I'm happier than I've been in months, Chantal, and I feel such peace about where my life is going now. Aren't you happy for me, too?"

Happy? You're living in sin with a con artist and I'm supposed to be happy for you? Chantal squelched the impulse to blurt out her thoughts and instead gave Brigitte another hug. "Sis, I'm glad to see you feeling and looking so much better," she said. "You really gave us a scare last night."

Brigitte nodded. "It's been a rough couple of weeks, I'll admit. Going for a week on nothing but water was a real test of my commitment, but now that the fast is over and I'm sure of my calling, I feel so much better. Do you think Mother and Father would appreciate it if Joseph and I paid them a visit? I want them to get to know him since we're together."

Chantal noticed even though Brigitte wore a wedding band, she never called Joseph her husband or said they were married.

She thought about Brigitte's question a few moments, then said, "I think you should drop by. Give Mother a call first, though, so you can make sure they're home. You know how busy they get this time of year."

Brigitte smiled. "I'll do that. Thanks for your support, sis. I need to get going now, but I wanted to let you know everything turned out okay." She said goodbye to the group, hugged Chantal briefly again, and walked away.

Mark slipped an arm around Chantal and guided her to the nearest bench while Sue and John returned to the booth to help the customers starting to gather and clear out the rest of lunch. Sue knew Chantal's appetite had fled and she wouldn't want what little salad she had left.

Chantal leaned into Marc as they sat under a fiery red maple. She watched Brigitte leave, then turned to Marc with a stricken expression. "What now? I thought it couldn't get any worse..." She closed her eyes as the tears flowed.

Marc shifted to straddle the bench and pulled her into his arms. Chantal melted into the comfort of his embrace for a few minutes, then straightened up and pulled away a bit. Laughing shakily, she remarked, "There seems to be a lot of this going on lately, huh?"

Marc smiled tenderly. "Hey, I don't mind a bit. Remember,

I know what you're going through. It will probably get worse before everything's done, but I promise you again, I will do whatever I can to make sure there's a happier ending for Brigitte and your family than there was for Jake and mine."

Chantal nodded. She turned so that her back was to him and pulled her legs up onto the bench. Scooting back into his arms, she sat in comfortable silence with her eyes closed for a few minutes. She could feel the warmth of his breath on the side of her neck, and she found herself thinking she'd like to stay like this forever...

Feeling Marc shift behind her, Chantal sat up and blinked. "Everything okay, Marc?" she asked over her shoulder.

"Yeah," he murmured. "I'd love to continue this, but Sue's about to wave her arms off trying to get our attention. Guess we'd better head over there..." He helped Chantal up and they strolled back with his arm around her shoulder and hers around his waist. Arriving at the booth, Chantal asked, "What's the emergency, cous?" *Remind me to kill you later for interrupting us,* she added silently.

"Hannah Swensen stopped by," Sue replied. "She said they announced the auction results and she got outbid on your set, so she'll need to get with you about a special order to go for the law officers' ball in December. She couldn't stick around, but she took one of your cards and asked me to tell you she'll call next week."

This information couldn't have waited? She stifled a glare and instead smiled and nodded. "Thanks for the update, Sue. Any action here in the last little while?" She picked up a double chocolate chunk cookie and bit into it with a force that betrayed her annoyance.

Sue noticed and lifted an eyebrow as she grinned. "As a matter of fact, we had a major influx of traffic right after John and I got back here. We barely had time to clear out our lunch dishes before the sales started racking up. If you'll notice, about half your inventory is gone."

Chantal gave her a genuine smile and a high-five. "Excellent! What about you? It looks like your inventory's fairly depleted, too..."

"It is. At this rate, we may be able to pack up tonight and skip the rest of the festival."

"Oh, no, that wouldn't be good. We committed to the whole festival, so we need to stay through 'til the end tomorrow afternoon." Chantal turned to Marc and John. "Looks like we're going to be busy for the next couple of hours. Do y'all want to bead, weave or sell?"

CHAPTER 30

The festival drew to a close the next day with an event Chantal had enjoyed watching since childhood – the annual Pumpkin Shooting in the vacant field near the park. The Shooting took place in two phases – first, there was a contest in which participants fired at pumpkins from increasing distances with the weapons of their choice. There were categories for bow and arrow, pistol, BB gun, rifle and even slingshot. In each category, the last contestant to hit a pumpkin was the winner. Awards ranged from gift certificates and merchandise donated by local businesses to a cash prize given by Gourds Galore, the local pumpkin farm.

The second phase of the Shooting was a bit more interesting, in Chantal's opinion. Two cannons, reproductions of Civil War models, were brought to the field for the Long Distance Pumpkin Shot contest. Small pumpkins, entered into the contest by individuals or by teams of up to four people, were shot into the field late in the afternoon. The festival crowd migrated from the park to the field to watch how far the pumpkins would fly before they landed with resounding splats. Whoever's pumpkin landed farthest afield was declared Big Shot of the Year and awarded a dinner for four at Taco Loco.

Around 4 p.m. Sunday, Chantal and Sue packed up their booth and the few remaining unsold items. The festival had started at noon because most of the town was in church that morning, so they'd only had four hours of selling time, but it was enough.   They lowered their prices slightly, which brought them more customers, some of whom had already bought things the previous two days.

"Is it always like this?" Chantal asked as she and Sue pulled their carts to the vehicles. Marc and John were close behind with the tent and furnishings.

Sue shook her head. "No, actually this was the best Festival I've had in the four years I've been doing it. I think it was because we shared the space. We gave people a greater variety to choose from, and our stuff was definitely different from anyone else's."

Chantal laughed. "And we have the awards to prove it." She waved a handful of blue ribbons.

The Festival's coordinating committee had commissioned an independent panel of judges from out of town to judge the booths and award ribbons for best in each category and Best in Show. While Best in Show had gone to their aunt Attie Mae and her gorgeous hand-made quilts, Sue and Chantal had both earned first place ribbons and cash prizes for best work in their respective categories.

"Good thing they brought in outsiders to judge this year," Sue commented.   "Otherwise someone might have claimed the judging was rigged, like they did last year."

"What happened?"

"You didn't hear? Oh my – it was all over town for weeks. I won the fiber arts category, but because Aunt Helene was on the panel, the second place winner raised forty kinds of Cain over the judges' decisions. She kept the ruckus stirred up until right before Thanksgiving. The Festival committee had to call in a gallery owner from Alabama to settle the dispute. He had never displayed any work by either of us, so everyone considered him an unbiased mediator."

"Mom never mentioned any of this. Who came in second?"

Sue tilted her head toward a slightly older platinum blonde striding past and whispered, "Constance Dupree, who else?"

Chantal rolled her eyes. "Gotcha. I almost feel sorry for her – she's tried so hard all her life to be the best at something, and she keeps getting edged out."

"Yeah, but the way she handles things doesn't make her any friends or bring her many opportunities." Sue shrugged. "On the other hand, I got more than a blue ribbon and a little cash out of the controversy. After the contest was settled, the gallery owner commissioned an exhibit of my work to run at his gallery. I accepted his offer, but only if he could wait until May. I wanted to let the furor die down so it wouldn't look like I was rubbing my success in Constance's face. The gallery owner agreed, and it's turned out to be a very profitable partnership for both of us. He asks for pieces on a regular basis, and so far nothing has returned unsold."

Chantal nodded. "That's great, Sue. I notice Constance didn't have a booth this year. Wonder why?"

"Don't know. She was telling people she had a prior commitment, but if that's the case, what was she doing here today? I think maybe she was embarrassed about last year's debacle."

Chantal grinned. "Good thing they brought in outsiders to judge this time, since Aunt Attie won Best in Show and we both won our categories. If Mom were judging, it would have been a disaster. You know Martha James never would have let her – or the rest of the town – hear the end of it."

Sue laughed at the thought of Martha - known as Magpie for her tendency to chatter about everything - giving Chantal's mother what-for every time she ran into her at a social function. "That would be a mess. Martha's quilting is good, but Attie has such a fine hand with the needle, and her eye for design is amazing. She could sell her work in the same galleries I do, but I can't get her interested in producing enough quilts to give it a shot."

"It does take her a while to do a quilt, especially these days. When I stopped by her booth yesterday, she said she didn't know how much longer she could keep quilting on account of her arthritis. I don't blame her one bit for slowing down and doing only enough for the Festival and gifts for friends and relatives."

"True, and she's also a member of the quilters' guild. Their projects keep her busy too – blankets for babies in the hospital and quilts for the fire and police departments to give to victims. I guess I can see why she isn't interested in selling through the galleries..."

The cousins put away their belongings, then joined Marc and John for the Pumpkin Shooting. They found a good vantage point and set up their chairs and cooler, and the guys excused themselves. Both were participating in the marksman contest, John in pistol and Marc in rifle. John won his category with a shot right between the eyes of his jack-o-lantern target from the very edge of his gun's range, but Marc missed his last shot and had to cede first place to Josh Thomason, a well-known local game hunter.

After the marksman rounds, the cannons were hauled out and set in place. The Ross brothers, a pair of Civil War buffs who took opposing sides in every battle re-enactment, were overseeing the pumpkin launches. They inherited the cannons from their father, David Ross, Sr., who had done the honors in previous years. Having passed the privilege on to his sons several years ago, he now watched as David Jr. and Dale readied the cannons for firing.

Chantal and Sue waited for Marc and John to reappear once the target shooting contests were finished, but they didn't show up right away. "You think they took their guns back to the car?" Chantal asked. Sue shrugged.

The cousins turned their attention to the launch preparations, noting the care with which the Ross boys loaded the cannons. Chantal had once written an article about the contest for the high school paper, so she was familiar with the process.

"They have to do everything exactly right," she said, "or the pumpkins won't make it out of the cannons. First, they place a two-ounce packet of coarse black gunpowder, called cannon grade powder, into the barrel and ram it down to the rear where the fuse hole is. David Senior told me they use cannon grade powder because it burns slower and allows pressure to build so the pumpkin will move along the barrel rather than blow up inside it when the powder ignites.

"Then, they put in a dry rag called wadding and tamp it down against the powder. The wadding helps keep the pumpkin from roasting or melting because of the burning powder. Next comes the pumpkin, which is pushed up against the wadding. Then they prick the powder packet through the fuse opening with a long pick called a gimlet. Finally, they put the fuse in the hole, light it and back off to a safe distance. If all goes well, the pumpkin launches intact. After the contest, they'll take the cannons home, clean the barrels and oil them to get out the black powder and pumpkin residue, then store the cannons until the next battle re-enactment."

"I'd never have guessed they had to be so methodical," Sue replied. "Makes sense, though – you don't want the cannon clogged with pumpkin parts."

They turned to watch as the first volley of pumpkins took to the air. A cheer went up as they hit the ground, and the cannons were reloaded. Several rounds of splatting pumpkins later, John and Marc showed up.

"You missed the excitement," Chantal said. "Some of those pumpkins grabbed big air."

Both guys were grinning widely, and Marc clutched a paper. "We didn't miss anything. We won. John and I are the Big Shots of the Year, and supper tomorrow night is on us!"

CHAPTER 31

Brigitte exited her suite and took the back stairs to the kitchen, anxious to check on the Thanksgiving preparations. The holiday was still three and a half weeks away, but she had never been in charge of a family meal, let alone a feast for some 40 people. The outreaches over the last few weeks had doubled the ministry's ranks, prompting the opening of two more sleeping rooms and the conversion of previously unoccupied rooms to classrooms so new disciples could receive the basic instructions necessary to become productive CUP members.

She smoothed down the front of her caftan, took a deep breath and stepped through the door at the bottom of the staircase. Two women, Gloria and Ruth, were at the stoves cooking breakfast. Hearing her enter, they turned and bowed. "Good morning, Mother," they greeted her in unison. Brigitte bowed and greeted them in return, wondering if she would ever get used to her new title or to calling people older than her "daughter" and "son." She would have preferred to continue calling everyone her brothers and sisters, but Joseph insisted that as his mate and co-leader of the ministry, she needed to operate within her authority.

"My daughters, after breakfast is complete, please come to the office. I need to discuss our Thanksgiving plans."

"Yes, Mother," they answered with another bow. Gloria handed Brigitte a plate of fresh fruit and scrambled eggs, and Ruth gave her a glass of milk. She thanked them and continued into the dining room, where several CUP members were finishing their morning meal. They greeted her deferentially and cleared their dishes, leaving her alone in the large room.

Brigitte paused to give silent thanks for the meal, then picked up her fork. Before she could get the first bite of eggs to her mouth, however, Joseph entered the house and caught sight of her. She put down her fork and smiled at him. To her surprise, he seemed upset. "Darling, is something wrong?" she asked.

Joseph scowled and pulled her to her feet. "Not here," he growled as he almost dragged her back through the kitchen and up the stairs. Once in their suite, he turned and demanded, "Why were you eating down there? And why are you wearing that robe?"

Brigitte backed up a step, stunned at his display of temper. "Joseph, I've eaten in the dining room every day since I moved in here, except of course when I was fasting. And as for the caftan, you gave it to me on our wedding night. Why shouldn't I wear it?" She stared at him as she waited for an explanation, a clarification, something to explain his sudden mood swing.

He turned to the bedside stand and picked up the house phone linking him directly to whatever room in New Canaan he wished to call. Pushing the button for the kitchen, he asked Gloria to bring Mother Brigitte's breakfast up from the dining room. Placing the phone back in its cradle with a care that indicated his first preference would have been to slam it down, he straightened and took several breaths while his back was still to Brigitte. She saw his reflection in her dresser mirror and the warring emotions scared her. She forced herself to remain calm and see what he would do next.

Finally, he turned as a knock came at the stairwell door. Brigitte moved to answer it, but he walked past her and opened it. Thanking Gloria dismissively, he took the plate and walked into the sitting room, placing it on a small table he'd had brought in Sunday while Brigitte was out. She followed and waited for him to say something.

Joseph finally looked at her. Seeing the fear she was unable to mask, his expression lost its steely glare. "Please forgive me, my love. I forgot you didn't know I brought this dining set to the suite for us to share our meals in private. I've had much on my mind lately because of the new influx of disciples." He reached out for her; after searching his eyes, she allowed him to embrace her.

"Of course I forgive you, Joseph. May I ask, though, why you were upset to see me wearing my bridal caftan?" Brigitte looked up at him.

He brushed her cheek with the back of his hand. "I would prefer you keep that particular robe for special ceremonies. It might be seen as prideful by the others if you walk around on a daily basis in such a richly embroidered gown when everyone else wears plain robes."

She blushed and ducked her head. "Of course, my darling. I didn't even think – I just love it so much I always want to wear it.

I'll take it off right now..."

Joseph reached down and took the sides of the caftan in his hands. "Oh no, my love, allow me..."

* * *

Brigitte's eggs were ice cold by the time she and Joseph finished making up, but she ate them anyway. His passion in apologizing had been greater than his anger, and she was ravenous. The fruit quickly followed the eggs, and she downed the milk without a pause even though it was a bit warm.

Joseph smiled and said he'd see her in the office shortly, after he attended to a couple of errands in town. She kissed him goodbye and went to her closet, where she pulled on a plain white robe and belted it with a blue sash. Slipping into her sandals, she picked up the breakfast dishes and practically skipped down the stairs into the kitchen. Seeing that Gloria and Ruth had finished and left, she did her own dishwashing.

She quickly covered the short distance to the office building, where Gloria and Ruth waited in the small sitting area. She invited them to make themselves comfortable while she started the computer and pulled up her notes for the Thanksgiving preparations.

She noticed the two women had exchanged uneasy glances and given her appraising looks when she entered, but she didn't ask them why. As the conversation progressed about plans for the meals and church services, Gloria and Ruth seemed to relax a bit.

By the time she finalized the shopping and task lists, they were smiling and nodding their approval.

"Now, my daughters, do we need to discuss anything else before we return to the day's tasks?" she asked, leaning back in her desk chair and stretching.

Gloria cleared her throat. "There is one thing, but we weren't sure it was our place to bring this up..." She looked at the door leading to Joseph's office, then back to Brigitte and bit her lower lip.

Ruth, who had been with the ministry from the beginning and had known Brigitte since she was a child, stepped in when Gloria trailed off. "Mother Brigitte," she said with raised eyebrows that revealed what she really thought of the title, "before we go further, may I inquire as to Father Joseph's whereabouts?"

"He's in town attending to some ministry business, Ruth. Why do you ask?"

"We want to be sure you're okay. We saw how he 'escorted' you upstairs earlier. Did he do anything inappropriate?"

Brigitte grinned at Ruth's bluntness. She shook her head and replied, "Thanks for your concern, Ruth, Gloria, but really, I'm fine. He was preoccupied with ministry matters and he forgot himself for a few moments. We cleared up the misunderstanding fairly quickly." She smiled at the memory of how well they had cleared things up, then added, "However, I do need to let you know Father Joseph and I will be taking morning meals in our sitting room from now on, unless we are joining the family for a special gathering. Ruth, could you please make sure the other women know that?"

Ruth's eyebrows shot up again, but she nodded without comment. Gloria also nodded, and the two women excused themselves, saying they needed to coordinate with the two sisters who would be preparing the noon meal. They assured Brigitte her lunch would be delivered to the office as expected, then bowed and wished her a blessed day.

"Thank you for meeting with me, daughters." She handed them the Thanksgiving plans and lists she'd printed, then turned her attention to answering the emails that had accumulated while she was at the festival.

Ruth and Gloria left at a brisk walk. When they put some distance between themselves and the office, Gloria said, "Do you believe her explanation?"

Ruth shook her head, looking grim. "Not for a second, Gloria. I think she believes it, though. We'll have to keep an eye on her. She's in over her head with him, and she doesn't even realize it."

CHAPTER 32

Chantal woke Monday still tired from the weekend, but she managed to drag herself out of bed and get to work on time. She brewed a double cup of her new favorite coffee and gulped half of it during the walk from the break room to her desk. Yawning, she opened the desk drawer to stow her purse, but stopped when she saw the folder from Pastor Barton. *Oh yeah, I told Ryan I'd get back on this today.* She pulled the folder and buried it at the bottom of her Inbox pile.

Her father had an appointment with his cardiologist in Natchez, so she didn't expect him to be in unless he got an emergency call of some sort. She decided to make quick work of the Inbox so she could get back to finding out something useful concerning Joseph Zacharias.

Half an hour later, Chantal was finished with the tasks her father had left. Most of it was simple scanning and filing that took less than ten minutes. The rest was correspondence. She followed her father's notes, typed and printed his responses, and put the freshly created pile of letters into his Inbox to be signed when he returned.

Walking back to her desk, she eyed the file from Pastor Barton. She knew she was procrastinating, but part of her dreaded what she might find out, so she headed for the break room to put away her coffee mug. As she washed out the cup and placed it in the drain rack, she considered the next step. So far, she hadn't come up with any real leads from the small amount of online research she'd done. *Pity I can't obtain a fingerprint or two from Zacharias for Marc to run.* She fished a Coke out of the refrigerator and walked slowly back to her desk, still pondering her options.

Dismissing the fantasy *CSI* scenario, she opened the file and looked at the seminary diploma. Pacific Northwest Theological Seminary in Oregon issued it, so she did a search for PNTS and found its website, then called the toll-free number on the Contact page.

To her delight, a live person answered instead of a computer spouting an options menu. "Admissions, please," she requested and was put on hold. After listening to a few bars of a contemporary take on *Amazing Grace*, she reached the Admissions office. The clerk who took her call redirected her to the Registar's office, where another clerk asked Chantal for more information about her inquiry.

"I'm working on a story for the *Atherton Gazette* in Mississippi, and I'm trying to verify some information about my subject. His name is Joseph Zacharias, and he holds a degree from your seminary. According to his diploma, he was awarded it about two years ago."

The clerk asked her to hold while she looked up his records, and Chantal heard the click of computer keys.

"Ma'am, I'm sorry, but we have no record of a Joseph Zacharias ever attending PNTS," the clerk told her a couple of minutes later. "Are you sure his degree was issued by us?"

"All I have is a copy, so although it appears to be from PNTS, I can't be certain it's legitimate. Is it possible he obtained a diploma somehow and altered it?"

"I suppose so, but I hope that's not the case. If you could fax or email it to me, I can see if there are any obviously incorrect details."

"I'll be glad to." Chantal fed the document through her desktop scanner, then asked for the clerk's email and sent her the pdf file. They chatted while the email transmitted and the clerk opened it.

"Oh, dear, this is definitely a fake. The logo and signatures don't match, and the person listed as seminary president has been dead for several years." Chantal heard rapid key clicking. "Thank you for bringing this to our attention. I'm reporting it to my supervisor right now. The seminary may need to get back in touch with you; if so, we'll email you and request a phone number. Meanwhile, I'm sending you my direct line in case you need to call me again."

Chantal thanked the clerk and hung up. *Thought so; wonder what else he's faked...* Shaking her head, she put the seminary diploma aside and picked up his résumé. Starting with the most recent employer, she started looking up numbers and making calls.

After a half hour of fruitless inquiries, she dropped the phone back in its cradle and picked up her cell. She sent Marc a text asking him to meet her at Kudzu Café for lunch if at all possible. Five minutes later, he replied he'd be there at noon.

Her next call was to Pastor Barton's office. His assistant said he was at the county hospital making visitation calls. When she asked if there were any message, Chantal requested that he stop by Midtown Bank in the afternoon if he could. The assistant pressed for details, but Chantal simply said it was a counseling matter and he would know why she called.

Opening a new word processing document in her computer, she spent the rest of her morning recording everything she had found out so far and all the new questions her search had raised. Topping her list: *Who is this Joseph Zacharias?*

* * *

When Marc arrived at 12:15, he found Chantal seated at a corner table, sipping a glass of iced tea while she waited for her cheeseburger and sweet potato fries to arrive. "Sorry I'm running late," he said. "We were held up on a call. I phoned in my order on the way here so we can talk without being interrupted until our food arrives. So, what's up?"

Chantal twirled the straw in her tea glass as she told him about her research on Joseph Zacharias. "Every trail dead-ended. It's as if he doesn't exist," she concluded. "Short of finding a way to lift his prints so you can run them, I don't know what to do from here."

"None of his references panned out, and the seminary has no

record of him?" She nodded, and he said, "If we could get hold of his fingerprints or his Social Security number, we could run a check, but I'm not sure how we can legally get either one unless we charge him with something."

"How about suspicion of murder?" She raised an eyebrow. "Who's to say he didn't kill the guy Sue found in the kudzu?"

Marc laughed, then stopped when he realized she was serious. "Now, Chantal, you know we can't go around making accusations like that without some evidence, and what we found at the scene isn't enough to justify charging anyone."

She scowled. "How about some kind of fraud charge, then? He misrepresented himself to First Baptist when they hired him, and now he's conning people left and right with this new 'ministry' of his."

"It's a possibility," Marc agreed. "We'll need someone to report it, though, and it needs to be someone who has actually been defrauded for us to build a solid case."

Chantal's cheeseburger and Marc's Reuben with fries arrived, and they paused to give thanks before resuming the conversation. Chantal could feel her frustration rising over the investigation's lack of progress, and she bit into her burger so hard Marc heard her teeth click. He gave her a knowing look as he took his first bite, and she shook her head and chewed.

Swallowing, she said, "I feel like I need to do something to rescue Brigitte, or at least present some concrete information so she can know what she's gotten into, but so far, finding anything out has been like trying to catch gnats with a butterfly net."

Marc nodded. "I know, but we'll catch a break sooner or later; criminals usually slip up at some point."

"Maybe that break will come this afternoon. I've put in a call to Pastor Barton and asked him to stop by my office. I want to ask if he noticed anything odd about the seminary diploma, if they bothered to run a check or just took his documentation at face value. I can't believe they hired him at all, given what I found out when I ran his references."

"If he stops by, ask him if the church still has anything with Zacharias's Social Security number on it," Mark suggested. "If so, it may give us something to work with. Also, ask him if he can think of anything Zacharias used during his time as youth pastor that hasn't been touched since he left the church. Maybe we can lift some prints and run them."

"Sounds like a plan." She signaled the waitress and asked for a carryout box, a cup with a lid, and the check. Marc protested, but Chantal insisted. "I invited you to lunch; I'm paying."

"Yes, ma'am. I guess you need to head back to the office. Don't forget, John and I are taking you and Sue to dinner tonight. I'll come by at 6 and we can walk over, okay?"

Chantal nodded as she boxed her leftovers and paid the waitress. After gathering her purse and food, she paused next to Marc and gave him a quick kiss. He smiled and waved goodbye, forgetting about his sandwich as he watched her exit the Café.

Sally, who was making the rounds with a fresh pot of coffee, gave him a playful punch on the shoulder. "Boy, you got it bad! It's all over that handsome face of yours..."

Marc grinned at her. "Don't I know it! Don't tell her, though; we're taking things slow."

Sally burst out laughing, and several diners turned their way to see what was so funny. "Slow, huh? Define 'slow,' Deputy Thibodaux."

"Now, Miss Sally, a gentleman doesn't-"

"If you say 'kiss and tell,' I will punch you for real," she retorted with a chuckle. "Besides, you two were seen hanging all over each other several times during the Festival, so don't bother trying to feed me those tired old clichés."

Marc blushed and rushed to explain, "That wasn't what it looked like." At Sally's skeptical look, he added, "Well, most of it wasn't. Actually, Chantal's been having a rough time lately with Brigitte and her involvement in CUP, and the last several encounters she's had with her sister have been really difficult. What you – or whoever told you about us – saw at the park was me comforting her after a couple of run-ins with Brigitte."

"Oh. Hang on a second; I want to hear more about this. Let me put the coffeepot up and take a quick break. Do you have time to talk?"

Marc looked at his watch. "John ought to be here in about 10 minutes."

"Ought to be long enough." She handed the pot off to her daughter Lisa, then sat down at Marc's table. "So, what's going on with Brigitte?"

Marc gave Sally a summary of the situation as he understood it, then told her about the last two times they saw her over the weekend. Sally shook her head and commented, "I had no idea she was so mixed up with those people. I haven't seen her much lately; I guess now I know why. Do me a favor when you see Chantal tonight; tell her I'll be praying for Brigitte, okay?"

She patted Marc's arm as she stood. "Gotta get back to the kitchen now, but I'll talk to you later in the week. I'm Chantal's Sunday school teacher, so I want you to keep me posted on this, if you don't mind. Sounds like the Atherton family needs some heavy-duty intercession, and that's something I know how to do."

CHAPTER 33

Back at her office, Chantal checked phone messages and email, then compiled a list of questions for Pastor Barton. A couple of minor account-related issues called her to the front of the bank, but otherwise the afternoon was quiet until Pastor Barton arrived at 3. The receptionist buzzed him into the back office and Chantal offered him a drink.

"Do you have any coffee? I'm running a bit low on energy this afternoon..."

Chantal chuckled. "Do I have coffee? Step this way, please, Pastor." She escorted him to the break room and showed off the single cup coffee brewer she considered her baby, since she was the one who talked her father into buying it.

"Goodness! Do you even go to Fuzzy Logic any more?" Pastor Barton teased her. "I know you were practically living there when you first got back to town."

"I still hit Jo up for an iced mocha now and again," Chantal said as she showed him how to brew a cup of the Kona blend he selected. He told her drinking Kona coffee was probably the closest he'd ever get to Hawaii. She laughed along with him, but caught the wistfulness in his voice and gave him a sympathetic glance while he watched the brew drip into his cup.

Chantal made a cup of French vanilla decaf for herself. They chatted about the church's Thanksgiving outreach and Christmas program plans as they went to the small conference room adjacent to Martin's office. Chantal had already placed her Zacharias file on the conference room table, along with two legal pads and pens.

She gave Pastor Barton a couple of minutes to settle into one of the comfortable leather chairs ringing the table. Sipping her coffee and glancing over her notes, she casually surveyed him for any indication he might know why she had called. From what she could see, he was alert and expectant, but relaxed.

Chantal thanked him again for meeting with her, then posed her first question. "Pastor, have you heard anything new about Zacharias or CUP since the last time we talked?"

"Same thing the rest of the town knows – they bought the old Hopkins place out in the county, renamed it New Canaan and moved in a few weeks ago. Why do you ask?"

Chantal struggled to keep her voice calm as she recounted the story of Brigitte's involvement with CUP and Zacharias. She told Pastor Barton everything she knew, watching him grow more alarmed with each new detail. She ended with a question: "Pastor, did you or the church board check him out in any way before hiring him?"

Pastor Barton looked at the table between them and shook his head. "The final hiring decision was up to the board, and I don't know what they may have done, since I don't attend the meetings. I can tell you I personally didn't do anything other than meet with him briefly and then recommend him to the board." He sighed and raised his eyes to meet hers, wincing at the anger and disappointment he saw there. "If you want, I can run his references now, see what I can find out."

Chantal took a deep breath and said in a tightly controlled voice, "I already did it this morning, Pastor. Neither the seminary nor any of his résumé references had any record of him. As far as I can tell, there is no such person as Joseph Zacharias."

* * *

On the walk to Taco Loco that evening, Chantal told Marc about her meeting with Pastor Barton. Nothing was resolved, but the pastor did pledge to bring her whatever documentation he could find the next day.

"I hope he can put his hands on a Social Security number or something to help us identify this man," Chantal said.

"I don't see why he shouldn't be able to, unless he's not allowed access to the church personnel files for some reason." Marc noticed her shiver and slipped his arm around her shoulder. "Let's try to forget about it for a few hours, okay? I know you're worried about Brigitte, but you've done all you can today, so let's enjoy the evening, all right?"

Chantal stiffened momentarily, then relaxed. "You're right. This is becoming an obsession with me. I'm afraid she's going to end up brainwashed, pregnant, abused or worse by the time this is all over."

"Yeah, it's a scary situation," Marc agreed. "We have to keep trying to get to the truth so we can show Brigitte what she's gotten into, and pray she listens. Meanwhile, if we can find something to substantiate a fraud charge, we can get Zacharias away from her, maybe get her straightened out."

"I don't want to pry, but what did y'all do when you found out your brother was involved in a cult?"

Marc sighed. "By the time we realized something was wrong, it was too late. He had stopped contacting us, but we thought it was another of his sulks. He was easily offended, and we never knew when something one of us said would set him off. The next thing we knew, he was gone. We didn't even get the letter explaining his intentions until he'd been dead for three days. It was in the mailbox when we got home from the wake that evening."

Chantal reached up and touched his cheek. "Forgive me for asking. I didn't mean to bring up such painful memories. I'm just looking for something to help me with all this. Dad says he's aware of the situation, but he doesn't seem to be doing anything about it, and I keep hitting one wall after another."

Marc hugged her. "I know. It's aggravating. But like I said, we've done all we can tonight. Let's let it go for now and enjoy our date, okay?"

Chantal laughed. "This is pitiful – even when I agree to let it go, I keep talking about it. Sorry, hon. Let's go eat."

Sue and John were at the restaurant when Chantal and Marc arrived a few minutes later. Sue waved them over to the booth and slid closer to the window so Chantal could join her. Marc joined John on the other side and signaled their waiter.

"So, how was your day, Sue?" Marc asked after placing their drink orders.

"Interesting," Sue replied with a raised eyebrow. "I have something for you, Chantal. I'm not sure who sent it to me, but it showed up in my mailbox today. I know you're going to want it..."

"What are you being so cryptic about?" Chantal asked.

"Well..." Sue produced a manila envelope and waited for Chantal to open it. As Chantal leafed through the half dozen pages, her eyes got wider.

"Marc," she said breathlessly, "I know we agreed to drop the subject for tonight, but you will not believe what this is!" She handed the envelope across the table, practically bouncing in the booth in her excitement. Marc opened the envelope and glanced at the papers inside. A satisfied grin spread across his face as he saw the First Baptist Church staff application and tax paperwork for one Joseph Zacharias inside.

"I don't know who our guardian angel is, but God bless him," Marc said with a laugh. He tucked the envelope inside his jacket and patted it. "I think this calls for a toast. To breaks and breakthroughs!"

CHAPTER 34

"Would you calm down? No one followed us." Ruth picked up a spaghetti squash and examined it.

"Why did we have to meet him here?" Gloria asked. "I'd be more comfortable with somewhere private..."

Ruth bagged the squash and reached for another. "This was where he asked me to meet him, so it's where I'm meeting him."

"Yeah, but no one will ever believe he's doing his own grocery shopping..."

"Good afternoon, ladies," a familiar voice greeted them. "Find any good bargains today?"

The women turned toward the owner of the voice. "Hello, Martin," Ruth replied. She extended her hand. He took it in both of his and held it for a moment, then turned toward Gloria and offered her his hand. She shook it without comment and glanced at Ruth, who smiled and asked, "What brings you to the grocery store? Doesn't Rosalie normally do the shopping?"

He chuckled. "Usually she does, but my daughter told me this morning we were out of coffee creamer at the office, so I offered to stop by and get some. Somehow my wife found out about my errand, so now I'm looking for bananas, ice cream and toppings in addition to the coffee creamer. I've never bought bananas before – do you have any tips for me?"

Ruth walked over to the bin and picked out a bunch whose skins were starting to spot. Handing them to him, she said, "You want them to be yellow with a few brown spots. That's when you know they're at their ripest and ready to eat."

"Thanks, Ruth. You shortened my shopping trip considerably." Martin tipped his hat to the women and went to find the rest of his banana split ingredients.

Gloria turned to Ruth. "What –"

Ruth gave a small shake of her head and asked what was next on their list. Gloria bit back a sarcastic reply and recited the part of the list they'd find in the produce department. The two silently resumed selecting and bagging items.

As they wheeled the cart toward the meat department, Ruth said she needed to visit the restroom. Gloria, still angry at being kept in the dark, nodded once.

When they arrived in the corridor outside the ladies' room, Ruth picked up both their purses, handed Gloria's to her and tugged on her sleeve. "But I don't need – "

"Yes, I think you do," Ruth replied.

Gloria shrugged and followed her into the two-stall restroom. Ruth turned and locked the door. "Sorry for the subterfuge, but you know..."

Gloria sighed through her teeth. "No, actually I don't. What the heck is going on?"

"A while back, Martin asked me to keep an eye on Brigitte, write down anything I thought he should know, and pass it along to him. We set up a schedule of meeting times and places that would look like random encounters to anyone seeing us together.

If I have anything, I initiate a handshake to pass my notes to him. If I don't, I smile and wave, make small talk for a minute and then go my way."

Gloria nodded. "Okay, I get it now. But why did you bring me into it?"

"I think Joseph or one of his inner circle might be on to me. If something should prevent me from meeting with Martin, I need someone I can trust to keep him informed. When you expressed your concern about Brigitte, I decided you might be the one. Can I count on you?"

"Of course. But why did Martin approach you in the first place?"

"I'm Brigitte's godmother."

* * *

Ruth and Gloria were silent on the ride back to New Canaan, each lost in her thoughts. Gloria was wondering if she would have to do something more than go grocery shopping on Brigitte's behalf at some point in the near future, and Ruth was questioning whether she had done enough so far.

Finally, Ruth cleared her throat and asked, "Gloria, why did you join CUP? I've wondered about it from the beginning, since you've never seemed to be an adoring acolyte of Joseph."

Gloria shot her a scared glance and looked around, gesturing with her hand at the same time. Ruth understood and shook her head. "There aren't any bugs in here. When I took the van for an oil change Friday, I had Martin call a contact of his who has the equipment to check for such things."

Gloria's eyes widened. "Dang! How long have you been doing this?"

"From the beginning. When Brigitte started getting involved in CUP, Martin asked me to join too and watch out for her. When I realized what Joseph had in mind for Brigitte, I knew I needed to let Martin know what was happening right away. Unfortunately, there wasn't anything I could do to prevent Joseph from taking her as his so-called wife."

Gloria shuddered. "So, there's no telling what might happen to the poor girl before this is all over..."

Ruth nodded as her lips tightened. "Look, I'm taking a huge chance telling you all this. You are on board with us, right?"

"No doubt," Gloria nodded.

"So, what about it?"

"About-"

"Why you joined CUP. You never answered me."

"Oh, that." Gloria looked out the van window. Ruth waited as several minutes passed. Gloria finally looked at her and said, "This isn't the first time Joseph has started a 'ministry.' Oh, it was under a different name in another small town, but he's run this con before."

"Daughter?"

Gloria gulped back a sob. "No, youngest son. He ended up dead. Everyone said it was suicide, a self-imposed hunger strike, but I don't believe it. I think he was starved, maybe for disobeying some edict of Joseph's. I haven't been able to prove anything yet, though. That's why I moved here and joined CUP – to try and find something we can use to stop this, this –" she put her face in her hands and cried.

Ruth reached over and touched Gloria's shoulder. "I'm so sorry to hear about your son. Knowing Joseph has done things like this before makes it all the more imperative we stop him as soon as possible." She put her hand back on the steering wheel. "We're almost at the farmhouse. If you need, I can turn off at the next road, drive a bit until you're ready to go back."

Gloria pulled a tissue out of her purse and dabbed at her eyes. Taking a quick look in the van's visor mirror, she saw her appearance wasn't too bad and shook her head. "Let's go on in. If anyone asks about my eyes, I can claim allergies. The leaf mold is heavy right now..."

Ruth nodded and glanced at Gloria again. She looked composed, and Ruth decided she'd have to trust Gloria to act as though nothing unusual had happened during their trip to town. As they passed the new front gate, Ruth said, "Remember, not a word about any of this..."

Gloria nodded and took a deep breath, then laughed. Ruth gave her a puzzled glance, and Gloria smiled. "Just trying to paste the appropriate look on my face. I figured if I laughed it would loosen the muscles around my mouth. They felt tight..."

"Well, merry heart and all." Ruth grinned. "Here we go –

show time, my sister."

* * *

Martin stopped in the office break room and deposited the Neapolitan ice cream in the freezer. The rest of the banana split ingredients stayed in the bag, which he set on the break room table. He put the coffee creamer in the refrigerator and grabbed a Coke. He knew his doctor would frown on that particular indulgence, but he hadn't had one in over a month, so he decided a little sugar wouldn't kill him.

Waiting until he had greeted Chantal and passed into his office, Martin shut the door, set the Coke on a coaster and pulled Ruth's note out of his jacket pocket with one hand as he put his hat on top of the coat tree with the other. He sat at his desk before he unfolded and read the brief message:

Joseph has convinced Brigitte they are married. We can't wait much longer to move.

He rubbed his eyes and picked up the phone. "Good afternoon. This is Martin Atherton. May I speak to the sheriff, please?"

CHAPTER 35

Marc pushed away from his desk and rubbed the back of his neck. He'd spent the entire morning at his computer and had very little to show for it. All he knew for certain was the Social Security number Joseph Zacharias used when he applied at First Baptist actually belonged to a dead wheat farmer from Kansas.

"We need prints," he muttered. "Then maybe we could find out more about this guy."

"Talkin' to yourself, Thibodaux?"

Marc looked up and found Sheriff Tom Aikers standing in front of him. "What's the good word, Deputy?"

"Wish I had one, sir." Mark shook his head. "So far I'm coming up empty on this investigation."

"And what investigation would that be, son?"

Mark grimaced. "You may not be happy with us, but John Borden and I have been checking into Joseph Zacharias and CUP, mostly on our own hours, but..."

"But what?"

"Yesterday we received some information we'd been hoping to get, so I ran it through the databases, but I'm not getting anything back on it."

Aikers scowled. "Do I want to know how you got this information?"

"Sir, I'm not entirely sure how we got it. A friend found it in her mailbox yesterday afternoon and she brought it to us."

"So, what's the problem?"

"The information included a Social Security number, but it doesn't belong to Zacharias. It belongs to a guy in Kansas who died four years ago."

Aikers nodded. "That explains why you want prints. You'll be interested to know I received a call a few minutes ago from Martin Atherton about this Zacharias character. Seems Mr. Atherton's younger daughter has gotten all mixed up with him and his group, and we're now being asked to investigate. So, I guess we're ahead of the game, thanks to you and Borden."

"I'm glad to hear it, sir. Chantal's been concerned – "

Aikers lifted an eyebrow and grinned. "Chantal, hmm? So the rumors are true, then?"

"What rumors would those be, Sheriff?"

"Don't bother trying to act innocent with me, Thibodaux. Everyone in town knows you two spend almost all your free time together."

Marc chuckled. "No point in denying it then, I guess. But just because we're dating, it doesn't mean I've been giving this case more attention than it deserves..."

Aikers guffawed. "Did I say that? Nah, son, I'm glad y'all took the initiative on this one. Now, if it turned out you and Borden were chasing your tails or shirking your other duties ..."

"Never, sir. Oh, there's another thing you need to know. We have reason to believe the apparent suicide back in September might have been foul play. Chantal and Sue found some evidence we missed at the scene ..."

"What, now the Atherton cousins are doing their own investigating?"

Marc shook his head. "Not really, Sheriff. They came across a CUP pendant on a broken chain a couple of weeks ago while harvesting vines for Sue to use. The chain showed signs of having been pulled off someone's neck, and the victim didn't have any corresponding marks, so we believe someone may have met him there, struggled with him and killed him. The victim may have grabbed the chain and pulled it loose during their tussle."

Aikers frowned. "I thought the coroner established cause of death as a drug overdose."

"Yes sir, there was fresh evidence of needle marks, but it could have been staged. Because it looked like an overdose-induced suicide, a tox screen wasn't originally ordered, but I've requested one and I'm waiting for it to come back for verification. Meanwhile, we need Zacharias's prints."

"We can't haul him in here without probable cause, and it's not going to be easy to get a search warrant for the same reason. Unless someone brings up charges or we can find concrete evidence he was involved in the death of Kudzu Man, we don't have anything to bring to a judge."

"Exactly." Marc shrugged. "On the other hand, if someone were to voluntarily give us something with his prints on it, we might be able to establish probable cause for a fraud charge. We have a start with the fake Social Security number, but we need something more solid."

"Any ideas how we might go about getting something, Deputy?"

"We've asked Pastor Barton if there's anything Zacharias might have used at First Baptist while he worked there, something no one has touched since he left, but so far we haven't heard back from the pastor. Other than that – "

" – we're stuck," Aikers finished his sentence. "Yep, unless Pastor Barton or Mr. Atherton's informant can produce something, we're dead in the water."

"A question, sir. Did you happen to mention it to Mr. Atherton?"

Aikers flashed Marc a grin. "I may have; I don't rightly recollect. We'll see what turns up in the next few days..."

* * *

Chantal closed her phone with a sigh. *So much for the breakthrough*, she thought. *At least now I know Dad has been paying attention to the situation.*

"Chantal, dear?"

She started at the summons from her desk intercom. Her father seldom used the antiquated device, and he rarely called her "dear" unless he was about to ask her to do something annoying or unpleasant.

"Yes, Father?" She walked into his office without knocking and sat down.

Several moments passed in silence. Finally, he extended his hand across the desk. In it was a small piece of paper. As Chantal took it, he said, "I need you to find a way to get this to Ruth Wills."

"Brigitte's godmother? How am I supposed to do that? Isn't she a member of CUP now? I can't exactly drive up to the front gate of New Canaan and tell them I need to pass Miss Ruth a note, can I?"

"No, indeed. I've been thinking about it, and I can't come up with any ideas. I know she did their grocery shopping yesterday, so she probably won't be back in town until next week, unless..." Martin picked up the phone and called the grocery store manager, Don Moss.

"Don, good afternoon... Yes, it's Martin; I need you to do me a favor and not ask any questions, okay? ... Excellent. I'd like you to call the office at CUP. Tell them who you are and that you need to let Miss Ruth know there's a problem with some of the produce she bought. ... I don't know, Don, e.coli on the lettuce or something. Anyway, tell whoever you talk to if she'll come back to the store you'll swap it out or give her a refund or whatever will get her there, okay? ... Thanks. Get a definite time from her and then call me back, will you? ... Great; I'll be waiting for your call."

Chantal stared at her father until he hung up the phone, then blurted out, "I had no idea you were such a schemer, Dad!" Martin looked taken aback. "I'm sorry, *Father*. You caught me off guard…"

"It's all right, Chantal. In fact, I think I like being called Dad. Not in front of your mother, of course; she'd have a fit…"

"Probably," Chantal replied with a grin. "So, you're going to let me know when Ruth will be returning to the grocery store, and I'll go bump into her there, is that the plan? Okay – how will she know I have something for her?"

Martin pulled open his center desk drawer and glanced inside, then said, "Ask her how the Thanksgiving preparations are going."

"What's in the drawer, Dad? Some kind of cloak-and-dagger code phrase list you two use when you 'accidentally' meet?" Martin's expression didn't change, but a flush crept up his neck. Chantal exclaimed, "You gotta be kidding me! How long has this been going on?"

"Since they moved into New Canaan. The only reason Ruth is in CUP is because I asked her if she would join and keep an eye on Brigitte for me. Close your mouth, daughter; you look like a dying fish. Why so surprised? I told you a while back I was aware of the situation."

Chantal shook her head. "I thought you were trying to placate me. I had no idea you had all this behind-the-scenes stuff going on. What about the letter you had me type to some guy in Natchez about his 'discretion' in handling something? Did that have anything to do with this?"

"In a way. I had him act on my behalf to buy everything

Brigitte was selling so I could save it for her without Zacharias suspecting I was aware of his manipulations."

Chantal brushed tears off her cheeks. "Dad, I owe you a huge apology," she choked out. "I thought you either didn't know what was going on or didn't think it was serious enough to do anything about..."

Martin came around the desk with a box of tissue from his desk. As Chantal blew her nose, he stroked her hair, triggering a fresh cascade of tears.

"It looks like I'm the one who owes you an apology, honey," he said. "I know it wasn't easy on you and Brigitte, growing up with parents who were so busy being the leading couple of this little town. I suppose it just became more comfortable for us over the years to hand out money and let Rosalie do the heavy lifting in the emotional department, since we had – since we took – so little time to spend with you girls.

"I am sorry for that. Maybe if we'd been more attentive, Brigitte wouldn't be in this mess..." He broke off and pulled a tissue out of the box.

Chantal watched him dab at his eyes and gave a small, shaky laugh. "Who knew? My little sister joins a cult, and we get a family breakthrough out of it. At least Zacharias saved us the psychologist's fees we'd have had to pay otherwise..."

Martin smiled grimly. "Don't forget, we still have your mother to bring up to date. She doesn't know about any of this. I wouldn't declare a family breakthrough yet..."

CHAPTER 36

Helene half rose from the chaise longue in the parlor where she'd collapsed after hearing Martin's account of Brigitte's situation. "My smelling salts, Chantal darling... I feel faint."

Chantal rolled her eyes and looked at her father, who gave a resigned shrug. "Oh, please, Mom – get over yourself!" she exclaimed.

"Mom? Mom!" Helene put a hand to her forehead and looked up at her husband. "Did I hear correctly, Martin? Did my daughter use the 'M' word to address me?"

"Yes, dear, she did. And it's about time, too." He glanced at Chantal, who'd turned away to hide her smile. "Don't you ever get tired of being Mr. and Mrs. Martin Atherton, sweetie? What would you do if someone were to call us Marty and Helen, hmm?"

"She'd probably faint dead away, Dad," Chantal piped up, unable to resist the chance to poke fun at her mother's pretensions. "I'm surprised she hasn't done exactly that, what with you calling her sweetie."

"Please, feel free to ridicule me in my hour of distress," Helene pouted.

Martin sat down on the chaise and put an arm around her shoulders. As she leaned into him, he kissed her on the top of her head and said, "Darling, you know we'd never ridicule you. But Chantal is right – we all need to get over ourselves and these silly roles we've been playing all these years if we're going to help Brigitte."

"Yes, Mother," Chantal said as she sat on Helene's other side. "This isn't simply some phase she's going through – this man has her convinced he's the patriarch of this group and she's their matriarch. You realize what this most likely means, don't you?"

Helene reached for Chantal's hand. "I don't want to face it, but yes. I do realize Brigitte has probably given herself to this man, whether voluntarily or – " she turned to stare at Martin, stricken by the thought she couldn't complete.

Several minutes later, Rosalie walked into the parlor to find the Athertons still sitting side by side on the chaise, staring at the fireplace without seeing it. She cleared her throat. "Excuse me, everyone? Should I serve dinner or put it in the refrigerator?"

Helene stirred first, focusing on the housekeeper with a haunted look in her eyes. "I'm sorry, Rosalie, I don't think I can eat a thing now..."

"Nonsense, Mom," Chantal declared. She grinned at Rosalie's startled expression. "Go on and set everything out, Rosie. I'll get Mom and Dad into the dining room, and I'm going to call in a few friends while I'm at it – if there's enough for six of us?"

Rosalie laughed loudly. "Child, when do I ever cook only enough for the three of you?"

Martin snickered; Helene giggled; and Chantal hopped up off the chaise and hugged Rosalie, adding to the housekeeper's confusion. "Thanks, Rosie. We needed you just now." She pulled out her cell phone as she turned to her parents and said, "I'm inviting Sue, Marc and John over for supper. I think we need a strategy session. We've waited long enough. It's time to rescue your daughter."

* * *

As the platter of fried chicken made the rounds a second time, Chantal, Sue and the guys chatted while Martin and Helene observed from opposite ends of the large table. They didn't miss the way Marc's hand brushed against Chantal's when she passed him the platter or the smile she gave him in response. Helene glanced questioningly at Martin, who nodded in return and gave Marc an approving look. Helene brushed a lock of hair off her forehead and sighed, then responded with her best hostess smile when Marc offered her the chicken.

"Chantal, dear, you called this gathering," Helene said as she passed the platter to John. "A strategy session, I believe you said? Did you have something specific in mind?"

Chantal set a half-eaten drumstick on her plate. "Well, Mom, I thought we should share what everyone knows so we can figure out what to do next."

Martin handed her the bowl of sour cream mashed potatoes. "Who wants to start?"

Chantal took a small spoon of potatoes and passed the bowl to Marc. "Is this an official investigation yet, guys? Is there anything you can't tell us?"

"It's semi-official, boo," Marc replied. Chantal blushed, but he continued as though he didn't realize what he'd said. "Sheriff Aikers told me today your father called and asked us to look into Brigitte's involvement in CUP." Marc looked past Chantal to Martin. "Mr. Atherton, did something happen to prompt that call?"

"Please, son, call me Martin. Yes, something did happen." He told the group about his encounter with Ruth and the information she relayed to him. Chantal and Helene, who had already heard the story, looked grim. Sue and the guys stared at Chantal in surprise.

"Yeah, I know, y'all. I was a bit stunned to find out about Dad's covert operation, too. I'm glad it's all out in the open now so we can start working together." Chantal took a sip of mint tea. "It turns out Dad is the buyer who relieved Brigitte of her possessions, too. Remember the letter I told you about, Sue? Dad went through an auction broker in Natchez." She smiled at her father. "He's been looking out for her all along, but like us, he didn't have anything concrete to work with until now."

Martin said, "True, but now we know Zacharias has caused Brigitte to enter into a so-called marriage I'm sure has no legal basis, and no doubt he did it through fraudulent means. Still, there's nothing about the situation for which we can press charges against him – Brigitte is an adult. So the question is, do we have anything prosecutable?"

Chantal nodded. "Exactly. Marc, would you tell everyone what you found out today?"

Marc related the story of the mystery package left in Sue's mailbox and how he'd hit a dead end on the Social Security search. "Chantal's said it all along – we need fingerprints to run through the databases. If this man has any kind of record, or if he's ever been bonded, we should be able to find out who he really is."

Chantal looked at her father. "Is that what the note you gave me is about? Are you asking Ruth to do some reconnaissance for you?"

"Ah, the sheriff implied something might be in the works," Marc interjected with a chuckle. "All he said was he'd suggested your dad's informant might be able to help us."

Martin nodded. "That about sums it up." He turned to Chantal. "I heard from Don right before the end of the workday. Ruth will be at the store tomorrow at 8 a.m., so you should go pick up some flowers for the office before you come to work. She'll be returning the bad lettuce and placing an order for the CUP Thanksgiving table centerpiece."

"I declare," Helene said, slipping back into drama queen mode out of habit, "all this intrigue! I don't know what to think..."

"I do," Marc said, offering Chantal and Helene each a hand. "I think it's high time we went to the Lord with all this, don't y'all?"

CHAPTER 37

Chantal picked up a silk fall flower arrangement, inspected it for a few moments, then returned it to the display stand and turned to a vase of cut flowers that had caught her eye the second she walked into the florist's section of the store. Featuring fiery red crocosmias, snowy white hydrangeas and mango orange calla lilies, the arrangement was colorful and exotic – the perfect touch for the very beige and brown office suite she and her father shared.

She waved to Marilyn at the florist's counter and pointed to the arrangement. Marilyn smiled mysteriously as she nodded and pulled out a vase to duplicate it.

"Good morning, Chantal! How are things at the bank?"

She turned at Ruth's greeting and smiled. "Fine, Ruth, and how are your Thanksgiving preparations coming?" She took Ruth's hands in hers, slipping her the note from Martin, then pulled her in for a hug. As they stepped back, Ruth slipped her hands into her pockets and gave the briefest of nods.

"They're going well, except for a few minor glitches. I'm here to swap out some produce Don called me about – " she gestured toward the lettuce in plastic bags, " – and to order a centerpiece for the head table. Any suggestions?"

The two women spent a few minutes discussing options while Chantal waited for her arrangement to be finished, then she told Ruth goodbye and took the arrangement to checkout. Ruth turned her attention to an arrangement of cut flowers in a pumpkin-shaped basket.

Chantal decided to walk through the front of the bank; with her hands full, it would be easier to be buzzed into the back than try to balance the flowers and fumble for her keys. Her friend Ryan left as she was entering, so he held the door open for her and murmured, "More from Marc?" as she passed. Blushing as red as the crocosmias and wrinkling her forehead in puzzlement, she shook her head and kept going, but a grin tugged at the corners of her mouth.

More good-natured teasing by staff and customers accompanied her through the lobby. By the time she reached the back office, she was giggling so hard the water in the vase started to slosh. Her father, who had made a cup of coffee and was on the way back to his office, heard the buzzer and caught the door as it opened. He nodded approvingly at her choice and asked where she planned to put it.

"Don't know yet," she replied as she surveyed the room. She stopped short at the sight of another arrangement already on her desk, this one with the same crocosmias and hydrangeas she'd chosen, but no calla lilies. She pivoted to look at her father, who was about to close his office door. "Dad?"

"Yes, dear?"

She looked at the vase on her desk with a lifted eyebrow, then back at him. "You know anything about those?"

His lips twitched, somewhere between a smirk and a grin,

and he shook his head. "They were at the front desk when I arrived. Jennifer called to tell me they were here, and I asked her to bring them back. That's all I know."

Chantal shrugged and walked to the end table between the loveseat and armchair in the small waiting area. She put the arrangement she'd bought on it and moved everything else off the table. The vivid flowers brightened the whole area.

Moving to her desk, she spied a card in the smaller arrangement and plucked it out of the plastic prongs of the holder. Reading the card, she smiled in understanding; suddenly Ryan's teasing and all the other comments made sense. The message simply read:

Thought you'd enjoy these. Sorry I missed you, boo.

Marc

Apparently he'd dropped them off on his way to work. No wonder everyone was ribbing her; they must have thought he'd gotten her the smaller bouquet, decided it wasn't big enough, and bought her a larger one.

She put the card back in its folder and caressed a crocosmia as she stared into space. *How did he know what flowers I'd pick?*

Coming back to the present, she realized her purse was still on her shoulder. She laughed at herself as she put it away and went to the break room for a cup of coffee.

On the return trip, she passed her desk and knocked on her father's door. She heard him hang up the phone as he invited her to enter.

"So, Dad, what's next, now that I've delivered the note?" Chantal sipped her French vanilla. "Does Ruth have a way to get in touch with you, or do we have to wait for the next scheduled 'accidental' meeting?"

"Our next meeting is – " he opened the desk drawer and consulted his list " – Thursday at 1 p.m. She's taking CUP's table linens to Perfectly Pressed for dry cleaning and I'll be there to pick up a suit I need Friday night. I'm hoping she'll have a glass or something bagged and ready to be tested for prints by then."

"Three days ought to be plenty of time to come up with something. If you want, I can run by the dry cleaner for you, then stop at Marc's office and drop off whatever she brings."

"I may let you. I have a hospital board meeting that day and was wondering how I was going to make it all work. Thanks for volunteering."

"No problem, Dad. I can thank Marc for the flowers." She grinned. "Right, like you won't be seeing him before then." He grinned back as she gulped in momentary shock. This less formal version of her dad would take some getting used to, she decided.

"It's settled, then. I'll let you get on with whatever you need to do – you have the Rotary Club today, don't you?"

Martin glanced at his desk calendar and nodded. "I also have a Heart Association committee meeting this afternoon. I know you can hold down the fort without me..."

Chantal nodded. "Won't be the first time," she replied with a chuckle.

"True." Martin paused and looked up at Chantal as she turned to leave. "You know, I don't think I ever thanked you for coming back home. I know you felt it was your duty, but you didn't have to, and I appreciate very much that you chose to take on this job. You've done an excellent job in the last few months, and if I could keep you here until I retire, I would."

Chantal turned back around. "What are you talking about, Dad? I don't plan on going anywhere. Do you know something I don't?"

"No, but I do know you didn't want to spend your career working as my office manager. It was selfish of me to ask you to give up a job you clearly loved."

"Don't go all sappy on me, Dad," Chantal sighed. "Of course I came back out of a sense of duty. And yes, I did enjoy my job as a reporter. But considering everything that's happened since I got home, I'm glad I returned. We all need to pull together to get Brigitte straightened out, and we couldn't if I were still several thousand miles away." She sat again. "Besides, I wouldn't have a budding career as a jewelry designer if Sue and I hadn't shared a booth at the Fall Fest, and I sure wouldn't have met Marc if I were still out west."

Martin smiled. "Are you serious about him, Chantal?"

"As serious as I've ever been about anyone, Dad. But we've agreed to take things slowly. I have no intention of making the same..." she trailed off and looked down.

"I'm glad you and Marc are approaching this sensibly.

There's nothing more devastating to a relationship – especially between Christians – than to go too far too fast."

"Not to mention how much fodder for gossip it would provide the local grapevine," she replied. Martin grimaced and nodded his agreement.

Chantal stood again. "Dad, thanks for letting me know how you feel. I'm glad we can finally talk about these things. Pity it took – oh, never mind. The past is done; no need to be catty about it." She walked around the desk, gave her father a one-armed hug across his shoulders and dropped a kiss on top of his head. "Okay, enough of this sentimental stuff – I'm going to work now, all right?"

He gave her a fatherly smile as she left, then turned his attention to the letters on his desk. Chantal reflected on the conversation as she returned to her desk. *Thank You, Lord, for all the good You're working out of this bad situation.*

* * *

Ruth delivered lunch to the ministry office for Brigitte and Joseph – chef salads with fresh greens from the morning's grocery store trip and boiled eggs from CUP's own henhouse, along with locally produced cheese and deli ham and turkey, accompanied by large tumblers of sugared mint tea – and said she'd come back in an hour to collect the dishes. Joseph, occupied with fund-raising phone calls, nodded distractedly. Brigitte thanked Ruth and promised to have the dishes on the lobby table for her.

"Oh, no, Mother Brigitte, no need to do that," Ruth assured her. "I can collect them without disturbing either of you – you won't even notice me."

"Nonsense, my daughter," Brigitte replied. "Father Joseph will be busy for the rest of the day with these calls, and it would be best if I were to collect his lunch dishes."

Ruth nodded and tried to conceal her concern. She decided there wasn't much to be done about it; she could only hope Brigitte didn't smudge any prints Joseph might leave.

As she moved toward the front door, a sound of breaking glass came from the inner office, followed by a muffled curse. Ruth and Brigitte traded a startled glance and rushed together toward Joseph's door. Ruth arrived a step ahead of Brigitte.

"Father Joseph, we heard something break. Are you injured?"

Joseph had the linen napkin from his tray wrapped around his hand. Through clenched teeth he said, "No, my daughter, but please remove this broken tumbler and bring me another glass of tea as soon as you are able."

"Father Joseph, please take my glass," Brigitte said, handing him the tea from her own tray. Ruth asked Brigitte for her napkin and used it to gather the large pieces of glass near Joseph's chair. Fortunately, the glass had broken almost in half, with only a few smaller pieces scattering on the carpeted floor. She quickly retrieved them all and put them into her apron, which she untied from her waist and bundled up.

"I'll return shortly with fresh napkins and more tea, Mother

Brigitte," Ruth said as she left the office. Practically running back to the kitchen, she told Gloria what had happened and asked her to bag the apron full of glass. Putting on a fresh apron, she quickly poured another tumbler of tea and grabbed two more napkins, then returned to the ministry office.

"Darling, it doesn't look too bad," she heard Brigitte say as she entered. "I don't think you'll need any stitches..."

"Quit fussing over me, Brigitte, and get back out front," Joseph snapped. Brigitte flushed and bit back an angry retort as she left his office, almost slamming the door. Catching sight of Ruth, she stopped. She put out a hand wordlessly, and Ruth gave her one of the napkins. Brigitte turned to walk back in and give it to Joseph, but the look on his face halted her. She closed the door and took a breath before turning to face Ruth.

"Thank you, my daughter. Father Joseph doesn't require this, so please return it to the linen closet."

"Mother Brigitte – "

A shake of Brigitte's head stopped Ruth, who gave her a mute look of sympathy and returned to the kitchen without another word.

"Is everything all right in the office?" Gloria asked as she walked through the door.

"Yes, Sister Gloria, but we might be a glass short for Thanksgiving dinner," Ruth said as Gloria handed her the bag with the apron and glass pieces in it. "I'm going to town to buy a few extras in case we have other breakage. If anyone asks, please tell them I'm seeing to some additional preparations. If I'm not back in an hour, please collect the lunch dishes from the ministry office. And tread lightly – Father Joseph is dealing with financial matters today."

Gloria handed her the van keys. "I'll take care of things here, my sister. Be blessed."

Ruth left without speaking to anyone else. Most of the CUP members were eating lunch in the main dining room or out in the garden, so no one noticed her departure.

Driving at a reasonable speed through the front gate of New Canaan, she waited until she was out of sight of the property, then accelerated to 60 miles an hour as she headed to town. *I hope Deputy Thibodaux is at the office*, she thought as she raced down the back roads into Atherton. Flashing blue lights in the rear view mirror caused her to glance back and sigh. She pulled over, cut the engine and rolled down the window.

"License and registration, please ma'am," the officer requested. She pulled her license out of her purse and handed it to him without looking. Telling him she'd have to get the registration out of the glove compartment, she started to lean toward the passenger side of the van but stopped short when she heard, "Miss Ruth?"

Straightening, she looked out the window and smiled. Deputy Marc Thibodaux stood at her door. "Yes, Deputy?"

"Miss Ruth, you know the limit here is 45, right?"

She nodded. "I apologize, Deputy. I was heading to town to

buy some new glasses for our Thanksgiving feast, and my mind was preoccupied." She glanced at the bag in the passenger seat, then looked up at Marc.

"Are y'all expecting extra guests or something?"

Ruth shook her head. "No sir. Father Joseph dropped a tumbler full of tea and it broke. He cut his hand, too, poor man." She reached for the bag and handed it through the window to Marc, who was beginning to rock on his heels and smile.

"I'll let you off with a warning, Miss Ruth, but slow it down, okay? The road crews are doing ditch maintenance a mile south of here. Wouldn't want you to rear end one of the mowers at 60 miles an hour..."

"Yes, Deputy," she replied as she cranked the van. She raised a hand in silent praise, then turned on the radio and sang along as she finished the short drive to the dollar store.

As she pulled back out into the road, Marc returned to the squad car and handed John the bag as he slid in behind the steering wheel.

"What's this?" John asked, hearing the tinkling of the shards as he put the bag on the floorboard.

"An answer to prayer," Marc replied with a smile so wide all his teeth were showing. "Let's go run some prints. We may even get some DNA evidence..."

* * *

"What in the world?" Martin rushed out of his office at the

sound of a shouted "Hallelujah!" from Chantal.

She jumped out of her chair and flung her arms around her father. "We got the prints!"

Martin hugged her back and asked what happened and how she knew about it. She held up her cell phone and said, "Text from Marc." Sitting back at her desk, she swiveled to face Martin and told him what Marc had relayed about stopping Ruth on the road outside New Canaan for speeding and getting a bag of bloody glass pieces from her.

"Wait a minute," Martin interrupted. "Did you say bloody glass pieces?"

Chantal laughed and nodded. "Apparently Joseph cut his hand when his tea glass broke. Not only do we possibly have prints, we may have DNA too. Let's hope the prints turn up in a database. Marc said DNA may take too long to analyze for it to be useful in bringing charges; it'll be more useful in court if Joseph is arrested and it goes to trial."

"You got all that from a text message?"

"Several messages, actually, but yes sir, I did." Chantal realized she was still clutching the phone and put it down. "Now we have to wait..."

CHAPTER 38

"Chantal, don't forget my suit, please," Martin called out from his office.

"Heading out now, Dad. Do you want me to bring it here or take it to the house?"

"If you're finished with your work, why don't you take the rest of the day off? The hospital board meeting was canceled, so I can hold down the fort for a change."

Chantal grabbed her purse, poked her head into Martin's office and grinned at him. "I like this new you, Dad! Thanks; I'll see you at home tonight."

"No plans with Marc?" Martin looked up from his writing.

"Actually, I invited him over for dinner with us. I've already cleared it with Rosie and Mom; sorry I left you out of the loop."

"No problem, honey. See you later." Martin went back to his letter and Chantal left before he could find something else for her to type. She texted Marc on her way to the cleaner, told him she was off work early and asked if he wanted to meet at Fuzzy Logic for coffee before they had dinner with her parents. He replied that he was out on a call, but he'd see her in about half an hour.

I wonder if Ruth will even be at the cleaner's since she gave that glass to Marc Tuesday, Chantal thought as she walked up the street to Perfectly Pressed. The November air was crisp and bracing, and Chantal smiled as she inhaled deeply.

Good afternoon, Chantal," Mr. Irias greeted her as she stepped into the dry cleaner.

"Buenas tardes, Señor Eduardo," Chantal replied. "How are things today?"

"Slow, but I expect that to change shortly. Many of the men in town are going to the benefit Thanksgiving dinner at the country club tomorrow evening, and I have suits waiting to be picked up. Your father's is one of them, sí?"

"Yes, sir, it is. He asked me to stop by and get it since he's tied up at the office."

While Eduardo retrieved Martin's suit from the rotating rack in the back of the shop, Chantal looked out the front window. She had no reason to hang around after she paid for her dad's suit, so she hoped Ruth would show up before then, even if they didn't have any information to share. She wanted to tell Ruth how much they appreciated her help.

Eduardo returned a couple of minutes later with the suit in one hand and the ticket in the other. "Here we are, Chantal. Please tell your father that burgundy stain was much easier to remove than he thought it would be."

"I will, thanks. I'm wondering – did Miss Ruth happen to stop in today?"

Eduardo shook his head. "Should I be expecting her?"

"CUP is having a pretty big feast for Thanksgiving, so I thought she might bring the tablecloths in to be cleaned before then. I bumped into her at the grocery store the other day, and I wanted to see if she made up her mind yet about the centerpiece she was ordering for the head table at New Canaan." *Shut up, Chantal! You're talking too much – dead giveaway that something's out of the ordinary.*

"Ah. If she should come in, I'll tell her you asked about her – unless you would like her to stop by the bank and see you?"

"No, thank you. I was just curious about how her preparations are coming along." She paid the bill and thanked Mr. Irias again for getting the stain out of Martin's suit.

Stepping out of the dry cleaner, she looked both ways but didn't catch sight of the CUP van anywhere on the street. Shrugging mentally, she headed to the Atherton house and left Martin's suit with Rosalie, then went to Fuzzy Logic, where Jo was offering a variety of seasonal flavored coffees.

Perusing the menu board, Chantal didn't notice the front door open. It wasn't until she heard "Hi, gorgeous," that she realized someone was standing next to her. Smiling, she turned.

"Oh, hi, Ryan," she replied, her smile slipping a fraction before she caught it.

" 'Oh, hi, Ryan?' I take it you were expecting someone else?"

She laughed. "Actually, yes. How are you this afternoon?"

"My ego's slightly bruised after that tepid response, but otherwise I'm fine. Gotta get some better caffeine than our break room sludge to fuel my journalistic drive. Anything new to report on the CUP story you asked me to let you do?"

She ducked her head slightly and glanced around before

replying. "Nothing I can tell you yet, Ry, but we have found out some interesting tidbits. As soon as I can put enough together for a story, I'll email you my copy, okay?"

"Why don't you do it old-school and bring the hard copy to me yourself – or better yet, come in and borrow one of our computers and type it up at the *Gazette* office? I miss seeing you in the newsroom..."

Chantal tilted her head and appraised Ryan's expression, then chuckled. "When was I ever in any newsroom where you worked? Okay, maybe the computer lab in high school, but that doesn't count. Besides, it would look odd if I suddenly start hanging around the newspaper office, don't you think? Someone might suspect something..."

"What, that we're dating?"

Chantal blinked. "No, goofy, that I'm investigating a certain ministry leader for a story."

"Hey, boo. Hope I didn't keep you too long." Marc walked up and slipped his left arm around Chantal's shoulders while extending his right hand. "Hi, Ryan. I've seen you around, and of course there's your photo on the editorial page, but I don't think we've ever formally met. Marc Thibodaux with the sheriff's department."

Ryan hesitated a moment before accepting Marc's handshake, and Chantal suppressed a giggle as she watched the two men. Moving away toward the counter, she said, "I've decided what I want. Jo, can I get a large spiced apple pie coffee with plenty of cream? Thanks."

She handed her money to the cashier and glanced back to see the deputy and the editor chatting as though they'd known each other for years. Her reporter-trained eyes told her another story, though; the posture and gestures of the two men gave away their tension. She turned back to Jo, who was handing her coffee over the top of the glass pastry case.

Jo's eyes twinkled; she had noticed the byplay too. "So, girl, how does it feel?"

"What?" Chantal asked as she sipped the coffee and gave a hum of approval.

"Don't give me that! You know dang well what – that display of testosterone back there."

Chantal clapped a hand over her mouth and sputtered, "Jo! Don't say stuff like that when I have a mouthful of hot coffee!" She glanced back over her shoulder and giggled. "It would be annoying if it weren't so flattering. Still, I better go intervene before their politeness gets any more forced. Thanks – the coffee is perfect. Tastes like hot apple pie a la mode." She turned to go, then moved back to the counter. "You got any Community back there?"

"Sure thing, doll. You want one?"

"No, make it two, large and black."

Jo handed her the coffees and refused payment. "Are you kidding? This is the most excitement I've had all day..."

"Slow day, huh?" Chantal grinned and took the cardboard

carrier of coffee cups over to the guys. "Hey, while y'all were getting acquainted I went ahead and grabbed you some coffee."

Marc thanked her with a peck on the cheek and an appreciative glance after his first sip. "CDM?"

"No, Community. Not quite Café du Monde, but I figured you could use a taste of home."

Thanks, cher." Marc took a gulp. "Black, too – exactly how I drink it."

Meanwhile, Ryan had taken a sip and discovered the coffee wasn't just coffee. "Maybe I should have stuck with the break room sludge! This stuff is strong – what's in it?"

Marc's eyebrows went up. "What, you've never had New Orleans coffee? That little extra zing you're tasting is chicory root. It's roasted, ground up and added to the coffee."

"Why would anyone do that?" Ryan asked, taking another sip and grimacing. He obviously didn't want to insult Chantal by not drinking it, but it was apparent he wasn't enjoying the brew.

Chantal said, "Using chicory or some other additive can help stretch your coffee supplies when your money is tight or coffee is hard to get. Also, it helps cut down on the caffeine content of the coffee, but not the intensity of the flavor. And it's reported that chicory has health benefits."

"I didn't know you were such an expert on chicory, Chantal," Marc commented with a smile.

"Learned about it a while back when I was researching an article on things people did in tough times to make do when they couldn't get coffee and other luxuries. Many people drank chicory straight back then; some still do."

"Well, informative as this has been," Ryan said, "I don't think chicory is my cup of coffee. Thanks, Chantal, but I'm going to have to grab something else."

"No problem, Ry. I'll get you that copy as soon as I can, okay?" Chantal turned to Marc. "So, how's your day been?"

Ryan moved to the counter and ordered something without chicory in it, and Chantal and Marc walked to the back corner of the shop and sat in the only booth, a round table surrounded by curved high walls with built in seating. Ryan sighed as he watched them walk away, then took his coffee and went back to the *Gazette*.

After a couple of minutes, Jo walked over and offered a tray of pastries to Marc and Chantal. "No thanks, Jo," Chantal said. "We're having dinner with my parents in about an hour and a half, and Rosalie would maim me if I let our appetites get dented before then."

"Now, Chantal, when has a cookie ever killed anyone's appetite?" Jo protested with a grin. "Stop channeling your mother and try a few samples on the house. Think of it as survey participation – try whatever you want and let me know which ones you like best, okay?"

"You had to drag my mom into the conversation, huh, Jo? Unfair tactic – but you talked me into it. Thanks." Chantal turned to Marc. "Split a double chocolate chunk brownie with me?"

"Don't mind if I do."   Marc picked one up, broke it and handed half to Chantal.

"So – mmm, this is excellent! – tell me, do you have anything new on your latest acquisition?" Chantal asked.

Marc shook his head and swallowed.   "That brownie will make you commit a felony, it's so good... No, we're still waiting on the handprint results."

"Handprints? I thought you only used fingerprints..."

"We recently acquired a digital scanning unit that records the whole handprint; it's a technology that's been in use in law enforcement for a few years now. We're part of a network of departments throughout the country. We can share our databases through the system since we all have the same type of scanners."

"So, shouldn't that make things a lot faster?"

Marc sipped his coffee. "Normally yes, but since we were dealing with a broken glass, it was a little harder to get a full handprint. What we ended up with was more like a print cut in half diagonally. We were able to patch it together, but it does mean the matching isn't as exact."

"Meanwhile, we're stuck. What about the homeless guy? Anything new on that?"

"Actually, there is. Right before I came over here, I got the tox screen back. There was no evidence of drugs in his system at the time of death."

Chantal's eyes widened. "So the needle tracks were a decoy?"

"Either that, or he was injected with a hypo full of air, which would kill him without leaving obvious evidence."

"There's no way to tell if that was what happened?"

"I'm not sure at this point. The coroner said if air embolism had been suspected at the outset, it could have been tested for, but by now the air bubbles may have dissipated. I've asked the coroner's office to do whatever they can to determine cause of death now that drug overdose has been definitely ruled out."

Chantal sat back in the booth and propped her legs up. Sipping her coffee, she thought about what Marc said for a minute, then shrugged and looked at him. "Not much we can do about it, then, except wait for results."

"And pray for a miracle of some sort." Marc broke off a piece of a Hawaiian cookie (white chocolate, macadamia nuts, toasted coconut and candied pineapple) and handed it to Chantal. "By the way, how was church last night? I had a last-minute call – more goat-related mischief at the Swensens' – and couldn't get back into town until the service was half over."

"It was more lively than it's been in a long time." Chantal chewed and smiled her approval of the cookie, then continued, "It seems like Pastor Barton has a fresh fire in him, and it's affecting everything from the music ministry's song choices to how Pastor prays before and after the message."

"That's great. I wasn't sure I wanted to go there after my first couple of visits, but I'm glad I stuck it out." Marc saw Jo headed their direction and gave her a thumbs-up for the dessert samples. She smiled and headed back to the counter, and Marc turned to Chantal. "By the way, I found out something you've been waiting to hear."

"Oh?"

"Yep – the reason behind the break-in at your place. Turns out the kid thought you took that folder from Pastor Barton home with you, and he was trying to get it before you had a chance to look at it."

"What? Why would he do that? Did Zacharias put him up to it?"

"Not according to what he said in his statement. Chief Swensen told me about it after I took the report on the latest attempt to scare the goats into falling over. Ted said Jim Bridges claimed God told him to retrieve the folder and that he acted alone, without anyone else's knowledge."

Chantal sat up and stared at Marc. Shaking her head, she protested, "That boy is a lot of things, and he's given his mother more grief over the years than I have time to tell you about, but a zealot carrying out the 'will of God' to the point of breaking and entering? I don't believe that for a second..."

"Neither does Ted, and since the break-in happened in his jurisdiction, the police and sheriff's departments are now partners in a joint investigation of CUP and Joseph Zacharias."

Chantal flung her arms around Marc and kissed him soundly. "That is the best news I've heard in a while, babe!" she exclaimed. "Maybe now we can make some real progress, if everyone's working on this."

Marc laughed and kissed her back. "I thought you'd like that news..." The rest of his comment was buried by another kiss from Chantal, and they quickly lost track of their surroundings and the time as they enjoyed the privacy of the booth.

The sound of a throat being cleared broke their lip lock, and Chantal looked over Marc's shoulder to find Jo standing at the booth's entrance. Picking up the tray, she grinned and said, "Ya know, I kick teenagers out of here on a regular basis for that much PDA – but I guess I'll let it slide this time." She looked at her watch. "Hate to break up the love fest, but you only have half an hour until you're due at the house for dinner. I'm not about to tell Miss Rosalie her cooking went uneaten because you two were makin' out like kids in my back booth..."

CHAPTER 39

"Mom, Dad, wait 'til you hear the latest!" Chantal yelled as she barreled through the front door with Marc following at a more leisurely pace.

"Chantal, why are you acting like you're ten years old and don't have any better sense than to be running in here screaming?" Rosalie said as she emerged from the kitchen.

"Sorry, Rosie, but I really need to talk to Mom and Dad. Shouldn't they be down here for a cocktail by now?"

Rosalie wiped her hands on her apron and took Chantal by the shoulders as Marc walked up behind her. "Honey, brace yourself. Your parents are at the hospital – "

"Why? What happened?"

"They got a call from the emergency room. Miss Ruth was in some kind of accident with that ministry's van, and she had your father listed as an emergency contact, so your parents lit out of here right away when they got the call."

"Accident? How serious was it?" Chantal felt Marc put his hands on her shoulders from behind as Rosalie released her, and she leaned back into his chest. He wrapped his arms around her and looked at Rosalie as they waited for her to continue.

She shook her head. "Miss Ruth is in a coma–"

"No!" Chantal turned and buried her head in Marc's chest.

Marc asked, "Did they say how the accident happened?"

"They said something about a blowout, but that's all the

hospital could tell them. I don't know any more than that..."

Marc pulled out his cell phone and hit the speed dial for the sheriff's department. After a couple of minutes of terse Q&A with the dispatcher, he had the details the hospital didn't provide.

"It happened on the road into town, not far from where I stopped her Tuesday for speeding. Her tire blew out and she plowed into the back of one of the mowers I'd warned her about that day. She had her seatbelt on, but the impact still caused her to hit her head pretty hard."

Chantal looked up and said, "What about the air bag? That was a late model van..."

Marc shook his head grimly. "It didn't deploy for some reason. What's worse, the evidence retrieved at the scene indicates that the tire was shot out and the airbag may have been tampered with as well."

Chantal's knees buckled and Marc caught her. Leading her to the chaise, he sat with her and held her until she regained her composure. Finally, she drew a shaky breath and asked, "What time did all this happen?"

"Shortly after 2 p.m., according to the report from the maintenance crew whose mower was damaged. That must be why she never made it to the dry cleaner. The dispatcher told me the report mentions a couple of linen tablecloths being found in the van."

Chantal looked up at Rosalie. "Why didn't we hear about this sooner?" she asked in a stricken voice. "We were killing time at Fuzzy Logic, when we could have been at the hospital with Mom and Dad..."

Rosalie walked over and patted her on the shoulder. "Honey, your daddy told me not to trouble you with this; he knew you and Marc were spending some time together, and he didn't want to interrupt with bad news that you couldn't do anything about."

Chantal glared at the housekeeper, who removed her hand and stepped back. Seeing Rosalie's reaction, Chantal immediately apologized. "I'm sorry, Rosie. None of this is your fault. You were carrying out Father's instructions."

"Now, Chantal, don't go back to calling him 'Father' because you don't agree with his reasoning. He was trying to spare you some unpleasantness and allow you two some time alone without all this cult mess intruding."

Chantal nodded. "I know Dad wasn't trying to patronize me or treat me like a little girl. It just felt that way for a moment." She wiped her eyes and turned to Marc. "Hon, can you take me to the hospital? I want to check on Ruth..."

Marc stood and pulled her into his arms. He looked at Rosalie and asked about the state of dinner. She said she'd already put everything away and they could heat it up later if they wanted it. Removing her apron, she told Chantal she was going home for the evening and would be praying for Ruth.

Chantal nodded and thanked her, then looked up at Marc. "Wonderful as this is, I still want to go to the hospital..."

Marc grinned ruefully and dropped a kiss on her forehead.

"Okay, cher. You go freshen up and I'll start the car."

* * *

At the hospital in Natchez, Chantal and Marc went straight to the waiting room of the critical care unit and found Helene and Martin, who had been there close to four hours. After exchanging greetings, foursome sat again and talked in hushed tones about what had happened to Ruth and her current status. Marc caught the elder Athertons up on the information he'd gleaned from the sheriff's dispatcher. They were shocked, as he'd expected.

Helene looked at the other three with widened eyes and whispered, "Do you really think someone tried to kill her, Marc?"

"Yes, ma'am, it appears that way. I don't know if someone suspected she was passing information to us because of her frequent trips to town, or if it was paranoia on Zacharias's part, but it definitely looks as though her tire was deliberately shot out."

He went silent as he noticed a doctor approaching the group.

"Mr. Atherton?"

Martin stood. "Yes, Doctor. Has she regained consciousness yet?"

The doctor shook his head. "No, but she is showing signs of responding to stimuli, so we're hopeful that she'll come out of the coma soon. If any of you want to visit with her for a few moments you may, but only one or two at a time, and if you visit in pairs, don't everyone talk at once. Even in a comatose state, a patient can be vulnerable to sensory overload."

"Dad, if you don't mind, Marc and I would like to go in first, okay?" Chantal looked at her dad, then glanced at Marc for confirmation. He nodded and so did Martin. Taking Marc's hand, she followed the doctor into Ruth's room.

"Remember, ma'am, only one at a time talking, and please limit your visit to five minutes or so." The doctor left, and Marc and Chantal walked to opposite sides of the bed. By unspoken consent, they each took one of Ruth's hands, bowed their heads and began to pray, with Marc starting.

Several minutes later, they both looked up and realized a nurse was standing in the entrance. She smiled and said softly, "I was supposed to come in and tell you your time was up, but I didn't want to interrupt your prayers. I know it works wonders for both the patient and the loved ones. She's blessed to have y'all in her life."

Chantal smiled and wiped away a tear. "You know, I think I felt her squeeze my hand a couple of times..."

"That's entirely possible," the nurse assured her. "We've noticed some improvement in her condition in the last hour or so. Perhaps your prayers will bring her the rest of the way back to consciousness."

"Ma'am," Marc said, "I'm going to make a call and see about getting a guard here, if that's not a problem." He showed her his badge as he explained that his department had reason to suspect attempted foul play. "In fact, we should have done this the moment she was brought in, but we weren't positive about the cause of the wreck until a little while ago."

The nurse nodded and showed Marc and Chantal to a phone he could use at the nurses' station. On their way, she paused and told Martin and Helene they could visit Ruth for a few minutes.

At the nurses' station, Marc called his own department and asked to be patched through to Sheriff Aikers. Explaining the situation to him, Marc asked the sheriff to call his counterpart in the Natchez police department and get someone posted outside Ruth's CCU room immediately. Marc told Aikers he'd stay until someone from either the city or state police arrived.

After hanging up, Marc turned to Chantal and suggested they step outside for a few moments. In the hospital parking lot, he said, "I think you should call Brigitte and tell her Ruth was in an accident and is in the hospital at Natchez. Tell her the van is in the county impound lot being inspected, and ask her if she can come to the hospital. Don't tell her about the tire being shot, though. If anyone is listening in, she could be in danger if we say anything about a suspected murder attempt."

Chantal rubbed her hands over her face and swept them back through her hair, then blew out a breath and nodded. Pulling her phone out of her pocket, she made the call and relayed the information about Ruth to Brigitte as Marc had scripted it, but with one addition. "Sis? Do you think you and Miss Gloria could come over to the hospital? Miss Ruth is in a coma in the CCU unit, and I think it would help if she could hear some familiar voices... Okay, see you in about 30 minutes."

She closed the phone and looked at Marc. "That's done. Now what?"

"Now we wait for them to get here, and then we tell Brigitte what really happened. What made you ask her to bring Gloria along?"

"Two reasons: Dad mentioned that Gloria was with Ruth the last time he bumped into her at the grocery store, which leads me to believe Ruth recruited Gloria into our little undercover op; and if Brigitte reacts like I think she will, she's going to need someone to drive her back to New Canaan."

Marc nodded. "Actually, I'm hoping this incident will shock her into reality and we'll be able to get her out of there tonight. But you're right – if Gloria is in on this with Ruth, she could be the next target, and either way, Brigitte shouldn't be alone if she does decide to return to the farmhouse."

"Marc, this is getting scary. Can we take a minute and pray before we go back inside?"

Marc held out his arms and Chantal walked into his embrace. They bowed their heads, his forehead resting on her crown, and prayed for the Lord's hand to be on them all and to guide them as they dealt with Brigitte and Gloria. Marc asked for a hedge of protection to be around everyone involved, and Chantal prayed that what was hidden in darkness would be exposed to the light. As they said Amen in unison, they hugged briefly and then walked back into the hospital hand in hand.

* * *

An hour passed and Brigitte and Gloria didn't show up. Chantal paced and prayed and finally told Marc, "I have to call her again. She should have been here by now..."

They started to head toward the elevator when an orderly flagged Marc down and told him there was a call for him at the nurses' station. He turned to the Natchez police officer who had arrived 45 minutes earlier and directed him not to let anyone into Ruth's room unless he checked their ID first and knew them to be family or hospital personnel. The officer nodded once and resumed his position in front of Ruth's door.

"Thibodaux here... What? Yes sir, immediately." He hung up and grabbed Chantal's hand. "Let's go – the stairs are faster."

"Marc, what-" the rest of her question was cut off as he dashed for the stairwell with her in tow. She pulled her hand free and strode alongside him, not sure what the urgency was, but certain she needed to keep pace with him. He blasted through the door and took the stairs two at a time to ground level. By the time they entered the emergency room, they were running.

Chantal slid to a halt and panted momentarily. "Marc – what – why – what is going on?"

He pointed wordlessly at the ER admitting desk, where Gloria stood supporting a battered Brigitte. As the sight registered with Chantal and propelled her toward the desk, two ER attendants rushed past her and took up positions on either side of Brigitte as they escorted her to an examining room.

"Gloria, what in the world happened to my little sister?"

Gloria turned to the admissions nurse and asked a question. The nurse nodded, left the desk and indicated that they should follow her. She led the trio down a side hall into a small unused consulting room and said she'd be back shortly with coffee for all of them. They thanked her and filed into the spartan room. Sitting around the small conference table, the women stared at each other in silence while they waited for the coffee.

Finally, with a few sips of strong hospital brew in their systems, they began talking at the same time – Gloria trying to recount what had happened while Chantal was asking the same thing. Marc put up his hand and they fell silent. "Chantal, let Miss Gloria talk. She's trying to tell us what you want to know." Chantal nodded and looked at Gloria, who began again.

"When Brigitte didn't appear in the kitchen to check on the progress of dinner, as was her usual habit, I decided to see if she might be ill or in need of something. I went upstairs to the suite she and Joseph share, and – " she stopped and shuddered. Breathing hard, she continued, "What I saw stopped me cold. Brigitte's cell phone was smashed on the floor and she was tied to her bed. She'd been beaten, and I feared worse. Joseph was nowhere around, so I took a chance that I might be able to get her out of the house unseen.

"I grabbed the key for Brigitte's Volvo, helped her down the back stairs and took off before anyone could miss us. On the way to the hospital, she told me about your call and that she was coming down to find me when Joseph stormed into their room raging about traitors in our midst.

"When she told him Ruth had been hurt in an accident and was in the hospital in Natchez, he forbade her to leave. Apparently that was the last straw for your sister, because she defied him. She said she told him if he didn't care about an injured member of his own flock, he was no shepherd and she wasn't going to continue as his partner. She flung her ring at him and turned to leave, and he grabbed her." Gloria broke off again, trembling. Chantal started to reach for her hand, but Gloria shook her head.

"I'm not shaking from fright, Chantal. I'm so mad that if I were to see that man right now, I couldn't be held accountable for what I'd surely do to him. Brigitte told me he not only beat her, he – he – he forced himself on her. She said she fought as hard as she could, but it wasn't enough. If I ever get my hands on him, I'll – "

Chantal turned to Marc and said through clenched teeth, "If you don't send someone out to New Canaan right now, I swear – "

Marc covered her hand with his. "Already on it, cher. I messaged the sheriff and John while Gloria was talking. They should have Zacharias in custody before the hospital personnel finish examining your sister." He stood. "I'll be right back; I need to go request that they do a rape kit – " Seeing Chantal crumple, he knelt and put his arms around her. "Baby, we'll get through this, and we'll see your sister through it, too. Will you be okay with Gloria until I get back?"

She nodded into his shoulder and he gave her a gentle squeeze before he stood up. Looking at Gloria, he said, "Can you take over here for a minute or two until I get back? Don't talk about anything else, okay? Just pray for her..." He strode out of the room.

In the examining room where Brigitte was resting, he tried to approach her gently. "Hey, sweetie."

Brigitte flinched reflexively as she opened her blackened eyes and saw a man standing over her. Marc saw her reaction and backed up a step. "Sorry, hon, didn't mean to scare you. Gloria told us what you said happened. I don't want you to suffer any more than you have, but I need to ask you to recount the events for me, okay? Hang on a second..."

He stuck his head out of the examining room and nodded to a passing nurse. "Ma'am, could you help me out?" He showed her his identification. "I'm Deputy Marc Thibodaux with the sheriff's department in Atherton, and this young woman was brought in here because she reported being assaulted and battered. I need a female witness here while she answers a few questions, and then we're going to need to have a rape kit run."

The nurse nodded and stepped into the room. She handed a tissue to Brigitte, who had started crying at the mention of a rape kit, and held her free hand. Marc stood at the right corner of the foot of the bed and asked Brigitte to tell him what she'd told Gloria. Between sobs, she managed to recount the whole ordeal.

"If she hadn't come in when she did," Brigitte finished, "I'd be dead. Joseph had left promising to come back with something that would make what had already happened feel like a friendly massage – his words. I don't know what he was planning to do to me, but I know I wouldn't have survived it."

Marc waited until she was able to stop crying, then he asked her if she'd be willing to press charges against Joseph.

"Absolutely!" she said through clenched teeth. "I don't know how I got sucked into his head games, but this tears it. Whatever hold he had on me broke when he did this..." She started to sob quietly again.

"I'd love to comfort you somehow, Brigitte, but I don't know what to do other than to tell you I already have people on the way to the farmhouse to apprehend Joseph." He looked at the nurse and nodded toward the examining room door. She followed him through and he told her he had to get back to the other witness, but he'd send someone to guard Brigitte in the meantime.

Motioning to a hospital security officer, he stationed the man outside Brigitte's room and walked outside so he could call the Natchez Police Department. A woman in an officer's uniform was walking toward him. She said, "Deputy Thibodaux? Your sheriff called my chief..." The woman produced her badge and identification.

Marc escorted her back inside, where she relieved the hospital guard in standing watch. Leaving the officer and nurse in charge of Brigitte, he went back to the consultation room, where he found Gloria hugging Chantal as she cried. Gloria started to disengage, but Marc shook his head and sat on the opposite side of the table.

Chantal looked up and saw Marc, wiped her eyes and asked, "How is she? Did he – ?"

Marc nodded and Chantal breathed a shaky sigh as she tried to stop the tears. "Go on, cher – cry it all out. Everything's under control now, and your sister is under guard. Get it all out of your system, and then we'll go find your parents. They need to know where Brigitte is..."

CHAPTER 40

"Sorry to hear that, John... Yeah, I know. Keep me posted." Marc sighed as he holstered his cell phone and turned to the Athertons. "When the deputies arrived at New Canaan, Zacharias was gone and the place was in chaos. No one would admit to knowing when he left or where he went, and since Brigitte was also missing, everyone was wandering around without a clue as to what they should be doing."

Helene shuddered. "That – that madman – he's still out there somewhere?" She turned to Martin with panic in her eyes. "You don't think he'd try to come after Brigitte, do you?"

Martin looked up at Marc. "Is it possible, son? Might Zacharias attempt to finish what he started with my daughter?"

Marc shook his head slowly. "He might, but unless he has some way of knowing for sure where she went when she left, it's unlikely he'd show up here. Still, we'll keep a guard posted outside Brigitte's room around the clock."

"So, what do we do now?" Martin asked.

"Be with your daughter. She's going to need a lot of counseling and family support. She wasn't attacked by a stranger – this man had her convinced they were married and worse, that he was some kind of modern-day messiah for this group. When he turned on her, the physical damage he did was the least of what happened. She's going to have some serious psychological, emotional and spiritual issues to get through, and she'll need to know she can count on all of us to walk through it with her."

Martin stood and extended his hand to Helene. "Come on, honey. Let's go see our baby." As they entered Brigitte's room, Marc sat next to Chantal on the waiting room couch and slipped an arm around her shoulders. She nestled closer and pulled her legs up on the couch, letting her shoes drop to the floor as she changed position.

"What a nightmare this has become," she murmured into his shoulder. "Marc, I don't know what to think. We no sooner pray for her to be protected than she's brought in here looking like he took a baseball bat to her. Where was God's protection while – while he was beating and raping her?" She started crying again, and Marc held her as she gave vent to her emotions.

When her sobs subsided, he handed her a tissue and stroked her cheek, drawing her gaze up to his. "Chantal, I realize you're angry and hurting, but you know the answer to your questions. God was with her the whole time. He kept her alive and He sent Gloria to rescue her. Yes, she got hurt, but that's not His fault. The responsibility falls squarely on the shoulders of that – "

"Evil megalomaniac?" Chantal said. Marc nodded and she continued, "I know, but it's hard not to wonder when things like this happen."

He stroked her hair. "Yeah, I agree. I see so much bad on a regular basis, it's often tempting to question God, if not blame Him. But we both know we're living in a fallen world, and horrible things happen, sometimes to the people we love."

Chantal reached up and touched his cheek. "How do you do it, Marc? How do you deal with all this evil without it messing with your faith, or your head?"

"I keep taking it to God. It's the best thing I can do."

Chantal sighed. "Sounds good. Will you do that now – help me take it to God?"

Marc nodded, and for the third time in as many hours, the two joined in prayer. When they opened their eyes, she sat up and embraced him. "Thank you for that. You know, you've been the best thing to come into my life since I moved back home."

He slipped his arms around her and smiled. "I know this is the absolute worst time for such things, but I've been wanting to tell you something for a while now..."

A shadow fell over them, and they looked up to see Martin standing in front of the couch. "Sorry to interrupt your conversation, but Brigitte is asking for you, Chantal."

"Come on, Marc, let's go – "

"No, dear. She wants to see you alone." Martin glanced at Marc apologetically.

"I completely understand. A male law officer is probably one of the last people she wants to see right now. I'd most likely make her uncomfortable." Marc let Chantal go and stood with her. "I'll put in another call to John and see if anything new has developed."

CHAPTER 41

Chantal sat next to Brigitte's bed, holding her hand and praying silently while she waited. Brigitte had burst into tears at the sight of her sister and was still crying ten minutes later.

Finally, she coughed and blew her nose. Peering at her sister through swollen eyelids, she chuckled ruefully. "We're a mess, huh, sis? You come back home to deal with a drama queen mother and a father who won't admit he has health issues, only to find your sister eyeball-deep in a cult. No wonder your eyes look as red as mine feel..."

Chantal laughed and squeezed her hand. "I'm glad you're joking about it, sweetie. That tells me you're going to be okay..." She glanced at the IV drip connected to Brigitte's arm, then turned her gaze back to her sister. "You know, there's no rush; you can tell me whatever you need to in your own time..."

"I want to tell you some of it now, if you're ready to hear it." Chantal nodded, and Brigitte took a moment to order her thoughts. "When I first joined CUP I thought we were going to do great things for God. Joseph talked about all these 'visions' he had for a new work of the Lord in our area, and I was excited to belong to something like that. My faith felt revitalized, and I thought I'd found a purpose beyond typing notes for Uncle Lawrence and fulfilling whatever role this town expected from the youngest Atherton daughter, you know?"

"I do know about the need for an identity apart from the

town. It's why I left home after college."

"Yeah, kinda wish I'd done that, too – gone away to college instead of getting my associate's locally and going to work at the law firm. I didn't have the drive, though – felt like it would have been wasting our parents' money if I'd gone to a university."

"That aimlessness was what got me into trouble. I was an easy target. Joseph played to my need to belong, to matter." Brigitte shook her head. "It didn't help that he was good-looking and charismatic. I see now I had a major crush on him, which worked to his advantage."

She looked at Chantal and sighed. "Amazing what insights you can gain into yourself in the aftermath of a beating."

Chantal bit her lip and looked away, fighting the urge cry again. Finally she turned back. "Now, sis, even if all the things you said about yourself are true, that doesn't excuse or justify his behavior. He's a fraud and a sex offender at the least, and possibly more..."

Brigitte sat up a little straighter. "What do you mean?"

"I didn't want to tell you this until you'd recovered a bit, but it's possible Joseph or someone under his direction shot out Ruth's tire earlier today – "

"What?" Brigitte started to tremble, and Chantal winced.

"Sis, I'm sorry – I don't want you to hurt any more than you are, but I think you need to know the truth about that man."

Brigitte took a deep breath. "Okay, Chantal – out with it. What else have you not told me?"

"Well, most of this we've discovered in the last day or two, and we were trying to gather enough evidence for either the police or the sheriff's department to apprehend him." She stopped, thinking about how to tell her sister everything without sending her into shock.

"Come on, Chantal – whatever you have to say can't be any worse than what he did to me."

"You may have a point there. Okay, here goes: We were able to get hold of the Social Security number he used when he applied as youth pastor at First Baptist, and it turns out to belong to a dead farmer from Kansas. Also, the seminary diploma he submitted with his application was fake. The seminary never heard of him."

"Identity theft – that's bad, but there has to be more to the story."

Chantal shook her head. "You're right; there is. Remember the guy in the kudzu a couple of months back? He was wearing a CUP t-shirt, and there was a broken silver chain with a CUP logo pendant near Sue tripped over him. Autopsy evidence indicates it wasn't an accidental overdose, either, as was originally supposed; there were no drugs in his system."

Brigitte pursed her lips and thought a moment. "Would a broken chain like the one that was found leave a mark if it were jerked off, say, in a fight?" When Chantal nodded, Brigitte said with a sigh, "Well then, add murder to the charges against Joseph, or whoever he is. I noticed a mark on the side of his neck a while back but didn't think anything of it. We were still at the drive-in at the time, and we had to set out furniture and put it back up for our meetings, so I assumed – oh wait, come to think of it, he never actually did any of that." She scowled and asked, "Is that it, or is there more?"

"Just a couple more things. You know Jim Bridges, Miss Terri's son? If you haven't noticed him missing from New Canaan, he has been. He's in jail awaiting trial for breaking into my cottage." Chantal told her all about the attempted burglary, including her use of the pepper grinder as a weapon.

"Why did he break in, sis? Has he told anyone, and does it have anything to do with CUP?"

"Yes, and it does. He claimed God told him to retrieve a file Pastor Barton gave me on Zacharias so the 'unbelievers' couldn't hinder the work God was doing through CUP. Of course, I didn't have the file at home at the time; I'd left it in my desk at the bank."

"Oh my – what nonsense!" Brigitte exclaimed. "I don't buy for a second that God would tell someone to commit a felony on His behalf. It's obvious that evil man put him up to it, probably by influencing him while he was on a fast. We did a lot of fasting around there, and it was always at *his* direction. Here's a question, though: how'd he know you even had the file?"

"I've wondered about that, too. Unless someone saw Pastor Barton bringing the file to me and assumed – but no, that doesn't make sense either." She bit her lower lip. "Is it possible there was a CUP plant in the First Baptist office?"

Brigitte raised an eyebrow and blew out a breath. "After today, I'd believe anything I heard about that man. Heck, I wouldn't be surprised to see horns sprouting from his head."

Chantal laughed at the image. After a moment Brigitte joined her, but quickly gasped to a halt. "Ow, that hurts my ribs. I know vengeance is the Lord's, sis, but I so want to beat that man down right now... Think I could borrow the replacement pepper grinder you gave Father?"

Chantal snorted. "I don't think so, girl – that particular birthday gift cost me close to $150 all told. I will promise you this, though – if they can find him, I'll hold him down while you do whatever you want to him..."

"What do you mean, if they can find him?" Brigitte almost hyperventilated as panic overwhelmed her.

"Oh, man! I'm so sorry, Brigitte – we didn't want to worry you, but he disappeared from New Canaan before they could nab him. There's an all-points bulletin out on him now, but he's still at large."

Brigitte swore loudly then clapped a hand over her mouth, but Chantal patted her other hand and said, "Totally understandable after what you've been through. Trust me, the only words I've had for that man lately are not one tiny bit Christian, and it's been really hard to keep them from slipping out of my mouth."

Brigitte smiled, then winced. "My face still hurts. When I'm completely recovered, I'm enrolling in a self-defense class. I don't intend to be anyone's punching bag ever again..."

"Count me in, sis. I'll take the class with you. Look out, world – the Atherton sisters are trained and dangerous..."

"Ouch! Don't make me laugh, Chantal..."

There was a knock at the door, and Chantal went to answer it. Seeing that it was Marc, she stepped aside and let him in, touching his shoulder as he passed by. He smiled at her and went to the other chair in the room. "Mind if we visit for a minute, Brigitte?"

She smiled and nodded. "Why don't you move that chair over by Chantal's? It'll be easier on my neck..."

Chantal waited for Marc to get settled, then told him, "I've caught Brigitte up on what we know so far..." She trailed off at his concerned expression, then asked, "Did I do something I shouldn't have?"

"No, boo. I thought it might be too soon to unload all that on her, but she seems to be handling it okay." He turned to Brigitte. "How are you doing, hon? Do you need anything?"

"Only to see that man behind bars for a very long time, Marc. I started to tell Chantal everything that happened, but we got kind of sidetracked. I know you've already heard a lot of it, but do you mind if I tell it again now?"

"Not at all; maybe some detail will come to you that we missed the first time around."

Brigitte took a deep breath and winced. "Forgot about the

ribs for a moment... Where was I? Oh yeah – I was feeling aimless and looking for a purpose in life, and he was charismatic, handsome and seemed to be on fire for God. So, I joined the group, and as I sank deeper into it, I sold off all my stuff to help finance the ministry, quit my job so I could manage the CUP office – again, at Joseph's direction – and moved into New Canaan."

"But why?" The question slipped out before Chantal could stop it.

Brigitte sighed. "Besides the whole business about looking for a purpose, at first I felt like he filled an emotional void – kind of a father figure, you know? After a while, I came to depend on him more and more to give me guidance and direction. Instead of listening to the internal voice cautioning me to run away from him and CUP as fast as I could, I only listened to him. Every time I began to doubt and wonder, something would happen that I took as a sign from God, and I got further into it."

Marc nodded. "That's typical of cult involvement. My brother's behavior was very similar – only he didn't get out..."

"Oh, Marc. I'm sorry to hear that," Brigitte said. "I take it he's still caught up in it, then?"

Marc shook his head and looked down. Chantal let go of Brigitte's hand and took Marc's as she said, "No, sis – Marc means he didn't make it out alive."

Brigitte gasped and blurted, "What happened?"

"Suicide cult." Chantal handed Marc a tissue and looked at

her sister. "Now you see why we were so worried about you?"

Brigitte nodded, too stunned to speak.

When Marc found his voice, he asked Brigitte if she could continue.

"I – I think so. Let me skip ahead a bit, to the weekend of the Fall Festival. When y'all saw me, I was on the tail end of a seven-day fast, water only – again, because Joseph said God told him I needed to do it to receive a word about what plans He had for me. I was exhausted and in serious need of some food when we bumped into each other.

"When I got back to New Canaan, I was too worn out to tell everyone how our festival outreach had gone. On top of that, I was upset after talking with you, Chantal – I was wondering if we'd ever see eye to eye on my involvement in CUP." She paused and lifted an eyebrow, acknowledging the irony in her statement. "So, there I was, sitting in the van, too tired to get out, when Joseph came out to check on me. He helped me into the house and up to the second floor, and I thought he was going to deposit me on my bed in the sleeping room the women shared..." A tear slipped down her cheek as she silently remembered what she could of the rest of that evening.

"Sweetie?" Chantal pressed a fresh tissue into her hand. "We don't have to keep going. There's plenty of time to talk about it..."

Brigitte nodded. "I thought I could do this, but it's still too raw. Could you send Mother in here? I suspect you won't be able to keep her out much longer, anyway."

"Sure thing, Midget," Chantal smiled as she used Brigitte's childhood nickname. "By the way, it's Mom and Dad now. If nothing else, this whole drama has knocked some of the façade off our family."

"At least something good has come of all this," Brigitte replied. "See you tomorrow?"

"Of course. Sleep well. We'll be praying for a peaceful night for you."

CHAPTER 42

Over the next several days, Marc, John and the rest of the Sheriff's Department were occupied with the Zacharias/CUP investigation. They scoured the county and sent out state and federal APBs for the man, but it seemed as though he disappeared as suddenly as he'd appeared.

Meanwhile, the department combed through New Canaan's property and computers looking for anything that would help the investigation, but they turned up very little. Apparently, before he disappeared Zacharias had stopped in the ministry office long enough to launch a virus that irretrievably crashed CUP's small on-site network.

After interviewing all the cult members, the deputies sent them back to their lives. Like Brigitte, some had given up their jobs and belongings when they joined the group. They now had to depend on families and friends for a place to stay and financial support until they could get back on their feet. A few had been transients and returned to the county shelters, having nowhere else to go. All of them were going to need counseling to repair the damage Zacharias had done to their psyches.

The night before Thanksgiving, Marc sat at his desk after another long day of fruitlessly pursuing leads. Rubbing his face, he reached out and poked the on button of his computer. As he waited for it to boot up, he felt his cell phone vibrate.

"Hello? Oh, hey boo... Yeah, I'm still coming over tomorrow

for dinner with y'all. How are Ruth and Brigitte doing?"

The hospital in Natchez released both women after two days. Ruth came out of her coma with very little trauma to her body and only vague memories of the wreck. The Athertons invited her to stay with them as long as she wanted.

The doctors also deemed Brigitte recovered enough to go home and be cared for by her parents' physician, one of the few doctors who still practiced general medicine and made house calls. Ensconced in her childhood bedroom and surrounded by the things she thought she'd lost when she sold them, Brigitte was beginning to heal physically. The emotional and psychological restoration would take much longer, they all knew. For now, when the nightmares caused her to wake up screaming, at least she was in familiar surroundings.

As Chantal recounted the signs of progress they were seeing in her sister, Marc smiled and looked at the picture on his desk. Someone had taken a candid portrait of Chantal and Marc at the park during the festival. He had no idea who it was from; it showed up in his mail a week or so ago. It was taken when they were sitting on the park bench and she was resting against him, and the photo brought back the feeling he'd had that day of wanting to stay like that forever...

As Chantal continued to talk, Marc found himself thinking that her voice was like a mug of cinnamon-laced hot chocolate after a brutal day like this: rich, sweet, a little spicy, and so comforting. He reached into his pocket and fiddled with the small box he'd picked up in Natchez earlier in the day. This was going to be some Thanksgiving dinner...

"Yeah, cher, it sounds like she's going to be okay; it's just gonna take some time and TLC... Hey, hang on a minute. There's new email in my box; let me see what it is..." He clicked open an encrypted email from the police department in Tyler, Texas. As he read it, he whooped.

"Oops, sorry babe. Forgot I still had the phone to my ear. An ID came back on that handprint. Seems we're dealing with one Roger Forrester, who's wanted in three states on a number of charges, including fraud, conspiracy to commit murder, attempted murder, rape, grand larceny... No, I don't know if it will help us bag him any faster, but at least we have a positive identification now. Let me get a revised APB out listing his real name and this whole slew of aliases he's used over the years... Okay, Chantal. See you tomorrow at 11."

CHAPTER 43

Chantal was placing the centerpiece her mother had ordered on the dining table when the doorbell rang. "I'll get it!" She plunked the flower arrangement down and smoothed her skirt as she headed for the foyer. Recent events might have stripped away some of the Atherton family's veneer, but Helene still insisted on some things, like everyone dressing up for holiday dinners.

As she opened the front door and admitted Marc, Chantal smiled her approval of his wardrobe. A charcoal suit with a light gray shirt and navy tie brought out his blue eyes and fit him with hand-tailored excellence. "Mmm, mmm – perfect. Mother will definitely approve," she purred as she hugged him hello.

He grinned and complimented her choice of lavender blouse and navy calf-length skirt. "It sets off those beautiful brown eyes, cher." Twirling her around, he smiled as he anticipated his plans for the day.

"What's that Cheshire Cat grin about, mister?"

Marc turned as Helene entered the foyer. "Hello, Helene. I was admiring this fine woman you've raised here."

Chantal blushed, and Helene actually tittered like a schoolgirl. *Oh my, she's as smitten with him as I am,* Chantal thought. *This is going to be an interesting day...*

Just then, Brigitte descended the staircase. She, Ruth, Chantal and Helene had gone shopping the day before in Natchez, and Brigitte was wearing a stylish but comfortable dress that covered her bandages and bruises without looking dowdy. An expert makeup job by her mother concealed the worst of the damage to her face, and she actually looked like she was going to be able to enjoy herself.

"Hi, everyone. Happy Thanksgiving," Brigitte said as she gave each one a careful hug. As she embraced Marc, her hand brushed against his jacket pocket and a smile stole across her face, but by the time she pulled back, her expression was blandly pleasant again.

"Mom, I know it's going to be a little while 'til dinner's ready. Is there anything I can nibble on in the meantime? I'm ravenous today for some reason..." Brigitte slipped an arm through her mother's and steered her toward the kitchen. As she left, she glanced back over her shoulder and winked at Marc.

Chantal caught the exchange and turned to Marc. "Now what was that all about?"

"Can we go someplace where we won't be drafted into helping set the table or something?" Marc asked.

"Why don't we go to the cottage for a while? If they need us they can call, and in the meantime I have something we can snack on while we wait for the main meal."

They walked through the kitchen with their arms linked and Chantal called out to the other women as they passed through, "We'll be out back if y'all need us..."

They strolled in silence to Chantal's cottage, each thinking about the events of the last few months. The door was unlocked, so Marc opened it, ushered Chantal in and locked it behind them as he followed her. She heard the click and turned to him. "Why – "

He pulled her into his arms and gave her a kiss that left her weak-kneed and breathless. "Oh..." she whispered. "Do that again..."

Finally, they separated and walked into the living room. Settling her on the couch, he sat and wrapped his arms around her. She curled up and leaned into him. "Hmmm, seems to me the last time we were sitting like this, you were about to tell me something and my dad interrupted us..."

He laughed softly into her hair and said, "Yeah, he did." He kissed her temple, and she turned her face to his. A few more minutes passed as they savored each other's proximity, and Marc finally broke lip contact and pulled away from her. "Aw..." she murmured with a flirtatious pout.

He stroked her cheek. "It's only a momentary delay, I promise." Slipping a hand into his right pocket, he cupped the box Brigitte had noticed earlier.

Holding Chantal's left hand in his, he said, "I know we haven't known each other very long, and we said we would take things slow, but – I've been wanting to tell you this for a while, Chantal, and every time I've gotten up the nerve to do it, there's been a crisis of some sort or an interruption. I figured with the door locked, we might get a little privacy..."

At that moment, his cell phone vibrated in his left pocket.

Chantal's eyebrow shot up as she tried to suppress a grin. "You gonna get that?"

He shook his head fiercely. "No, it can wait..."

On its charger base, Chantal's phone rang. She stood to go answer it, but Marc wouldn't let go of her hand. "Marc, what if it's the sheriff's department with news about Zach – I mean, Forrester?"

"I don't care!" She plopped back onto the couch and stared at him, nonplussed. "I'm trying to tell you –"

The doorbell rang and Chantal rose again and started to walk past him. "Now Marc, I really can't ignore – "

Still holding onto her hand, he pulled her back toward him and exclaimed, "Dang it, woman! I love you! Will you marry me?"

Chantal collapsed into his lap and stared at him. "What? I'm sorry – did you just yell a proposal at me?"

With the doorbell ringing and two telephones clamoring for their attention, Marc laughed and hugged Chantal tight. "Yes, I did. So, you want to yell an answer back at me or what?"

- END OF BOOK 1 -

A PREVIEW OF **BRIGITTE'S BATTLE**, *BOOK 2 OF THE WOMEN OF ATHERTON (SCHEDULED FOR RELEASE IN MARCH 2013)*:

As Brigitte left her bedroom, the doorbell rang and Chantal yelled, "I'll get it!" Pausing on the stairs, Brigitte laughed as her 30-year-old sister ran through the parlor, skidded to a halt in front of the foyer mirror to check her dress and makeup, then sedately opened the front door.

"Merry Christmas, Marc!" Chantal wrapped her arms around him and planted a long kiss on his lips.

"Joyeux Noel, boo!" he replied with a laugh when he caught his breath. "Can I come in now?"

"Had to break in the mistletoe," she said, pointing at the top of the doorframe. "Want some eggnog?"

As the couple moved into the dining room where the eggnog sat in a crystal punchbowl on the sideboard, Brigitte descended the staircase unnoticed. She watched them stroll away, joined at the hip, and sighed. *If only I hadn't...*

Shaking her head to dismiss the ever-present regrets, she headed for the kitchen to see if anyone needed help with Christmas dinner preparations. She'd only gone five paces when the doorbell rang again. "I got it this time," she called out and turned around.

She hesitated before grabbing the door handle, but relaxed when she saw Sue and John through the peephole. "Merry

Christmas, y'all! Come in - presents can go under the tree in the parlor; we'll be opening them after Aunt Attie arrives."

The trio exchanged pleasantries as they deposited gifts under the ten-foot spruce and stepped back to admire the tableau. For years, a professional designer had decorated the tree. This time, though, the Athertons had a tree-trimming party the weekend after Thanksgiving, inviting Marc, John and other family friends. The spruce was loaded with items from the family attic and new ornaments contributed by partygoers.

Brigitte smiled as she saw her childhood hanging from the branches. Sue put an arm around her shoulders. "It's beautiful, isn't it, cous? All those good memories, the fun we had, right there on display. Remember the day we made those?" She pointed to a set of three macaroni-and-glitter masterpieces, each featuring a photo of an Atherton girl in her Girl Scout uniform. "It was one of those rare occasions when the Brownies and Cadets got to mingle..."

"I remember the macaroni fight that erupted, and how much Rosie fussed when we came home with noodles and glue stuck in our hair." Brigitte chuckled.

Laughter broke out behind them, and they turned to see Marc and Chantal entering the room. "Noodles, huh, cher?" Marc teased Chantal. "Pity no one got that on film..."

"Oh, hush." She gave him a playful slap on the shoulder. "It's funny now, but boy, did Rosie give us what-for. It took about a week for all the glitter to go away..."

"What about your parents? Didn't they have something to say about it?" John asked. The entire group turned and looked at him in disbelief. He smacked his forehead. "Oh yeah – forgot who I was talking about for a moment there..."

Brigitte patted him on the arm. "It's okay, John. They've changed so much in the last month or so I sometimes forget what they used to be like, too."

"Is someone casting aspersions on my character in here, and on Christmas Day at that?" a pleasant rumble came from the dining room. Brigitte and Chantal's father Martin entered with a cup of warm spiced tea in one hand and a celery stick in the other. "Your mother, bless her, won't let me anywhere near the sausage balls. Celery sticks – it's Christmas, for pity's sake!"

"Now, Dad, we all know you've managed to sneak at least one sausage ball already. Mom's trying to look out for your health; she wants you around for a long time – although I'm not entirely sure why..." Chantal grinned, squeezed his shoulders and kissed him on the cheek.

Brigitte moved in for a hug from her dad, lingering a bit longer than her sister had. Martin set his snack on a side table and held his youngest daughter. "Merry Christmas, sweetie."

Sue and John wandered into the dining room for eggnog, and Chantal gave Marc a tour of the downstairs rooms, showing off the decorating the Atherton women had done together for the first time in over a decade. They ended in her father's study, where a handmade quilt from Chantal's aunt, Attie Mae Smith, was the focal item.

"Looks good in here, boo." Marc drew Chantal down onto the antique loveseat.

"Can't take credit for it." She curled up next to him. "Mom and Dad did this room by themselves. Dad said if it had to be decorated, he didn't want it all girly. They spent a lot more time in here than the decorating warranted, too..."

"Ah, so the spark is rekindling?"

"Yes indeed. I caught them necking like teenagers this morning, right out on the front porch in full view of the entire town."

"So we didn't truly break in the mistletoe..."

"Not really... I don't think you mind much, though, do you?"

He pulled her into his lap and kissed her soundly. "Not one bit..."

"Oops, sorry, didn't mean to disturb y'all." Brigitte stepped over to a shelf and pulled down a thin book. "When you're ready to rejoin the family, Dad's waiting to start."

"I didn't hear Attie arrive," Chantal said.

"She came through the kitchen entrance with a double armload of food. She's in the parlor now. *Everyone* is in the parlor now..."

"Okay, sis, I get it; we'll be right there." She chuckled and shook her head as Brigitte closed the study door. Chantal started to stand, but Marc kept his arms wrapped around her.

"Honey, you heard her; they're waiting on us."

"I need to ask you something..."

She sighed. "I thought you agreed not to bring that up for a while."

A pained look came into his eyes. "I know I did, and I'm trying to be patient, but it's been a month. I don't understand – why won't you give me an answer?"

She stood and drew him to his feet. "Marc, you know I care for you a great deal. But your proposal came so soon after we met and everything else that happened. I want us to take a little time, get to know each other better – that's all. I want to make sure what we're feeling is real and not just a response to the drama we went through earlier this year."

"Is that really all it is?" He pulled her close and searched her eyes. "It's not because of anything – or anyone – else, is it?"

She stroked his cheek. "It's not because of anyone else, certainly not Ryan, if that's what you're thinking. We dated briefly in high school, but that was over years ago..."

"The way I've seen him looking at you, I don' t know..."

"Trust me, there's nothing but friendship between Ryan and me. I do need to deal with something, though, and until I can find peace about it, I can't give you the answer you want."

Marc moved to a bookshelf and ran a finger over the spine of a leather-bound volume. Chantal noted with amusement that it was Jane Austen's *Persuasion*. "I wish you'd share whatever it is with me," he finally said. "That's the kind of thing couples are supposed to handle together, isn't it?"

She put her hands on his shoulders. "I can barely think about it. I'm not ready to talk about it yet. Can you please give me a little more time?"

"How much?"

She blew out a breath and backed away as a tear escaped. "I don't know! Trust me, I'd love for this to be settled in my heart, but I can't snap my fingers and make it be. I know this isn't fair to you, but I can't – not yet." She opened the door as Brigitte was about to knock again.

"Everything okay, sis?"

She nodded and wiped her cheek. "Yeah, Brigitte. We'll be there in a minute." She turned to Marc. "Please be patient with me. I promise it'll be worth the wait."

Marc tried to smile, but it didn't reach his eyes. He joined her at the door and gave her a brief kiss. "I'm tryin', cher – believe it or not, I am trying."

As they returned to the parlor and looked for a place to sit, Martin realized there wasn't enough seating for everyone, so he had John and Marc move the loveseat out from the study temporarily. Sue and Brigitte exchanged looks as Marc and Chantal settled next to each other. Both were smiling and they were holding hands, but a noticeable reserve had come over them. Sue cocked an eyebrow and Brigitte shrugged the tiniest bit. *We'll talk later*, she mouthed. Sue nodded and turned to Martin, who was waiting for everyone to give him their attention.

"Now, it has long been a tradition in our family to read a

Christmas story before we open gifts," Martin said as he looked around the group. "We usually read Luke's Nativity narrative from the Bible before we go to church on Christmas Eve, and we pick another story for Christmas Day. This year, in honor of Marc's Louisiana heritage, I bought a new book for our collection when I was at Cover 2 Cover the other day. I'd be honored if you would read it to us." He handed Marc a copy of *Cajun Night Before Christmas*.

Marc smiled widely as he opened the book. "I haven't heard this one in years..." He cleared his throat and began:

> "'Twas the night before Christmas
> An' all t'ru de house
> Dey don't a t'ing pass
> Not even a mouse
> De chirren been nezzle
> Good snug on de flo'
> An' Mamm pass de pepper
> T'ru de crack on de do'."

By the time Marc got to the verse about the eight alligators everyone was chuckling, and he and Chantal had relaxed.

As he read the final verse – "An' I hear him shout loud as a splashin' he go: 'Merry Christmas to all... Till I saw you some mo'!' " – Helene passed a tissue box around the group; everyone was breathless and tear-streaked from laughing. Martin led a round of applause for the reading, and Chantal gave Marc a kiss on the cheek.

"Now, let's see what's under the tree," Martin said. Leaning over and picking up a package, he called the name on the tag and handed Brigitte the present to deliver. "Please, everyone wait until we're done passing out the presents before you open them. Around here we take turns so we can enjoy each other's gifts as much as our own."

The process of calling out names and distributing gifts continued until there was only one left, a manila envelope with a red bow on it. Martin picked it up and looked at Chantal. "Daughter, I want to give you this one myself, and I want you to open it first."

Giving her father a puzzled look, Chantal took the envelope and opened it as she returned to the loveseat. She tipped the contents into her lap and stared at the three business-size envelopes, pen and set of keys that fell out.

"Go on, open the envelope marked #1."

She read the letter inside silently and looked up in shock at her father. "Wha- why – what is going on, Dad?"

Marc took the letter from her and read it, then looked at Martin with an expression that almost matched Chantal's. "Martin, why are you having her resign from the bank?"

Chaos broke out as everyone started asking questions at once. Martin waved his hands, then his arms, and finally resorted to shouting, "Calm down, everyone! Chantal, now that I have your attention, please open the envelope marked #2."

Glaring at her father, she opened the second, bulkier

envelope. She unfolded the document inside and gasped as she passed it to Marc. He skimmed it and laughed.

"He gave her Cover 2 Cover as a Christmas gift!" he exclaimed, waving the deed papers.

Chantal dumped the contents of her lap into Marc's and rushed to hug her father. Laughter and congratulations replaced the chaos and questions, and once again Martin had to quiet everyone down. "Go on, daughter, go back to your seat. We're not quite done. The keys, as you may have guessed, are for the bookstore, and the pen is for you to sign the resignation letter. Now are you okay with doing that?" She grinned and signed the letter. "One other thing I need you to do, dear. Give that last envelope to your sister."

She glanced at the envelope, and sure enough, a note – "For Brigitte" – was written on it. She shrugged and passed it to her sister.

Brigitte opened the envelope, read the letter and smiled. It was her turn to hug her father while questions erupted.

She turned to the group and explained, "He offered me a job at the bank – Chantal's former job – and he deeded the duplex to me. The side I used to live in is unoccupied again; I can move back in whenever I want."

Acknowledgments

This book took a while to go from "what if?" to finished story. I'm grateful to God for everything and to all the folks He put in my path who contributed to the novel's completion:

- My family and English teachers for supporting my lifelong interest in writing; all those literary Christmas gifts and good grades were greatly encouraging.
- Shepherd's Way Church and the members of my Spiritual Studies class about Christianity, cults and world religions; your participation and questions inspired the premise of *Chantal's Call*.
- My offline friends who kept asking how the book was coming; if you hadn't continued expressing an interest, I might not have finished writing it.
- My online friends on Facebook, at ChristianWriters.com and IndieAuthors.com, whose encouragement and advice kept me going. I'm especially grateful to the members of the CW blog chain gang, who read the excerpts I posted and said they couldn't wait for more.
- Christine Henderson of the blog *TheWriteChris*, whose interview about my participation in NaNoWriMo (National Novel Writing Month) was the final nudge that got this story out of my laptop and into cyberspace. Thanks, Chris!
- My beta readers – Lynne Breland, Jordan Fisher Morris and Rose Donaldson – whose enthusiastic responses convinced me the novel was worth sharing.
- Chris Baty, whose wild idea of writing a novel in a month became the impetus for NaNoWriMo, which started me on this journey. Although *Chantal's Call* is not officially a NaNo novel, if it weren't for that annual exercise in literary insanity, I never would have started writing the

story you just read.

And as any author who's honest about it will tell you, no story ever gets written without assistance from people who know more about stuff than the writer does. So, my thanks to:

- Neil Thomas, whose blog *Natural Baskets* taught me the basics of cutting kudzu and preparing it for use in basket making, and Virginia Tech for its *Vines for wreaths and other natural products* fact sheet, which answered some of my questions about the botany and uses of kudzu.

- David Ross of Cannon-Mania LLC, for his invaluable instructions on safely firing a pumpkin from a traditional cannon.

- Fuller Theological Seminary for publishing its directory of theological seminaries of North America, which helped me create a fictional name for the seminary in my story.

- All the organizations and individuals who have posted their cult research online; your information helped shape the scenes involving CUP.

- The legal and medical chat forums that helped with information about air embolisms and handprint scanning. Unfortunately, I didn't save links to or copies of the pages, but I greatly appreciate being able to find them.